A Land Apart

A LAND APART

A South African Reader

Edited by André Brink
and J. M. Coetzee

faber and faber

LONDON · BOSTON

First published in 1986
by Faber and Faber Limited
3 Queen Square London WC1N 3AU
This paperback edition first published in 1987
Reprinted 1987

Photoset by Parker Typesetting Service, Leicester
Printed in Great Britain by
Richard Clay Ltd, Bungay, Suffolk
All rights reserved

British Library Cataloguing in Publication Data

A Land Apart: a South African reader
1. Short stories, South African (English)
I. Coetzee, J. M.   II. Brink, André
823'.01'08968[FS]   PR9367.3

ISBN 0–571–14824–7

CONTENTS

INTRODUCTION

This anthology has been compiled amid the tumult of the uprisings of 1985 across the face of South Africa. The meaning of 1985, as seen by the writers of this country, has yet to emerge in print, and is not reflected in the collection we have made.

It has not been our ambition to give a full picture of the wealth and range of contemporary writing, by writers both Black and White, working in English, Afrikaans, Xhosa, Zulu, Sotho and the other languages of South Africa. The collection is offered as the personal choice of the editors who, restricted by space even within the liberal limits set by the publisher, present a mere sample of the variety and quality of South African writing in English and Afrikaans of the past ten years or so.

If the outlines of a map of contemporary South African writing do seem to emerge, the map should be used cautiously and within the limits very cursorily sketched in this introduction.

1

In selecting works for the 'English' section of this reader, we have used an impure set of criteria, and in certain cases have relaxed even these. As a rule we have gone back no further than 1976; but we have relaxed the rule to include one or two telling (and prophetic) pieces from the early 1970s. We have confined ourselves to work originally written in English, but have made an exception in the case of Mazisi Kunene, a major presence in South African poetry, who writes in Zulu and translates into English. We have looked beyond the genres of poetry and fiction to include diary and autobiography. We have not set out to define, isolate and excerpt the best that has been written in the past decade, doubting whether there is any generally acceptable standard of absolute literary excellence by which writers of various ambitions, working in diverse genres, addressing themselves to different audiences, in a time of acute ideological tension and political polarization, can be judged. What is therefore presented in the English-language section of the book is no more (and no less) than a constellation of seventeen writers engaging with the reality of life in South Africa at a particular juncture in its history, and reworking that engagement upon the page.

Of the writers represented, only Nadine Gordimer and, to a lesser extent, Mazisi Kunene and Christopher Hope can be said to have an international reputation. If anything, the bias in selection has been toward younger writers, in particular toward the 'generation of 1976'. The generation that went (or was forced) into exile in the 1950s and 1960s is represented only by Kunene. Many of these exiled writers are still active: Alex la Guma, Lewis Nkosi, Dennis Brutus, Bessie Head, Es'kia Mphahlele (who has returned to South Africa). But, as one might expect, for them history froze when they departed: they can no longer be said to give voice to contemporary South Africa.

A more synoptic anthology would include many writers working in English for whom we have not found space. Whether or not it cast its net so wide as to include expatriates like Dan Jacobson and C. J. Driver (and even, going further back, Doris Lessing), it would certainly include such older but still vigorously productive writers as Alan Paton and Jack Cope. The generation that came into its own in the 1950s is represented only by the commanding figure of Nadine Gordimer. Among writers who began to make their reputation around 1970, Christopher Hope is present, while other notables like J. M. Coetzee, Patrick Cullinan, Douglas Livingstone, Peter Wilhelm and Rose Zwi are not. Of the writers who emerged into prominence around the time of the 1976 Soweto uprising, we have included Mtutuzeli Matshoba, Christopher van Wyk and (slightly later) Jeremy Cronin, while omitting many of equal achievement. Among the latter, we might name the poets Mongane Serote, Mbuyiseni Mtshali, Sipho Sepamla, Mafika Gwala and Ingoapele Madingoane; and, working in prose, Miriam Tlali, Mothobi Mutloatse, Njabulo Ndebele, Achmat Dangor, as well as (again) Serote and Sepamla. Finally, there is a considerable body of drama which we have not taken into consideration: the plays not only of Athol Fugard but of Black dramatists like Zakes Mda, Moise Mapanya and Fatima Dike.

2

Afrikaans literature, barely a century old, initially was no more than the means to an end, that end being the political emancipation of the Afrikaner. Until well into the twentieth century writers also fulfilled the function of philosophers and prophets for the national cause; in many instances they were political and/or religious leaders of their people as well, a phenomenon which exacerbated the situation when poets in the 1930s and fiction writers in the 1960s began quite simply to express themselves as individuals.

True to literary patterns in most evolving societies, Afrikaans poetry was the first genre to emancipate itself from the constraints of derivative, colonial forms. It was more than a decade after the Second World War that fiction followed suit. (Afrikaans drama, severely inhibited by censorship soon after it began to show its first stirrings of new developments in the 1960s, is still distressingly lagging behind). At that stage a group of young writers, most of whom had spent shorter or longer periods in Europe, and more specifically in Paris, consciously introduced the then current vogues of experimentalism, existentialism and post-modernism into a literary scene still largely determined by nineteenth-century techniques and by the severely localized expression of themes like drought, locusts and poor-whites. The enthusiasm with which this new wave of writing was received by younger Afrikaans readers soon added unexpected dimensions to the work of these so-called 'Sestigers' ('Writers of the Sixties'): as a result of the conventions and taboos broken in their work, mainly in the fields of religion, morality, sex and narrative tradition, political implications were attached to what had started as a purely cultural, literary movement. The Afrikaner establishment, threatened by the new sophistication in indigenous writing, branded as traitors writers like Chris Barnard, Breyten Breytenbach, André Brink, Abraham de Vries, Etienne Leroux, Jan Rabie, Adam Small and Bartho Smit, and tried to ostracize them from their community: books were burned publicly, authors were denounced from the pulpit and in parliament, cultural organizations tried to boycott productions of plays, pressure was exerted on printers and publishers not to publish certain books.

Towards the end of the 1960s, inspired by the early example of Jan Rabie and Adam Small, some of the writers from the group – notably Breytenbach and Brink – began to extend the scope of their work in attempts to come to grips, quite explicitly, with the socio-political context within which they worked. Within a few years practically all the Sestigers were exploring at least the fringes of a more overtly 'committed' form of literature. This development led to a head-on collision with the political authorities who, previously, had appeared reluctant to use the censorship act (first introduced in 1963) against fellow Afrikaners. After the banning of Brink's *Kennis van die Aand* in 1974, published in English as *Looking on Darkness* later that same year, the hunt was open. Within a few years Afrikaans books by Breyten Breytenbach, Welma Odendaal, André le Roux, John Miles, Etienne Leroux and others were banned. This crusade, encouraged by constantly more draconian revisions of the censorship act, had a devastating effect on Afrikaans letters. After the abundance of new writing in the 1960s only a single new fiction writer of note, John Miles, made his début during the 1970s. (Poetry, on the other hand, flourished, presumably because by its very nature poetry is less accessible to a large public and consequently is deemed to be potentially less 'harmful': even so, several volumes of poetry also fell prey to the omnivorous censor.)

One positive reaction to this menace was the establishment of the Afrikaans Writers' Guild in 1975 (which, in spite of its name, was open to writers of all races and languages), and an increasing sense of solidarity among all the writers in the country. By late 1979, after the banning of Nadine Gordimer's *Burger's Daughter*, André Brink's *A Dry White Season*, Mtutuzeli Matshoba's *Call Me Not a Man* and Etienne Leroux's *Magersfontein, O Magersfontein*, a total showdown with the government threatened to take place, with a real possibility of writers going underground, emulating the Russian practice of *samizdat*. To the amazement of most, the authorities backed down: not because they felt intimidated by any means, but because an open clampdown on writers would be disastrous to a government which, in the wake of the Soweto riots of 1977, the death of Steve Biko in 1977, and the escalating schools boycotts of 1978 and 1979, desperately needed such allies as Mrs Thatcher (newly arrived in power in Britain) and Reagan (hovering in the wings in the USA).

That proved to be a turning point in conventional censorship, and since that date most literary works previously banned in the country – including those by Black militant writers – have been released. It should be made very clear, of course, that this move has had nothing to do with liberalization as such: at most it reveals a growing sophistication in the methods of a government that is finding constantly new means to disarm critics and enemies without relinquishing an ounce of its repressive powers.

Sadly, certainly as far as the novel is concerned, much of the vitality and resourcefulness of the 1960s seemed to have become dissipated in the course of the following decade, possibly, and among other reasons, because the direct struggle for survival made so many exhausting demands on writers that little creative energy was left. However, a resurgence of the short story has become spectacularly evident in recent years, as has the activity of poets.

It is difficult to generalize about 'trends' in Afrikaans fiction over the past decade, as the historical perspective is still lacking. But it certainly would be true to say that the spectrum of writing is remarkably wide, ranging from the exploration of the most private of aches on the one hand to a blunt and brutal dessection of the military situation, in ways and forms reminiscent of writing in the US at the height of the Vietnam crisis.

Introduction

There are many refinements in the exploration of the private inscape. In addition to the often almost Chekhovian subtlety of Hennie Aucamp and the quiet melancholy of M. C. Botha represented in this volume, mention should be made especially of Karel Schoeman (whose novel *Promised Land* has been published in English translation): although his work sometimes degenerates into a vague and unfocused *Weltschmerz*, Schoeman at his best offers haunting evocations of loneliness, outsidership, nostalgia for a lost paradise, and a yearning for human contact.

Woman, and the feminine experience, has been a focal point in much recent Afrikaans fiction (while Afrikaans poetry has been wholly dominated by female figures in the past decade: Wilma Stockenström, Sheila Cussons, Antjie Krog, Marlene van Niekerk, to name only a few). Several quite different nuances of this experience are represented in the present anthology: the pathos of defeat which, through the incomprehension of the male narrator, becomes poetic victory in Jeanette Ferreira's story; female solidarity undermined by politics in Elsa Joubert's; a grim struggle for survival which results in the opening up of constantly new frontiers of private experience in Lettie Viljoen's; fierce vengeance in Dalene Matthee's; the agony and disillusionment of love in Ina Rousseau's . . . These should be seen against a much more variegated background. In *The Expedition to the Baobab Tree* (published in Afrikaans in 1981, and in English in 1983) Wilma Stockenström explores the life of a female slave in universal terms of freedom and bondage, resulting in one of the most hallucinatory and poetic probings of the female condition in post-modernist fiction: Petra Muller's short stories offer an extension of the everyday world into that of intimations, symbols and the supernatural; Eleanor Baker uses the form of a fairytale in *Weerkaatsings* (*Reflections*), (1984), to reveal archetypal meanings in ordinary human relationships; Henriette Grové, with exquisite literary refinement, explores interactions between 'story' and 'life' . . .

Inevitably, South African racial politics and policies pervade much of what is being written in Afrikaans. Sometimes it is

Introduction

obfuscated by literary gymnastics (J. C. Steyn); sometimes it is a brutal and direct indictment, as in much of Adam Small's dramatic writing. George Weideman's story in this collection, like Abraham de Vries's, concentrates on some of the more devastating ironies in human relationships brought about by apartheid. Possibly the most brilliant ironist in Afrikaans fiction is Etienne Leroux (not represented in this collection as no excerpt from a novel can do justice to the flair of his phantasmagoric imagination), and in his recent work he has turned more and more towards the specific ironies of the South African political situation – as opposed to the more universal myths of humanity explored in his earlier work – for inspiration.

Underlying almost everything written in Afrikaans today, even texts which on the surface appear tranquil and tender, is an intimation of violence and death, whether portrayed as an intensely private experience, as in John Miles's 'Lucy', or directly linked to apartheid or the South African military experience (Etienne van Heerden's 'My Cuban', Haasbroek's 'Departure', Prinsloo's 'Crack-Up' . . .), or examined as an inescapable part of human experience as such (Cloete's 'Disaster', Kotzé's 'Day of Blood' . . .). This forms part of a crucial dimension in contemporary Afrikaans fiction. In one form it emerges as a series of relentless explorations of war, conscription, border skirmishes, incursions into neighbouring territories, the invasion of privacy, in works by Elsa Joubert (*Die Laaste Sondag: The Last Sunday*, 1983), Louis Kruger (*'n Basis Anderkant die Grens: A Base Beyond the Border*, 1984), Alexander Strachan (*'n Wêreld Sonder Grense: A World Without Borders*, 1984) and others. More generally, it is expressed as an intimation of apocalypse, which implies not just the death of the individual or the end of his hopes, but the destruction of the entire known world or a way of life.

Quite often this kind of fiction acquires its peculiar significance because it is portrayed through the eyes of a child. Possibly because of the Afrikaner's very recent rural past, childhood reminiscences have always formed an important part of Afrikaans literature (whether evoked with nostalgia,

13

as in work by F. A. Venter, or with a true sense of the myths embedded in the lost worlds of childhood, as in M. I. Murray's *Witwater se Mense: Witwater's People*, 1974); more recently, much of this work has become informed by an awareness of the intrusion of evil and violence within this precarious little paradise. This certainly happens in several stories written by George Weideman, Pirow Bekker, Hennie Aucamp, John Miles, Henriette Grové and others. And perhaps even the grimly delightful 'magic realism' in the clown stories by Fransi Phillips reflects something of a child's dream world invaded by a sense of destruction and of doom.

In making the selection for the 'Afrikaans' section, nothing but fiction has been considered; and for obvious reasons fragments from longer works have been restricted to a minimum, in favour of short stories which provide a rounded-off reading experience and also makes it possible to include more texts. Although some of the most important recent writing in Afrikaans has been in the form of poetry, it has been decided to exclude this category altogether because of the problems inherent in the translation of verse. And as extracts from plays are seldom satisfactory, this category, too, has been excluded a priori, even if it meant depriving the volume of major contributions by a new generation of 'Coloured' writers using Afrikaans as their medium (Peter Snyders, Melvyn Whitebooi, etc.).

In only one case could permission for the inclusion of a text not be obtained – a story from Breyten Breytenbach's *Mouroir* – because the author believes it requires the context of its original volume fully to be appreciated. But this exclusion should remind the reader that, as in the case of the 'English' section of this volume, a whole group of important and stimulating writers had to be omitted purely for reasons of space. And to the eighteen names of those authors included in the volume it would not be difficult to add another eighteen which would serve as equally significant place-names on a map of contemporary Afrikaans fiction.

14

Because any reader of South African writing must contend with the effects of censorship – not only the prohibition of the publication or distribution within the Republic of specified works, but the banning of the entire written production of specified individuals – we must place it on record that we agreed at the commencement of the project that we would proceed as if the apparatus of censorship did not exist. If the consequence of that decision was to be that our book would be prohibited in South Africa, we would live with that consequence. Banned works, and the works of banned writers, were therefore considered on the same basis as any other writings.

Primary responsibility for the English-language selections has been undertaken by J. M. Coetzee; for the Afrikaans selections, by André Brink.

André Brink
J. M. Coetzee
October 1985

Postscript Since this Introduction was written, the deaths have occurred of Alex la Guma and Bessie Head.

PART ONE

NADINE GORDIMER

A Lion on the Freeway

Open up!
Open up!
What hammered on the door of sleep?
Who's that?

Anyone who lives within a mile of the zoo hears lions on summer nights. A tourist could be fooled. Africa already; at last; even though he went to bed in yet another metropole.

Just before light, when it's supposed to be darkest, the body's at its lowest ebb and in the hospital on the hill old people die – the night opens, a Black Hole between stars, and from it comes a deep panting. Very distant and at once very close, right in the ear, for the sound of breath is always intimate. It grows and grows, deeper, faster, more rasping, until a great groan, a rising groan lifts out of the curved bars of the cage and hangs above the whole city –

And then drops back, sinks away, becomes panting again.

Wait for it; it will fall so quiet, hardly more than a faint roughness snagging the air in the car's chambers. Just when it seems to have sunk between strophe and antistrophe, a breath is taken and it gasps once; pauses, sustaining the night as a singer holds a note. And begins once more. The panting reaches up up up down down down to the awe-ful groan –

Open up!
Open up!
Open your legs.

In the geriatric wards where lights are burning they take the tubes out of noses and the saline-drip needles out of arms

19

and draw the sheets to cover faces. I pull the sheet over my head. I can smell my own breath caught there. It's very late; it's much too early to be awake. Sometimes the rubber tyres of the milk truck rolled over our sleep. You turned . . .

Roar is not the word. Children learn not to hear for themselves, doing exercises in the selection of verbs at primary school: 'Complete these sentences: The cat ...s The dog ...s The lion ...s.' Whoever decided that had never listened to the real thing. The verb is onomatopoeically incorrect just as the heraldic beasts drawn by thirteenth- and fourteenth-century engravers at second hand from the observations of early explorers are anatomically wrong. Roar is not the word for the sound of great chaps sucking in and out the small hours.

The zoo lions do not utter during the day. They yawn; wait for their ready-slaughtered kill to be tossed at them; keep their unused claws sheathed in huge harmless pads on which top-heavy, untidy heads rest (the visualized lion is always a maned male), gazing through lid-slats with what zoo visitors think of in sentimental prurience as yearning.

Or once we were near the Baltic and the leviathan hooted from the night fog at sea. But would I dare to open my mouth now? Could I trust my breath to be sweet, these stale nights?

It's only on warm summer nights that the lions are restless. What they're seeing when they gaze during the day is nothing, their eyes are open but they don't see us – you can tell that when the lens of the pupil suddenly shutters at the close swoop of one of the popcorn-begging pigeons through the bars of the cage. Otherwise the eye remains blank, registering nothing. The lions were born in the zoo (for a few brief weeks the cubs are on show to the public, children may hold them in their arms). They know nothing but the zoo; they are not expressing our yearnings. It's only on certain nights that their muscles flex and they begin to pant, their flanks heave as if they had been running through the dark night while other creatures shrank from their path, their jaws hang tense and wet as saliva flows as if in response to a scent of prey, at last they heave up their too-big heads, heavy, heavy heads, and out it comes. Out over the suburbs. A dreadful straining of the bowels to deliver itself: a groan that hangs above the houses in a low-lying cloud of smog and anguish.

O Jack, O Jack, O Jack, oh – I heard it once through a hotel wall. Was alone and listened. Covers drawn over my head and knees drawn up to my fists. Eyes strained wide open. Sleep again! – my command. *Sleep again*.

It must be because of the new freeway that they are not heard so often lately. It passes its five-lane lasso close by, drawing in the valley between the zoo and the houses on the ridge. There is traffic there very late, too early. Trucks. Tankers, getting a start before daylight. The rising spray of rubber-spinning friction on tarmac is part of the quality of city silence; after a time you don't hear much beyond it. But sometimes – perhaps it's because of a breeze. Even on a still summer night there must be some sort of breeze opening up towards morning. Not enough to stir the curtains, a current of air has brought, small, clear and distant, right into the ear, the sound of panting.

Or perhaps the neat whisky after dinner. The rule is don't drink after dinner. A metabolic switch trips in the brain: open up.

Who's that?

A truck of potatoes going through traffic lights quaked us sixteen flights up.

Slack with sleep, I was impaled in the early hours. You grew like a tree and lifted the pavements; everything rose, cracked, and split free.

Who's that?

Or something read in the paper... Yes. Last night – this night – in the City Late, front page, there were the black strikers in the streets, dockers with sticks and knobkerries. A thick prancing black centipede with thousands of waving legs advancing. The panting grows louder, it could be in the garden or under the window; there comes that pause, that slump of breath. Wait for it: waiting for it. Prance, advance, over the carefully tended please keep off the grass. They went all through a city not far from this one, their steps are so rhythmical, waving sticks (no spears any more, no guns yet); they can cover any distance, in time. Shops and houses closed against them while they passed. And the cry that came from them as they approached – that groan straining, the rut of freedom bending the bars of the cage, he's delivered himself of it, it's as close as if he's out on the freeway now, bewildered, finding his way, turning his splendid head at last to claim what he's never seen, the country where he's king.

JEREMY CRONIN

Walking on Air

Prologue

In the prison workshop, also known as the seminar room;

In the seminar room, sawdust up the nose, feet in plane shavings, old jam tins on racks, a dropped plank, planks, a stack of mason's floats waiting assembly, Warder von Loggerenberg sitting in the corner,

In the prison workshop, also and otherwise named, where work is done by enforced dosage, between political discussion, theoretical discussion, tactical discussion, bemoaning of life without women, sawdust up the nose, while raging at bench 4, for a week long, a discussion raging, above the hum of the exhaust fans, on how to distinguish the concept 'Productive' from the concept . . . 'Unproductive Labour';

In the prison workshop, then, over the months, over the screech of the grindstone, I'm asking John Matthews about his life and times, as I crank the handle, he's sharpening a plane blade, holding it up in the light to check on its bevel, dipping the blade to cool in a tin of water, then back to the grindstone, sparks fly: 'I work for myself' – he says – 'not for the boere';[1]

In the prison workshop, with John Matthews making contraband goeters,[2] boxes, ashtrays, smokkel[3] salt cellars of, oh, delicate dovetailings;

Over the months, then, in the prison workshop, I'm asking John Matthews, while he works intently, he likes manual work, he likes the feel of woodgrain, he doesn't like talking

---

1 *boere* warders   2 *goeters* things   3 *smokkel* contraband

23

too much, the making and fixing of things he likes, he
likes, agh no, hayikona,[4] slap-bang-bang, work for the
jailers;

In the prison workshop, then, I ask John Matthews, was he
present on the two days of Kliptown . . . 1955? . . . when
the People's Congress adopted the Freedom Charter?

Actually

No he wasn't

He was there the day before, he built the platform

In the prison workshop, then, over the hum of exhaust fans,
between the knocking in of nails, the concept 'Productive',
the concept 'Unproductive Labour', feet in plane shavings.
John Matthews speaks by snatches, the making and fixing
of things he likes, though much, never, much you won't
catch him speaking;

But here, pieced together, here from many months, from the
prison workshop

Here is one comrade's story.

Born to Bez Valley, Joburg
into the last of his jail term
stooped now he has grown

In this undernourished frame
that dates back
to those first years of his life.

He was nine
when his father came
blacklisted home

From the 1922
Rand Revolt,
and there with a makeshift

---

4 *hayikona* no

Forge in their back yard
a never again to be employed
father passed on to his son

A lifelong
love for the making
and fixing of things.

From Bez Valley it was,
veiled like a bride in fine
mine-dump dust

He went out
to whom it may concern
comma

A dependable lad
comma
his spelling is good.

At fifteen he became
office boy at Katzenellenbogen's
cnr. von Wielligh

And President streets
where he earned: £1 a week,
where he learned:

   – Good spelling doesn't always count.
   – The GPO telegram charge is reckoned per word.
   – A word is 15 letters max.
   – You have to drop ONE *l* from Katzenellenbogen Inc or
                        HEAR ME BOY?! nex' time
                        YOU'S gonna pay extra one word
                        charge your bliksem[5] self.

And the recession came
but he got a book-keeping job
with Kobe Silk

On the same block
   – John Edward
Matthews

---

5 *bliksem* swear-word

Mondays to Fridays
on that same block
for 37 unbroken years until

The security police
picked him up . . . But first
way back to the Thirties.

WEEKENDS IN THE THIRTIES:
church and picnics
by Zoo Lake.

And later, deedle-deedle
– Dulcie, heel-toe,
his future wife

Whom he courted with
(he can still do it)
diddle-diddle: the cake-walk

And always
on Sundays it was
church and church.

And then to Kobe Silk
there came
a new clerk

Myer Chames by name
a short little bugger who talked
Economics at lunch-break

And Myer Chames talked
of all hitherto existing societies,
the history of freeman

And slave, lord, serf,
guildmaster, journeyman,
bourgeois, proletarian and

In a word
John Matthews stopped
going to church.

Walking on Air

His name got inscribed
inside
of a red party card.

He'd sell Inkululekos[6] down by
Jeppestown
Friday nights

While the bourgeois press wrote
RUSSIA HAS GONE SOFT ON HITLER
He learnt to fix duplicators and typewriters.

He was still selling
Inkululekos in 1943
when even the bourgeois press wrote

RED ARMY HAS BROKEN
BROKEN
THE BACK OF HITLER

In the year 1943 – born
to Dulcie and John
a daughter

Their first child
first of seven.
And now

Into the last months
of his 15 years
prison term

At nights in his cell
he peeps down at his face
in a mirror

In a mirror held low, about
belly-height,
wondering how he'll seem

To his grandchildren
from down there
next year when he comes out.

---

6 *Inkululeko* Freedom

Jeremy Cronin

But that's later . . . back
to 1950
The Suppression of Communism Act

Membership becomes a punishable crime.
But laws only
postpone matters – somewhat.

There were still duplicators to fix
and typewriters to mend
through the 50s

Passive Resistance, the Congress Alliance, Defiance Campaign,
    Pass Burnings, Bus Boycott, Potato Boycott, the Women's
    March, the Treason Trial, the Freedom Charter, until

Until 1960: the massacre
        Sharpeville
            and Langa.

And people said: 'Enough,
                our patience, it has limits' . . . and so
it was no longer just typewriters and duplicators to mend.
A man would come to the backyard and whisper: 30 ignitors.
And John Matthews would make 30, to be delivered to X.
And a man would come in the dead of night
These need storing comrade, some things wrapped in water-
    proof cloth.
                TERRORISTS BOMB POWERLINES
He would read in the bourgeois press, or
                MIDNIGHT PASS OFFICE BLAST
He'd sigh a small sigh
– Hadn't been sure
Those damned ignitors would work.

Finally.
1964.
After a quarter century in the struggle

A security police swoop
and John Matthews was one
among several detained.

Walking on Air

White and 52
so they treated him nice.
They only made him stand

On two bricks
for three days
and three nights and

When he asked to go to the lavatory
they said:
        Shit in your pants.

But the State needed witnesses
So they changed their tune.
Tried sweet-talking him round.
Think of your career
      (that didn't work)
Think of the shame of going to jail
      (that thought only
      filled him with pride)
You really want kaffirs to rule?
      (like you said)
Think of your wife
      (Dulcie. Dulcie.
      7 kids. Dulcie.
      She's not political at all).

And there they had him.
On that score he was worried, it's true.
And they promised him freedom.
And they pressed him for weeks on end
Until finally he said:

Okay, agreed.

– But first I must speak with my wife.

Barely an hour it took them to find
and rush Dulcie Matthews
out to Pretoria Jail.

Then looking nice, because they let him shave, let him comb
his hair, looking nice then, chaperoned by smiling, matri-
monial policemen, shaven and combed, John Matthews got

led out to his wife. and holding her hand, they let him hold
    her hand, he said
– Do you know why they've brought you?
And she said
– I do.
And he said
– Dulcie, I will never betray my comrades.
And with a frog in her throat she replied
– I'm behind you. One hundred per cent.

So back they hauled John Matthews then and there,
back to the cells,
that was that, then, but
all the way down the passage
toe-heel, heel-toe, diddle-diddle
ONE HUNDRED PER CENT
I mean, he was high
off the ground man.

He was walking on air.

MODIKWE DIKOBE

Episodes in the Rural Areas

1

'Baas I want to get married.'
'What do you want me to do for you?'
'To help me with eight head of cattle.'
'How will you pay back?'
'I shall work for you until I have recovered their price.'
'All right Jan, I shall advance you eight cattle. Piet will play father for you. Piet see that you get me a receipt. Nothing else must be written on the receipt except eight head of cattle.'

Piet heads the bogadi[1] to Jan's parents-in-law. Mary, Jan's bride, accompanies him. She's immediately engaged for domestic chores. Jan is on outdoor duties. During the day Captain Smythe has sexual intercourse with Mary. Jan is told by others who had noticed the boss's misdeeds. Jan deserts the farm in the evening with his wife. Capt Smythe reports him to the district magistrate. He appears in court for desertion. He is asked to plead.
'Mokolo[2] sleeps with my wife.'
The magistrate is astounded.
'What!'
'Yes baas, Mokolo sleeps with my wife.'
'Did you not promise to work for him until you've recovered the price of eight head of cattle you paid for bogadi?'
'Yes, but he sleeps with my wife.' The magistrate remained adamant.
'You must go back and work for him.'
'Haaikona[3] baas, he sleeps with my wife.'

---

1 bogadi dowry   **2** Mokolo master   **3** Haaikona no

31

2

On a farm in Rust De Winter are squatters working on option for a farmer. Mr Mackay has a son primed for farming duties. The only children nearby are squatters' ones.

Mr Mackay plays with them. On a certain day one of the squatters obediently greets Mr Mackay.

'Baas, I want to talk to you.'

'What is it about, Piet?'

'Young baas has spoilt my daughter.'

'What! My son spoilt your daughter? Do you mean he has got your daughter pregnant?'

'Yes, baas. She is in her third month. She says the young baas got her like that.'

'Look, Piet. Your kaffir children have been coming here. Do you think a bull will leave a bitch if it exposes itself. It is your daughter that has spoilt my son. Get out of this place.'

3

'Hans, my ox has disappeared. Do you perhaps know who has stolen it?'

'No, baas.'

'Have you perhaps sold it as yours by mistake?'

'I sold no ox, baas.'

'What about the one slaughtered for your niece's wedding?'

'I have not been to the wedding.'

'You're a bad uncle not to attend your niece's wedding.'

Hans remains silent.

'I am attending the wedding this afternoon. Will you come with me?'

Hans drops his head.

Mr Post leaves without Hans. He squats at a beer-drinking group. He asks to see the skin of the slaughtered beast.

'I buy skins,' he tells the father of the home.

'The skin is for the uncle of my daughter,' he is reminded.

'All right, I will take it home for him.'

Mr Post has it loaded on a horse-cart.

'Hans' he calls out, 'I've brought your skin. Come and see it.'

Hans comes, his hands folded; avoiding to look at the skin.

'Hans don't worry. I won't call the police for you. Go and

fetch sixteen of your oxen. I shall choose one to replace mine.'

The sixteen oxen are driven to Mr Post.

'All right Hans. Thank you. All these sixteen replace mine. You and I are old friends. We don't want police intervention.'

4

Geelbooi and Thomas arrive on a farm late in the afternoon. Thomas is neatly dressed. He looks sophisticated. He seems to be following the farmer as he tells Geelbooi that the sale of livestock is tomorrow. Geelbooi now and then nods foolishly. 'Yaa, baas, yaa, baas,' he keeps on repeating.

The trouble comes when the farmer asks: 'Waar vanaf kom julle?' ['Where do you come from?']

'Skilpadfontein,' replies Thomas.

'Wat! Nie "Skilpadfontein baas" nie?' ['What! Not "Skilpadfontein, baas"?']

Geelbooi is shown a hut for night shelter.

'Maar nie vir daardie Engelse kaffir nie.' ['But not for that English kaffir.']

5

Thomas has not yet received a lesson that this is the Platteland.

'Kaffirs' are not allowed just to speak without respect to a White person. He enters a novelty shop and examines authors' names on the books.

'Hoekom vra jy nie wat jy soek nie?' ['Why don't you ask what you want?']

'Sorry, madam. I have already found one that I want.'

'Ja! Jy praat nog Engels.' ['So! You speak English.']

'A bit of Afrikaans, too, nooi.'

'Wat is jy?' ['What are you?']

'An author.'

The shop owner changes to English.

'I would like to see what you've written.'

A month later Thomas arrives with the book he has written.

'Can I have it for reading?'

The next following month, Thomas calls again.

'Your book is down-to-earth. You should add to what happened in the later life of your heroine. She is such a marvellous girl to have braved shame by not discarding her baby.'

MOTSHILE WA NTHODI

South African Dialogue

Morning Baas,
Baas,
Baas Kleinbaas[1] says,
I must come and tell
Baas that,
Baas Ben's Baasboy[2] says,
Baas Ben want to see
Baas Kleinbaas if
Baas don't use
Baas Kleinbaas,
Baas.

Tell
Baas Kleinbaas that,
Baas says,
Baas Kleinbaas must tell
Baas Ben's Baasboy that,
Baas Ben's Baasboy must tell
Baas Ben that,
Baas says,
If Baas Ben want to see
Baas Kleinbaas,
Baas Ben must come and see
Baas Kleinbaas here.

Thank you
Baas.
I'll tell
Baas Kleinbaas that,

1 *Kleinbaas* young master   2 *baasboy* boss-boy

35

Baas says,
Baas Kleinbaas must tell
Baas Ben's Baasboy that,
Baas Ben's Baasboy must tell
Baas Ben that,
Baas says,
If Baas Ben want to see
Baas Kleinbaas,
Baas Ben must come and see
Baas Kleinbaas here,
Baas.
Goodbye Baas.

Baas Kleinbaas,
Baas says,
I must come and tell
Baas Kleinbaas that,
Baas Kleinbaas must tell
Baas Ben's Baasboy that,
Baas Ben's Baasboy must tell
Baas Ben that,
Baas says,
If Baas Ben want to see
Baas Kleinbaas,
Baas Ben must come and see
Baas Kleinbaas here,
Baas Kleinbaas.

Baasboy,
Tell Baas Ben that,
Baas Kleinbaas says,
Baas says,
If Baas Ben want to see me
(Kleinbaas)
Baas Ben must come and
See me (Kleinbaas) here.

Thank you
Baas Kleinbaas,
I'll tell

Baas Ben that,
Baas Kleinbaas says,
Baas says,
If Baas Ben want to see
Baas Kleinbaas,
Baas Ben must come and see
Baas Kleinbaas here,
Baas Kleinbaas.
Goodbye
Baas Kleinbaas.

Baas Ben,
Baas Kleinbaas says,
I must come and tell
Baas Ben that,
Baas says,
If Baas Ben want to see
Baas Kleinbaas,
Baas Ben must come and see
Baas Kleinbaas there,
Baas Ben.
Baas Ben,
Baas Be-ne . . .
Baas Ben
Goodbye
Baas Ben.

GCINA MHLOPE

Nokulunga's Wedding

Mount Frere was one of the worst places for a woman to live. A woman had to marry whoever had enough money for lobola[1] and that was that. Nokulunga was one of many such victims whose parents wholeheartedly agreed to their victimization. She became wife to Xolani Mayeza.

By the time Nokulunga was sixteen years old she was already looking her best. One day a number of young men came to the river where she and her friends used to fetch water. The men were strangers. As the girls came to the river, one of the men jumped very high and cried in a high-pitched voice.

'Hayi, hayi, hayi!
Bri – bri mntanam uyagula!'

He came walking in style towards the girls and asked for water. After drinking he thanked them, went back to his friends and they left. This was not a new thing to Nokulunga and her friends, but the different clothes and style of walking left them with mixed feelings. Some were very impressed by the strangers but Nokulunga was not. She suspected they were up to something but decided not worry about people she did not know. The girls lifted their water pots on to their heads and went home.

In late February the same strange men were seen at the river, but their number had doubled. The day was very hot but they were dressed in heavy overcoats. Nokulunga did not see them until she and her friends were near the river. The girls were happily arguing about something and did not recognize the men as the same ones they had seen before. Only when the same man who had asked for water came up

---

1 *lobola* dowry

to them again did they realize who the strangers were. Nokulunga began to feel uneasy.

He drank all his water slowly this time, then he asked Nokulunga if he could take her home with him for the night. She was annoyed, and filled her water pot, balanced it on her head and told the others she had to hurry home. One of her friends did the same and was ready to go with Nokulunga when the other men came and barred their way.

Things began to happen very fast. They took Nokulunga's water pot and broke it on a rock. Men wrapped Nokulunga in big overcoats before she could scream. They slung the bundle on to their shoulders.

The other girls helplessly looked on as the men set off. The men chanted a traditional wedding song as they quickly climbed the hillside, while many villagers watched.

Nokulunga twisted round, trying to breathe. She had witnessed girls being taken before. She thought of the many people in the neighbourhood who seemed to love her. They couldn't love her if they could let strangers go away with her without putting up a fight. She felt betrayed and lost. She thought of what she had heard about such marriages. She knew her mother would not mind, as long as the man had enough lobola.

The journey was long and she was very hot inside the big coats. Her body felt so heavy, but the rhythm of her carriers went on and on . . . her lover Vuyo was going back to Germiston to work. He had promised her that he would be away for seven months then he would be back to marry her. She had been so happy.

Her carriers were walking down a very steep and uneven path. Soon she heard people talking and dogs barking. She was put down and the bundle was unwrapped. A lot of people were looking to see what the newcomer looked like. She was clumsily helped to her feet and stood there stupidly for viewing. She wanted to pee. For a while no one said anything, they all stood there with different expressions on their faces. The children of the house came in to join the viewing one by one and the small hut was nearly full.

She was in Xolani, her 'husband's', room. She was soon left alone with him for the night. She sat down calmly, giving no

39

indication that she was going to sleep at all. Xolani tried to chat with her but she was silent, so he got undressed and into the big bed on the floor. He coughed a few times, then uneasily invited her to join him. She sat silent. He was quiet for a while, then asked if she was going to sleep that night. No. For a long time she sat staring at him. She was watchful.

But Nokulunga was tired. She thought he was sleeping. Xolani suddenly lunged and grabbed her arm. His eyes were strange, she could not make out what was in them, anger or hatred or something else.

She struggled to free her arm, he suddenly let go and she fell. She quickly stood up, still watching him. He smiled and moved close to her. She backed off. It looked like a game, he following her slowly, she backing round and round the room. Each round they moved faster. Xolani decided he had had enough and grabbed her again. She was about to scream when he covered her mouth. She realized it was foolish to scream, it would call helpers for him.

She still stood a chance of winning if they were alone. He was struggling to undress her when Nokulunga went for his arm. She dug her teeth deep and tore a piece of flesh out. She spat. His arm went limp, he groaned and sat, gritting his teeth and holding his arm.

Nokulunga sat too, breathing heavily. He stood up quickly, cursing under his breath and kicked her as hard as he could. She whined with pain but did not stand up to defend herself.

Blood was dripping from Xolani's arm and he softly ordered her to tear a piece of sheet to tie above the bite. She did it, then wiped blood from the floor. Xolani got under the bed-covers in silence. Nokulunga pulled her clothes together. She did not dare to fall asleep. Whether Xolani slept or not, only he knows. The pain of his arm did not make things easier for him.

Day came. Xolani left, and Nokulunga was given a plate of food and locked in the room. She had just started eating when she heard people talking outside. It sounded like a lot of men. They went into the hut next to the one she was in and came out talking even louder. They moved away and she gave up listening and ate her food, soft porridge.

The men sat next to the big cattle-kraal. Xolani was there,

his father Malunga and his eldest brother Diniso. The rest
were uncles and other family members. They were slowly
drinking their beer. They were all very angry with Xolani.
Malunga was too angry to think straight. He looked at his son
with contempt, kept balling his hands into fists.

No one said anything. They stole quick glances at Malunga
and their eyes went back to stare at the ground. Xolani shifted
uneasily. He was holding his hurt arm carefully, his uncle
had tended to it but the pain was still there. His father sucked
at his pipe, knocked it out on the piece of wood next to him,
then spat between his teeth. The saliva jumped a long way
into the kraal and they all watched it.

'Xolani!' Malunga called to his son softly and angrily.

'Yes father,' Xolani replied without looking up.

'What are you telling us, are you telling us that you spent
all night with that girl and failed to sleep with her?'

'Father, I . . . I . . .'

'Yes, you failed to be a man with that girl in that hut. That
is the kind of man you have grown into, unable to sleep with
a woman the way a man should.'

Silence followed. No one dared to look at Malunga. He
busied himself refilling his pipe as if he was alone. After
lighting it he looked at the other men.

'Diniso, are you listening with me to what your brother is
telling us? Tell us more, Xolani, what else did she do to you,
my little boy? Did she kick you on the chest too, tell me,
father's little son?' He laughed harshly.

An old man interrupted. 'Mocking and laughing at the fool
will not solve our problem. So please, everyone think of the
next step from here. The Mjakuja people are looking for their
daughter. Something must be done fast.' He was out of
breath when he finished. The old man was Malunga's father
from another house.

The problem was that no word had been sent to Nokulunga's family to tell them of her whereabouts. Thirteen cattle
and a well-fed horse were ready to be taken to the family,
along with a goat which was called imvulamlomo, mouth
opener.

The sun was about to set. Nokulunga watched it for a long
time. She was very quiet. She stared at the red orange shape

as it went down into the unknown side of the mountain.

By the time the colours faded she was still looking at the same spot but her eyes were taking a look at her future. She had not escaped that day. She felt weak and miserable. A group of boys sat all day on the nearby hill watching her so that she did not try running away. She was there to stay.

She did not know how long she stood there behind the hut. She only came to when she heard a little girl laughing next to her. The girl told her that people had gone out to look for her because they all thought she had managed to get away while the boys were playing. She went back into the house. Her mother-in-law and the other women also laughed when the little girl said she'd found Nokulunga standing behind the hut. More boys were sent to tell the pursuers that Nokulunga was safe at home.

She hated the long dress and doek she had been given to wear, they were too big for her and the material still had the hard starch on it. The people who had gone out to look for her came back laughing and teasing each other about how stupid they had been to run so fast without even checking behind the house first.

Nokulunga was trembling as it grew dark. She knew things would not be as easy as they had been the night before. She knew the family would take further steps although she did not know exactly what would happen.

She was in her husband's room waiting for him to come in. The hut suddenly looked so small she felt it move to enclose her in a painful death. She held her arms across her chest, gripping her shoulders so tight they ached.

The door opened and a number of men about her husband's age came in quietly. They closed the door behind them. She watched Xolani undress as if he did not want to. His arm did not look better as he stood there in the light of the low-burning paraffin lamp. She started to cry.

She was held and undressed. Her face was wet with sweat and tears and she wanted to go and pee. The men laughed a little.

One of them smiled teasingly at her and ordered her to lie down on the bed. She cried uncontrollably when she saw the look on Xolani's face. He stood there with eyes wide open as if he was walking in dreamland, his face had the expression of a lost and helpless boy. Was that the man she was supposed to look upon as a husband? How was he ever to defend her against anything or anyone?

Hands pulled her up and her streaming eyes did not see the man who shouted to her that she should lie like a woman. She wiped her eyes and saw Xolani approaching her.

She jumped and pushed him away, grabbed at her clothes. The group of men was on her like a mob. They roughly pulled her back on to the bed and Xolani was placed on top of her. Her legs were each pulled by a man. Others held her arms.

Men were cheering and clapping hands while Xolani jumped high, now enjoying the rape. One man was saying that he had had enough of holding the leg and wanted a share for his work. Things were said too about her bloody thighs and she heard roars of laughter before she fainted.

'The bride is ours
The bride is ours
Mother will never go to sleep
without food
without food

'The bride is ours
The bride is ours
Father will never need for beer
will never want for beer . . .'

The young men were singing near the kraal. Girls giggled as they sang and did Xhosa dances. Soon they would be expected to dance at Xolani's wedding. They were trying new hairstyles so each would look her best. The young men too were worried about how they would look. Some of them were hoping for new relationships with the girls of Gudlintaba. That place was known for the good-looking girls with their beautiful voices. Others knew too that some relationships would break as a result of that wedding. Everyone knew the day was in their hands, whether fighting or laughter ended the day.

Women prepared beer and took turns going to the river for water, happy and light-footed in the way they walked. Time and again a woman would run from hut to hut calling at the top of her voice, ululating joyfully:

'Lilililili . . . lili . . . lili . . . liiiiii!

To give birth is to stretch your bones!

What do you say, woman who never gave birth?'

Nokulunga spent most of the time inside the house with one of her friends and her mother's sister tending to her face. They had a mixture of eggs and tree barks as part of the concoction. All day long her face was crusted with thick liquids supposed to be good for her wedding complexion. Time and again her mother's sister would sit down and tell her how to behave now that she was a woman. How she hated the subject. She wished days would simply go by without her noticing them.

'Ingwe iyawavula amathambo 'mqolo.

The leopard opens the back bones.'

She heard the girls happily singing outside. She hated the bloody song. The only thing they all seemed to care about was the food they were going to have on that day she never wanted to come. Many times she would find herself sitting there with her masked face looking out of the tiny window. She hated Xolani and his name. She felt that he was given that name because he would always do things to hurt people, then he would keep on apologizing and explaining. Xolani means 'please forgive'.

The day came. Nokulunga walked slowly by Xolani's side with lots of singing and laughing and ululating and clapping of hands around her. She did not smile, when she tried only tears came rolling down to make her ashamed.

It was the day of his life for Xolani, such a beautiful wife and such a big wedding. He was smiling and squeezing her hand when Nokulunga saw Vuyo. He was looking at Xolani with loathing, his fists very tight and his lips so hard. She pulled her hand from Xolani's and took a few steps. She began to cry. Xolani went to her and tried to comfort her. A lot of people saw this, they stood watching and sympathizing and wondering . . .

Months passed. Nokulunga was sitting by the fire, in her arms a five-day-old baby boy was sleeping so peacefully she smiled. Her father-in-law had named it Vuyo. How thankful she had been to hear that, she would always remember the old Vuyo she had loved.

Nokulunga now accepted that Xolani was her lifetime partner and there was nothing she could do about it. Once she saw Vuyo in town and they had kissed. It had been clear to them that since she was already pregnant, she was Xolani's wife, and Vuyo knew he would have to pay a lot of cattle if he took Nokulunga with the unborn baby. There was nothing to be done.

AHMED ESSOP

Dolly

'If any of you rich Indian bastards try to joll[1] my wife I will put a knife into your guts. What you know is to show off, talk big, ride in your big cars . . .'

That was Dolly (Dooly) speaking in one of his violent, dangerous moods to bearded Mr Darsot, the spice and grain merchant. Mr Darsot dreaded meeting Dolly in the street. Yet when Dolly's scurrilities against Indians exploded, he could hardly move away, fearing a loss of dignity in ignominious retreat. Nor could he utter a word in defence, fearing to rouse Dolly's temper further. Trapped by his self-esteem and feebleness, he would listen to Dolly's unsavoury oratory:

'You Indian dogs, there were not enough bitches in India so you came to South Africa. Now you look for our wives. You lock your wives up and want to joll ours. Bring your wife here. I will show you, you Indian bastard . . .'

Dolly would go on in this vein until he tired, or one of his friends pulled him away. Mr Darsot, displaying a tepid smile in moral victory, would hurry to seek refuge in his mansion, happy in the knowledge that he was physically unscathed.

Dolly was a small very dark man, athletic and wiry in build, and extraordinarily tough. I once saw two burly policemen vainly trying to pull him away from a railing to which he clung – and he only released his grip when one of them crushed his fingers with a brick. His black hair was always liberally oiled to combat its intractability. He was very ugly. His first wife had run away, unable to bear his inordinate jealousy and maniacal rages. His second wife Myrtle received a regular beating. There were times when he beat her so savagely that the police had to be called. At other times she

---

1 *joll* fuck

was forced to go out with him and point out some lover (Myrtle felt that if her husband was jealous he might as well be justifiably jealous) somewhere in Fordsburg or Vrededorp. As they walked Dolly uttered menacing howls like some predacious animal. What ensued one would know after his return. If his revenge had been slaked he would shout coarsely: 'Indian swine, busted his guts, showed him what Dolly is made of, the bastard!' If thwarted, he would scream obscenities at everyone in the street and bang his fists against several doors, terrifying the people within.

Myrtle was a blowzy woman, tall, frizzy-haired, with thrusting buttocks. She believed in the attractiveness of her body and she flaunted it: one would see her sitting on a balustrade, her legs daringly outstretched; or bending over a tap in the yard, her raised skirt revealing the ample flesh of her legs; or dancing, her thighs and mons Veneris embalmed in tight-fitting slacks. She had two voices: an original voice, coarse and ebulliently vulgar, which one heard during bouts of altercation with her husband, or when she reviled some woman who dared to look at her 'as though I have taken your husband's you-know-what!' Her other voice was cloyingly euphonious, imitative of some woman's heard over the radio: 'Oh, you're a darling honey. You do look super today, don't you?' She was often abusively referred to by women as 'that Bushman bitch'.

One day Bibi arrived to board and lodge with Mrs Safi, the next-door neighbour of the Dollys. She caused a sensation the day she arrived. She was the most beautiful woman to set foot in our suburb. Black-haired and blue-eyed (she was the offspring of an Indian father and a Dutch mother) with the complexion like the white flower of the gardenia, her sylph-like beauty was at variance with the earthiness of our suburb.

Dolly was mesmerized by Bibi. He expressed his adoration to us in these terms: 'If any of you touch Bibi I will eat your livers.' One day she was hanging up some washing in the yard when she turned around and saw him. He was gazing at her in open-mouthed rapture from beside a tap, his dark face frothing with soap.

Dolly's behaviour underwent a transformation. He no longer

roamed the street Caliban-like (though he drank and smoked marijuana as usual), nor involved himself in turbulent feuds with his wife. The presence of Bibi seemed to work like alchemy in him – he was seized with a sense of shame.

And Myrtle who had once inspired so much jealousy in him (jealousy which to her was a testimony of love) and had weathered the storms of his sadistic rages, found herself cauterized by jealousy. She would scream uncouthly and accuse him of deceiving her with Bibi in a vain effort to trigger his natural turbulent response, but he remained placid. Her jealousy then found vent in threats against Bibi. She would speak coarsely, in the presence of other women: 'That half-caste bitch will not get away with it. Who does she think she is? Because she has a white skin and blue eyes she thinks she is someone great. One of these days I will get even with her.'

And she got 'even' with her. One day she waited for Bibi to arrive from work, grabbed her as she passed by her doorstep, and began assaulting her. Bibi screamed and various people rushed to her assistance. When I reached them Myrtle was in the grip of several strong hands. Bibi was cowering next to a wall, her clothes torn and her hair disarranged.

When Dolly came home someone told him of the assault on Bibi. He went next door. He saw her bruised cheek, her inflamed eye, her nail-scratched neck.

That day hideous screams reverberated through the streets as Dolly, in a rampant mood, took Myrtle into the house and turned on her with his fists.

The police were called, but tired of the feud between man and wife stood around looking bored. We waited in the street. At last Myrtle stopped howling.

Dolly unlocked the door and saw Bibi amongst us. He burst into wild laughter.

'Beauty! Beauty! Come inside. She will never touch you again.'

He took Bibi by the hand and we followed them into the house.

CHRISTOPHER VAN WYK

It is Sleepy in the 'Coloured' Townships

It is sleepy in the 'Coloured' townships.
The dust clogs in the rheum of every eye
The August winds blow into all the days
Children play in a gust of streets
or huddle in tired dens like a multi-humped camel.

It is sleepy in the 'Coloured' townships.
Wet washing semaphore, then don't
and the dirt is spiteful to the whiteness
A Volkswagen engine lies embalmed in grease and grime
(the mechanic has washed his hands and left)
but the car waits patient as rust.

It is sleepy in the 'Coloured' townships.
Heads bob around the stove of the sun
The sleepiness is a crust harder than
a tortoise's shell.

It is sleepy in the 'Coloured' townships.
A drunk sleeps lulled by meths
Children scratch sores – sleep
bitten by the tsetse flies of Soweto
of June 16
(Noordgesig lies on the fringes of Soweto).

It is sleepy in the 'Coloured' townships.
A pensioner in Coronation
lies dead for a week
before the stench of her corpse
attracts attention through keyholes
and windows.

In Detention

He fell from the ninth floor
He hanged himself
He slipped on a piece of soap while washing
He hanged himself
He slipped on a piece of soap while washing
He fell from the ninth floor
He hanged himself while washing
He slipped from the ninth floor
He hung from the ninth floor
He slipped on the ninth floor while washing
He fell from a piece of soap while slipping
He hung from the ninth floor
He washed from the ninth floor while slipping
He hung from a piece of soap while washing

MARIA THOLO

from Diary of Maria Tholo

Wednesday, 18 August 1976

What a miserable weekend. Nothing interesting. We didn't even go out Saturday evening. We went to church in the morning but no one would say a word about all that's happening because we have this informer, Jason, in our congregation. We know he's an informer because he's tried to get others to join up. In the afternoon we went to see the family of that boy I saw in hospital Thursday night but they already knew of his whereabouts.

I had quite a shock later. Arthur came to tell me that the schoolboy who was shot at Langa was one of the Mosi family, Xolile. I know his brother and his family well. Xolile was a student at Langa High. His mother is alone here as the father is somewhere in the country. They stay in one of those shacks in Elsies River. She can't get a house in Guguletu because her stay here is not legal. The funeral is on Saturday.

There are several stories of what happened. One person there said Xolile was armed with a short axe and charged an African policeman. It was an African who shot him. Others say he opened his shirt and just ran at them shouting, 'Well, if you have got my friend, take me too.' So they shot him at point-blank range because one of the girls behind him was hit by the same bullet. Who knows? I suppose they felt he was asking for it.

The children are really organized now. They meet every day. Langa High is the gathering point. The newspapers are saying that school attendance is up but that is nonsense. These children are not attending classes. They are only there for the meetings to decide what action to take next. I hear they spent Sunday going from church to church collecting for bail and for the funerals of the Mosi boy and another one who went to Intshinga. At the Langa Baptist church alone they got R26.

51

Each school held a collection and the principals handed it on to the bereaved families. Then, Sunday, the children divided themselves into two groups. One went to the Methodist church until after the collection. Reverend X. was outside when they left and he overheard one say, 'Right, comrades. We are going to the Anglicans this afternoon.' So another piped up, 'No, let's go to the Catholic church.' The first one replied, 'No, these Roman Catholics are very stingy with their communion. They stick to their special members but in the Anglican church we are all going to get communion. Let's go there.' So that's where they went and sure enough they all got communion. And the Anglicans were also distributing bread because there are no bread vans coming into the township.

They went everywhere, these students, even as far as Silvertown. In all they've collected over R800. Can you imagine?

They are wearing their uniforms all week now, even on Sundays, because the police are denying that the Mosi boy was a student. They've decided the police must shoot them in their uniforms.

Sunday, 22 August

Yesterday was a day of funerals. The first one was that of the Mosi boy. Now because he was the first student to be killed in the riots the police were worried that there would be trouble at the funeral so they told Mrs Mosi that only very close relatives could attend, not more than twenty people. I hear that they threatened her that if she allowed a crowd she would be endorsed out of Cape Town because she is here illegally. I don't know why she is not living with the father. He is from Kingwilliamstown but he came here for the funeral.

Now with Africans twenty people is impossible. Who can decide who is a close relative? Why, when I got married to Gus he had to adopt my whole family. If you keep counting his people and her people and her sister's people and their people's people you'll never stop counting. Everybody who belongs to that clan or that totem belongs to the family.

The students insisted that they were going to be at the funeral even though the teachers had told them that the police had forbidden this. We heard this from Arthur. Because he knows I know the family he came to ask me what they must do about catering. He is a close friend of the older brother. I told him I'm sick of large funerals. You can't tell whether it's a wedding or a funeral, there is so much cooking and preparation. But seeing the mother was struggling on her own I thought we should make sandwiches and tea.

So even though I knew of the restriction on attendance, seeing that I was going to help with the catering I thought we should at least try and force our way to the ceremony.

The trouble was no one was sure when the funeral was due to take place. First we heard ten o'clock, then nine o'clock, then one and so on. The authorities kept on changing it. So instead of going to early morning service at church we went to the graveyard. As we turned the corner from Jungle Walk past the Langa High School I noticed that the school grounds were deserted. This meant something funny because that is where the children have been meeting and if they intended going to the funeral they must have been collecting some-where. Police were watching the stations and the bus term-inals to see that the children didn't gather together. Because they wear their uniforms they are easy to spot.

But the children were too clever for the riot squad. The girls put their mothers' overalls over their uniforms and the boys took off their ties and blazers and only when they were safely in Langa, away from the eyes of the police, did they strip and get into uniform. I don't know where they did it but as we turned the car into the road that runs straight to the grave-yard, we saw a whole crowd of children dressed in the uniforms of all four township high schools, and some of the higher primary ones as well.

They seemed to be in quite a hurry. I thought perhaps we were late and that the funeral had started already. Everyone along the road had come out of their houses to watch. Gus's cousin lives there and we saw her at her gate, still in her gown, as she's just had a baby. Her eyes were red and puffed from crying and we noticed all the people along the road were crying too. When she heard where we were going she just nodded her head and said, 'OK, sisi. I don't think you'll get there but anyway you go, you go.'

We parked and followed the students through the knots of curious people flanking the side of the road till we came in sight of the actual grave. You could see from this distance that there were very few people there, a handful. There was nobody at the gate, no sign of riot cars or police.

Out of nowhere they appeared. All you could see were camouflage uniforms charging for the gate. One policeman, dressed in proper light blue, appeared in front shouting, 'Stop, or we shoot.' I thought wow, they really are all armed. They had those big guns on slings and revolvers. We quickly slunk into one of the gates but stayed in the yard, watching.

The children didn't stop. One of the boys called out, 'They say they don't shoot school children. Let them prove it today.' The policemen crowded together to stop them entering the gate.

And then as if a switch had been pulled the girls started wailing. You know how Africans can scream. 'Wah, wah, wah. It's not a dog that's being buried. We want to see our comrade. We want to see our fellow student.' The people around took up the chorus and the next moment it was just pandemonium with everybody screaming 'Yes! Yes! Yes!' and then the teargas shot out. One minute Gus was screaming 'You can't shoot children. Let them go!' and the next he was diving away. I saw him dodging the canisters, off down the road.

Everyone was watching the canisters go up, watching to see where they fell and quick as anything the women around were organized. Some tore off their doeks, others had buckets of water. As the canisters fell they were doused with water. They pulled nappies, clothes off the lines, dipping them in water and throwing them to the children to cover their noses.

The boys had thrown a cordon around the girls, cautioning them to stand firm and sit out the gas fumes. I looked around just in time to see Gus driving off around the corner. He had dodged, dodged, disappeared and left me to myself. That's a fine husband for you, leaving me there in the lurch with all the teargas.

from Diary of Maria Tholo

The children were carrying a big wreath to put on the grave but there was no way to get through, so eventually they moved off slowly towards Langa High. I ran to where I'd seen the car disappearing. It was a couple of streets away. Gus says he left to protect the children. I know better.

Either way he was not having any more of Langa. He wouldn't even go to church. We drove straight out and back to Guguletu. There was still another funeral to go to. This one was of the boy who had gone to Nomsa's school. We didn't expect trouble because they had a permit to be in Cape Town and there were no restrictions on the number of people attending. I don't know why there was a difference, possibly because he was only a primary school boy.

There were no incidents. The police kept far away, just watched from a distance. The only funny thing was watching the change in the attitude of the adults to the children. There were well over eighty children present though the teachers had tried to restrict it to just the standard fives. Even the high-school children turned up in numbers. They hitch-hiked from Langa and collected together.

There was a tremendous moment of tension as we saw the horde of children approaching. By now they were the fear of the township. You could see everyone's eyes turn but they just came in quietly and the bigger men gave way for them.

Now at most African funerals everyone who wants to make a speech does so but the M.C. asked that because this was not an ordinary funeral he'd appreciate it if they would stick to the programme and just hear the appointed speakers.

He couldn't stop one old man from jumping up. 'I'm not in the programme,' he said, 'but I just want to say that I have learned something in my old age when my hair is turning grey. We have always said that Christianity is what is asked of us in the Bible. I have learned the truth from these children. I'm sure all the parents here will tell you that they can get nothing out of their children. They will not tell what the others have been saying. They are as one. They speak as one and they act together. Christians are supposed to be people who are united, who are brother and sister to each other. Whereas we turn around and gossip about each other, these children cry together, laugh together.

'We must learn a lesson from them. According to African custom this is not a boy lying here. This is a man because we say that a man shows that he is one by his deeds. Here lies a hero. He has died for you and me.' Before he could go on the M.C. jumped up. 'Please friends, can we just stick to the verse that is in front of you and not flounder.'

But the man had said his piece. At least one person stood up for the truth. When we went back to the house for refreshments it was the children who were given first preference. I never thought I'd see that. The graveyard was quite full. There must have been four or five riot deaths buried at once.

We heard about another death today. This Miss Gobile who teaches at Nomsa's school. Her brother had been missing since the first day of the riots and however many times they'd been to Tygerberg Hospital and the mortuary they'd never found him. (What happens is that they put all the unidentified bodies in one place and you have to search through them like a pile of old clothes to find yours.)

Well, at the Intshinga funeral yesterday someone told the mother that they had seen Christopher's body among the bodies at Tygerberg. This person had gone to look for her own son. So Miss Gobile and the mother went there and even though they were told at first there was no such person, they insisted and, sure enough, there was the corpse.

But someone said, 'No. That looks too fresh a thing.' So they investigated and finally were told he had died only yesterday morning. Imagine after searching and being put off for all that time, to miss him by only one day.

Tuesday, 24 August

Last night was my Tupperware party. I didn't want to cancel it because Angela would have been upset, but because of all the unrest I had a lot of difficulty making up my ten people. Quite a few let me down. In the end I got Shelley, Nomsa and Gus to buy things so that I could get the free gift. Gus's cousin, Agnes, came, together with her sister Noncebe. I hadn't invited Noncebe but Agnes brought her anyway. I suppose it was to keep her occupied since her shop was burned down. She had a fishery in the Langa complex. They lost a lot because they own all that machinery. They had a good stove for frying and very good refrigeration. And they thought they had almost finished paying their accounts and could start living. They weren't insured or anything.

Noncebe wouldn't know anything about something like that. She's very slow. The husband can even have a girlfriend in his car and she won't go and peep. She'll accept anything that the husband says without argument. A real country girl. But that fish shop had brought her out of herself a little so it was really a pity.

Ruth offered her sympathies. She was quite indignant about the senselessness of destroying African people's property. Someone else said it wasn't really African things because these shops, like our homes, belonged to the Board, not to us. But not everybody had their things insured so it's very casual to dismiss it like that.

There wasn't much time for talk because Angela was anxious to get selling. She's become very greedy with this Tupperware. She's out every night selling and her children are being neglected. She's also become quite a nuisance, always asking for lifts to these parties. But it's interesting to see how this selling has made her learn to talk, because she's always been a very quiet person.

Everyone bought something so I got my present. Ruth is having the next party but it won't be for some time. She is really worried about what is happening because of her boys. She's terrified that they will be picked up by the police if they are anywhere near the scene of any action. Or even that they will get excited and start to throw stones. So she's been locking them inside while she's at work.

6–14 September

It's difficult to describe or understand the kind of excitement everyone is feeling. There is danger around but you still want action all the time. I think that in Belfast they must be feeling the same thing. But not in Kampala. Even though you are not quite sure you will be coming home, you want something to happen. You don't like it to be too quiet.

Maria Tholo

It's as if people are looking forward to results and if it's quiet there can't be any results so they don't want things to stop. Once it touches *you*, you don't like it, like this stayaway, because then you lose your pay. But if *they* go on fighting, OK let them. I think this is the way everyone is feeling.

Everyone wants to know what's new, what's happening. We all enjoy talking about it. And when a different story comes out in the papers we hate it. 'Liars, they are trying to cover up,' you hear. What they are saying about Soweto must be the same thing, not the full story, just a half truth.

For instance they mention looting, and all they say is just that – 'Looting'. They weren't there. They just heard about it but not how extensive it was, or what exactly happened. No newspaper can describe the excitement of watching looting. You stand apart; you enjoy seeing the people take things. After all, let them have something free for a change. They don't have the money.

The owners are insured so they won't lose a thing. The minute it happens to someone from the township you don't like it because our people have got nothing anyway. But those delivery vans are insured so let the people have something free. You brush it off like that.

There was a butcher's van, a S.A.U.M. truck that was looted. Shelley alerted us. She was on watch. When we got outside we saw that someone had got into the van and was throwing the meat to anybody passing. 'Catch, catch,' he called.

It wasn't even as if he wanted it for himself. Whoever was passing took whatever was thrown and ran. There was one whole big sheep carcase. A man picked it up from the sand, dusted it off, put it over his shoulders and he ran. It was quite funny.

The lorry people just stood away from the van. There was nothing they could do. It's best not to resist but just stand back and watch. Most of the time you find the drivers are not injured. The youths stop the vans, say 'Get out,' and start taking things. Sometimes they wait for the driver to go into a shop and then they climb in.

But it wasn't nice when Nontshongwe's paraffin lorry was looted. I am really sorry about that because it was his own

lorry, not a company's, and there it is, completely burned
out. Not all the shops could afford to fetch their own paraffin
so he took drums to Caltex or wherever, filled them up and
sold them to the shopkeepers. I think he charged two rand
more than at the BP centre, something like that.

His lorry was on its way up 108 just between the Methodist
and the Seventh Day Adventist churches. Suddenly the
driver jumped out. There were two others in front of the lorry
with him and they also jumped and ran. A bunch of youths
got into the back. The next thing they were pushing the
drums on to the street. They rolled them down, calling,
'Anyone who wants, come and get' – the usual thing when
there is looting.

Even old people came to fetch paraffin. You just heard
'I-umboomboom!' and everyone came running, even some
mothers. Some people took whole 20-litre tins. They rolled
them down the street. Others used whatever containers they
had.

The police were there very quickly but by the time they
came the lorry was on fire. The people who had rolled the
drums home were the first to be caught. The police just
followed the paraffin trails and came back with the drums but
they didn't arrest the people who had taken them. The children disappeared when the police arrived.

I don't know what happened to the driver. He was
nowhere to be seen. No one could stop the fire so they just
pulled the van to one side so it didn't block the street. I didn't
see anyone come to collect the drums either. Earlier on a
crowd used to collect if they saw anything happening but not
any more. The police have become too ready to shoot.

Our school is really in the thick of things. We've been lucky
that the police have never chased youths in here or even
come in to see whether there are older children hiding. I
suppose this is why the older ones use this as a refuge when
the vans are passing. They can always say they came to fetch
their younger brothers or sisters. We ask, 'Anything we can
do?' and they shake their heads and say, 'No. I'm just
waiting.' We just smile at them. You can't throw them out.

The children get very excited by the vans. Not a day goes
by when they don't come scurrying along past here. The

children cry 'Amabhulu', when they see them and sing that horrible song about 'Amabhulu zizinja' which terrifies me in case the police hear it and come in, but children are natural mimics and we can't do a thing to keep them quiet.

One thing I've noticed and enjoyed is that since the riots even people who were not on speaking terms have unexpectedly found themselves talking. It must be because of the many shocks and frustrations. We especially noticed it with the Coloureds. They have always been divided into two groups. Those very well-off people who vote and do all those things, and the working class who have nothing to do with those small luxuries because they are not content with that.

Before the riots the Coloureds used to keep us away from them. But now, even if you don't know a person, he behaves warmly towards you. It's as if you are fellow sufferers. The fact is we are all under one blanket. We are all non-White.

In spite of this I'm not looking forward to the day when I find myself under Black rule. I might be wrong but our people can be hard to those under them. Some time ago I was in the Langa Post Office. It was Saturday morning and there were long queues, mostly of African men from the zones. The assistants behind the counter were rudely yelling at those who were not sure how to send money by telegraph or register parcels.

One unfortunate man in front of me was really nervous as this was now the third form he was presenting for a money order. He'd made mistakes in the first two and the assistant had just torn them up and sent him away to try again. This time the assistant told him to get out of the post office. I beckoned to him to wait for me and when my business was finished showed him how to do it correctly. He was so grateful he wanted to give me money.

Hospitals are not the same since we have had Black nurses in the wards. They are impatient and rude and are always trying to short-cut their duties.

During the pass raids the African police are the worst. A White policeman can be forgiving but the African can be vicious. The only time a person is talked to decently at any administration office is when you know the assistant or you are a well-known personality.

Even for domestics it is worse to work for a Black than a White madam in terms of kindness and time off. My neighbour is one example. She expects her helpers to work seven days a week with no set time off and is always packing them off at a moment's notice when she is not satisfied. I could go on and on. We seem to absorb all the bad lessons from the Whites.

Whatever people's opinions, we have all developed a tremendous respect for the youth. Within a day they showed such power, and without weapons. They call us cowards, only concerned for our own positions and unable to say 'no' to Whites. That's why they won't tell their mothers anything. As someone said, 'If Madam asks you what is going to happen you will say, "The children are going to march," because you must tell Madam everything. Therefore we won't tell you.' People respect someone who can keep a secret like that.

You would think everyone would be cross with the stone throwers because it makes travelling by bus so unsafe, but all criticism is directed at the police or riot squad. I hear time and again how the stonethrowing and rioting was the result of police interference and that it was the only way the children could fight back. I wish I knew the truth.

Frankly I have seen a lot of the unfairness of the riot squad. To begin with there is Ouma Swartbooi who has a cracked arm because she was beaten up by a policeman on her way from school. I won't even mention Connie who still has 58 bird pellets to be taken out from her bottom.

I had my own taste of bird pellets the other day. Nomsa was outside. She often goes around to Angela. I was busy in the kitchen when I heard shooting. Oh, I was out of the front door calling before I realized I'd even opened it. As I ran out the front Nomsa came charging in the back but I didn't see her. Then I heard 'Shwoowa' and something hit me under the arm. I was sure I was dead. But they didn't injure me, just made lots of little holes in my jersey. I got back inside very quickly.

Why is there all this shooting? Children are shot at, even a nine-year-old. Why not arrest them and interrogate them or give them a beating? Nobody here is prepared to call this justice. If anything, it proves we Blacks are treated differently, and this has just cemented racial hatred.

In spite of the riots, our neighbours have been doing themselves proud in acquiring new things for their homes. Agnes and Thabo have at last bought a three-piece for their sitting-room. It is a modern suite, a soft-cushioned leather thing in brown. It must have cost a fortune. They've also installed new brass curtain rails which cost R120 for three windows and new curtains. To top it all there is a handwoven karakul mat for the middle of the floor.

Agnes is so happy again. Now she prefers having guests because she cannot show off by just talking about it. Well, being such a popular person we must all have visited her by now to congratulate her. As she's Gus's cousin I had to bring a present so I gave her R2 to buy ashtrays.

Now Ruth and Sidney have bought a TV. What excitement. It's a black and white model and she's placed it in her crowded sitting-room. The sitting-room acts as a bedroom for her two boys and is not as tidy as it could be by any means. There is not even leg room when you all sit facing the set. Ruth is not such a wonderful housekeeper. She always has too many bright colours that clash with her furniture. Actually I am inclined the same way. She bought the TV because her children were always watching at a nearby shebeen. Now they will stay at home. A shebeen is no place for children.

29 September

One little boy, Zukile, came to sit with me while I was writing. His sister is at a high school. I think it is I.D. Mkize. I asked him if his sister was going back to school.

'No, she's not.'

'Why not?'

'Don't you know?' he said. Remember he's four and a half. 'We want our blood, we want our people, we want our school and we don't want to learn the rubbish. And we don't want the umboomboom.'

At that age!

Though I must say at that age he's old enough to be shot. I got such a fright last week. There were ten children left, all of whom live in Section 4. So when one of their fathers arrived, I asked him, if I helped as far as NY 5, could he carry on with the lot from there. We left, me with about six kids and he with four.

We were just at the corner of 108 and NY 6 when I saw a bus coming along NY 6 towards us. Now on that corner there is a grassy patch and a whole lot of little kids had gathered. Very young kids, the age of those at the school – from two upwards. They were playing with bicycle tyres and a couple of them had gathered some stones.

And there came the bus. One little girl got excited. A really little thing. She didn't even have panties. There she was shouting and suddenly I realized she was about to throw stones at this bus. These children stay along 108, they've seen what's been happening and the stonethrowing at cars and buses and all. And now they wanted to copy it.

I pushed the children over to the Mr N., grabbed a big stick and rushed across the road shouting, 'Go home,' beating the stick on the ground as if I was about to hit them. So they ran and one of the mothers came out to see what the shouting was about and why I was scaring her children. She wouldn't believe that they had been about to throw stones.

Just then a riot car came along. If they had seen that they would have fired. They don't care about the age group of the children.

Wednesday, 8 December

Nyanga is quiet again but there are still fires burning in Guguletu. I nearly didn't get to Claremont today. I thought that seeing that the buses were running again I wouldn't need to arrange to have the car. But I ended up waiting at the bus stop for over an hour. While I was waiting, Shelley came running to tell me that the house on our right was on fire. The place is teeming with riot squads yet the fires go on.

I know the woman who stays in that house. She is not selling liquor so they must be saying that she is an informer. She owns a lovely new Chev, a 1975 model. They've always owned two cars. She and her husband built themselves up very quickly. That's what makes people suspicious. But I think in the long run these accusations are going to be shown to be real untruths – that either people were jealous, or they sent those hooligans to burn down someone's house simply because of dislike.

Can there be as many informers as houses that have been burned down? I doubt it. That's why we're in such a state. You don't know what people think of you. Jealousies and personal fights are being decided by petrol bombs.

We held our end-of-year Christmas party at the school. We kept it very small with just a few parents invited because of all the threats against Christmas celebrations. The children had made lovely decorations but I didn't dare hang them up. We did all the baking ourselves and the parents also contributed. I tried to keep everyone as quiet as possible but by the end of the afternoon quite a few uninvited guests had turned up and we were all singing folk-songs and dancing. Fortunately there was no trouble.

I am very relieved that the school is closed. Keeping it open was like holding a hot potato.

The teachers are upset. Department schools officially closed today but they are due to reopen on 5 January – two weeks early – though they don't think there'll be any students attending. It makes it a very short holiday for them. I suppose the education people felt that because they've had no pupils they've had their holiday. But they still had to be at their posts all that time and were under great strain.

It's a very strange school holiday. Usually there are extra buses at this time of year for all the mothers to take their children Christmas shopping but because we aren't supposed to shop, or paint or do anything this Christmas, it's all quiet. There are no long queues at the bus stops and most people don't dare be seen with large parcels. I've heard that people carrying parcels are searched at Claremont terminus and if the youths find new clothes they tear them up. Of course shoplifters and pickpockets are taking advantage of the situation by pretending to be comrades and confiscating things for themselves.

I don't know what to do about my monthly food buying. I always buy in bulk but I'm having to get it all in bits and pieces now. I hate the expense of buying meat in small portions.

Some mothers are thrilled by the no-shopping campaign as it means saving money, but most of us are worried because it also means no share of our husbands' Christmas bonus. African men do not give money easily for clothes, and Christmas is the only time they let go. I've never cared for decorating the house with all that rubbish but I do like to dress the girls properly once a year and also to paint the house. If we don't paint now it won't get done till next Christmas and I miss the luxury of a freshly painted house. Even in the country Christmas is the time to mend cracks and remodel and paint the mud huts.

My neighbour's cousin has a son at Fezeka. The son had warned the father about the no-painting rule but he was not going to be told what to do in his own house, so he went ahead and painted. The comrades arrived, stripped him of all his clothes and painted him from head to toe. He was made to parade outside his gate to warn others of what could happen to disobedient people.

I've also heard of people who have had paint splashed over their furniture. Some still go ahead but it's all done at night. New furniture is also delivered only at night-time. I wasn't going to risk painting, but on Tuesday Shelley and I closed up the front of the house as if we were out and washed down the kitchen and dining-room walls. We did it very quickly, taking turns to watch and see if anyone was coming. I haven't put up any cards though. They are hidden in a drawer.

The youths have declared that 16 December is to be our Black Christmas. 25 December is for Whites only. Ours must be what used to be called Dingaan's Day because Boer blood was shed on that day.

25 December

I thought it was time we went to the graveyard. Gus wouldn't budge. 'I'm not going anywhere. I'm not sticking my neck out another minute.' So we did our own sort of Sabbath service in the house and just lay around. But I was feeling miserable.

Finally, I got up and went around to Angela – only to find

that she and Linda had gone off to the graveyard, and without inviting me. One of her neighbours was outside. She had just returned. 'The whole town's there, sis,' she said. 'You'd better go. People are afraid that those who haven't gone are being marked. It's safer to go because there's nothing there, no riot squads, nothing. Nothing but people, but I don't want to tell you the whole thing. Seeing is believing. Go yourself.'

I collected Grace's mother and my own and together we went off, all wearing something black. Gus was still stubborn. We met Linda and Angela on their way back. They had thought I was already there. They'd also been told that it would be hell if they weren't seen. They told us the procedure. First we had to go to the graveyard to tidy up the graves and then to a house in NY 78 which had suffered the most recent bereavement in these troubles.

It was one thing hearing it. Arriving was still a shock. I have never seen so many people. I hadn't understood what they meant about tidying up the graves. I thought perhaps we had to clean the graveyard or something. But what it was was that we had to mould the graves, make the mounds of earth on top, because these graves were flat. They weren't like the usual ones, rounded on top. These graves were separate, in three long rows of about fifty in each line. There were so many I couldn't count any more.

Usually at a new grave there is a cross with the name of the deceased, age and date of birth and death. But the graves in these lines were just marked with a stake and a number. Every gravesite has a stake but it's only when someone gets buried that a metal tag with a number is clipped to it. And these were all numbered graves with no names on them.

Unknown graves. I was too scared to openly ask questions, but you start feeling your way and people start talking. These graves, we heard, were riot deaths who were buried by the police in the night. Some of the comrades used to come and watch. The people of Section 4 said they used to see the police coming along with big plastic bags, those rubbish bags, and bury them there. Some of the comrades dug them up to find already decomposed bodies, sometimes more than one in a bag. So, it was said these were the graves of the unknown people who were just shot at random during the riots.

Well, you couldn't know whether there were also Coloureds buried there, or even convicts. But it was still terrible to think that so many people could be buried like that without the parents or people or relatives or anyone knowing.

At the beginning of each line of graves there was a man with a spade with earth on it. You took a handful and put it on to the grave. Now all day from six o'clock in the morning people had been coming to put a handful on each grave. You could tell how many people must have been there, from all the townships, Nyanga, Langa, Guguletu and all, because these mounds were growing.

I counted two out of all those graves that had a flower on them, a lousy little plastic flower, where the family had been to the police station and discovered the number of the grave. All over people were crying. There were those who had lost their relatives or who still didn't know where their children were. They couldn't help but cry to think that maybe it was their child on whose grave they were throwing earth, but which one, which one? There were so many.

All the time there was this low singing, the sad hum of the freedom songs, and all the time more people, coming, coming. I am used to going to funerals but it had never felt so heavy, people milling around singing, others crying quietly.

Some youths stood, lecturing. 'This is what they do to us. This is what they do to us. This is the treatment we get and still when we say to you people, "Co-operate with us," you don't understand. You won't say "Shoo" when someone stands on your corns. You smile and say, "That's good."'

It was quite an effort, all that bending and throwing. It was too much for Mother. We were getting so tired that we tried to dodge the last row. We went on to the house in NY 78. The owner of the house was filling basins with water with which to wash your hands and everyone who passed put down a few coins.

MAZISI KUNENE

The Rise of the Angry Generation

The great eagle lifts its wings from the dream
And the shells of childhood are scattered
Letting the fierce eyes focus on the morning
As though to cover the earth with darkness.
The beautiful bird builds its nest with old leaves
Preparing the branches of the birth-plant
Covering them with red feathers
As though to warn the earth against its anger.
The once proud planet shrieks in terror
Opening a vast space for the mysterious young bird
For the merciless talons of the new generation
They who are not deterred by false tears
Who do not turn away from the fire
They are the children of iron
They are the fearless bees of the night
They are the wrath of the volcanic mountains
They are the abiding anger of the Ancestral Forefathers.

Changes

The feet of strangers pass our home
Trampling on our grounds with fierce footsteps
Stones break, fragments of lightning explode
Hope for escape is impossible.
The shadows of birds frighten our children
Layers and rings of sand strangle the river.

The swelling of the earth shutters the ocean
It disturbs the silence that is old.
It brings the broken bone from the river.
It crushes the leaves
It breaks the mountain.

The ears are treacherous
They hear things that are meant for death
Then they follow these sounds into remote time.

But how wonderful when the tale is told,
And the message that is meant for us
Opens like the scents of a mountain-flower!
Then the rivers echo with bird-song
New life travels through the veins of the earth.

There are those who came before us
Who saw a gigantic cloud rise from the ocean
Who planted the round seeds of the lucky bean
Vowing to give us its abundance.
From them comes the harvest-basket.
Yes nothing has been lost
Not even the fragments of a dream.
These are the pure gifts of the Ancestral guardians;
They who are always ready to take each other's place.
The earth is said to be the opposite of water
Eternally the twins embrace
And the summers throw their fruitfulness to the sand.

After the Death of Mdabuli, Son of Mhawu

Part One

Silence walks slowly through the dark forest
Giraffe-plants sway and dance to the mourning song.
Before us a mountain heaves and sighs
It is as if it shall touch the bending sky
And proclaim the eternal bonds with the milky way,
For the ultimate order of life is a cycle.
Life begins but does not end.
People must talk now and tell their story
They must move without fear
Nor should they raise their voices to the hurricanes
But must with their power command them to silence.
It is us, the descendants of the lions
Who must rule, without us the earth itself would end.

Our flame cuts through the clouds of darkness
We walk to the mountains with our own sun.
We have created the night and flashes of lightning
To raise the proud manes of our children.
We have composed a song to accompany the sun
To him we sing from the valley of the palm trees.
People must walk without fear
Like us who have created a legend
Who have opened our gates to the stranger
We said, let him enter and be free.

Part Two

A bluebird fell before us
It had lost its ability to fly.
It shall open its eyes and raise its wings.
It shall fly into the infinity of the sky.
We shall give it power to live again.
We stopped our procession for the hero

70

After the Death of Mdabuli, Son of Mhawu

And said to the young of our clan: 'Bring water
Bring the pure herbs of cleansing
This is a sign, our clansman lives!'
It is always wise to know: birds sing at dawn
They fear no violence from the huntsman.
Great minds do not succumb to fear.
The flower that is spreading
Once was buried under the earth.
So shall our race rise from the nightmare
And their shadow shall cover the earth.
From this wound we shall live again.
Our House shall continue forever and ever.
The Pleiades is my witness:
The night shall not triumph over our House
Nor shall any creature
Cast its shadow over our foreheads.

On the Nature of Truth

'People do not follow the same direction, like water'
Zulu saying

Those who claim the monopoly of truth
Blinded by their own discoveries of power,
Curb the thrust of their own fierce vision.
For there is not one eye over the universe
But a seething nest of rays ever dividing and ever linking.
The multiple creations do not invite disorder,
Nor are the many languages the enemies of humankind.
But the little tyrant must mould things into one body
To control them and give them his single vision.
Yet those who are truly great
On whom time has bequeathed the gift of wisdom
Know all truth must be born of seeing
And all the various dances of humankind are beautiful
They are enriched by the great songs of our planet.

In Praise of the Ancestors

Even now the Forefathers still live
They are not overcome by the power of the whirlwind.
The day that sealed their eyes did not conquer them.
Even the tall boulder that stands over them
Casts only a humble shadow over their resting place.
They are the great voice that carries the epics.
The Ancestors have come to listen to our songs,
Overjoyed they shake their heads in ecstasy.
With us they celebrate their eternal life.
They climb the mountain with their children
To put the symbol of the ancient stone on its forehead.
We honour those who gave birth to us,
With them we watch the spectacle of the moving mists.
They have opened their sacred book to sing with us.
They are the mystery that envelops our dream.
They are the power that shall unite us.
They are the strange truth of the earth.
They came from the womb of the universe.
Restless they are, like a path of dreams,
Like a forest sheltering the neighbouring race of animals.
Yes, the deep eye of the universe is in our chest.
With it we stare at the centres of the sky.
We sing the anthems that celebrate their great eras,
For indeed life does not begin with us.

BEN J. LANGA

For My Brothers (Mandla and Bheki) in Exile

You have seen part of the world
Met some very nice people
Experienced the hardships of fresh air
Longed for the warm home-fires
Around which we sat on winter nights
Listening to pa tell us stories
Or reading passages from the Bible.
Those were the days, my brother Mandla,
Some days they were, my brother Bheki.
Do you remember those days?
When we were young and happy together
Playing cops and robbers, hide and seek,
Pinching bottoms whilst in hiding –
Young and happy together?
One day it would rain
And before the night was out
We'd be carrying brooms, sacks and buckets,
Urging the water out of our house.
You do remember those days?

Maybe I do not know where you are.
You left in the stealth of the night
Maybe hiked miles in fear but determined
To finally reach new worlds unknown.
Some days I happen to clean house
Exploring every nook and cranny.
I find here and there memories of our youth
Written on scraps of black and white photos.
I shake my head in pain of loss,
Say to myself, 'Gone are those days.'

For My Brothers (Mandla and Bheki) in Exile

The old woman is still around, brothers,
Heavy creases run down her mahogany face;
They are dry rivulets opened by heavy rains of pain.
At night, alone in the vaults of darkness,
She prays. In her prayer she talks about you.
Mama cries at night – by day she laughs,
Tending sisters' small children.
I know she longs to catch but one glimpse
Of her flesh and blood. Of her own womb.
Sometimes she talks about it,
Swallowing lumps, hiding tears behind eyes.
Mama is strong. Very tough. She was carved in teak.
In the evenings when we're together, she sometimes
Sings the songs we used to sing together.
Then she goes to sleep. I wonder if she'll sleep.

On Xmas Day mama makes custard and jelly,
Reminds us of how we all looked forward to Xmas
Because that was about the only day
We have tasted custard and jelly.
Big bowls of jelly would be made
Then taken to the kindly butcher
(Remember, we didn't have a fridge).
Some time before our big meal
She'd send one of us to collect the bowls.
I remember we would handle those bowls gingerly
As though our whole life depended on them.

I do not know, maybe, what you're doing out there.
I know you're alive, yet longing for the home country.
You loved this country deeply,
So much that you could leave only to come back
When it has gained more sense.
Our neighbours (the ones you knew so well) are still there.
We meet at the tap (it's still outside) and chat.
They ask about you. They care about you.
Those days you do remember.

Ben J. Langa

In all our pain and agony we rejoice,
For the tensile steel strength of our souls
Transcends border and boundaries.
However far apart our bodies may be
Our souls are locked together in a perpetual embrace.

JOEL MATLOU

Man Against Himself

*We must work before the sun goes down. The life of a man is very
heavy in his bones and his future is a deep unknown grave.*

One day when I was alone, struggling to get money, and far
away from my home where no one lives or grows, I met a
man from Zululand called Dlongolo. He told me to try for
work at the offices of Rustenburg Platinum Mine (RPM) in
Bleskop, 8 km from where I was living.

The following day I went to the offices of RPM. I found
work. The man who hires labourers was a Black man with
three missing upper teeth. I was told to come on Monday.
Before I left the premises I saw the sportsground, the mine
hospital, a bar, a café, trucks, vans, buses and a compound
with many rooms and toilets. But I left because I was sleeping
at the hostel in Rustenburg and my home was in Mabopane,
Odi.

On Monday morning I returned to the offices with others.
At about 9.30 a.m. our passes were taken and looked into.
They told me to fill in the forms they gave me in Ga-
Rankuwa. So, with the little money that I had, I arrived in
Ga-Rankuwa and my forms were filled in, but I was surprised
when they told me to pay R1 for the forms. I paid it and left.
So I was short of money for the train back to Rustenburg. I
had only 85 cents in my pocket, and the journey would cost
R1.10. It was 9.30 a.m. and the train left Ga-Rankuwa at
10.00 a.m. I was far from the station and I lost hope of catch-
ing the train. I thought of begging for money, but decided I
was too young to beg.

My second plan was that I should sleep somewhere in
Ga-Rankuwa and at about 4 a.m. I would walk to the station

of Wolhuterskop where my 85 cents would be enough for the train. At about 8 p.m. I chose myself a toilet to sleep in at a certain school in Ga-Rankuwa, Zone 4. I went into the toilet at night but it was very dark inside. There were lights all over Ga-Rankuwa roads. I walked slowly to the back of the toilets where I found a big stone. I sat on it trying not to think of dangerous snakes under the stone. At midnight I heard barking dogs. All the people in Ga-Rankuwa were asleep. At about 3 a.m. I heard cars hooting all over Ga-Rankuwa. I thought I was in danger. But those cars belonged to newspapers and were calling for their employees. And there were two buses hooting. I thought they were staff buses for drivers. People started to walk on the roads then, to catch trains and buses to Pretoria and Rosslyn. At about 5.15 a.m. I felt cold. I was wearing a shirt, a jersey, trousers, and shoes without socks. The sun rose and I left Ga-Rankuwa early so that I could catch the 11.30 a.m. train at Wolhuterskop. I ran until De Wild were I started to walk and beg a lift to Brits or Rustenburg.

On the road to Brits I saw a Black man sitting on the white government stone indicating bridges. I greeted him and he greeted me. As I passed he called, and stood up. He begged 20 cents from me. With shame I told him my story and showed him the forms I'd filled out in Ga-Rankuwa. He was wearing sandals, black trousers, a red 'hemp',[1] a black jersey and a scarf. He had a camera in his hand. I continued to tell him my story. I told him to beg a lift to Brits, where he was going. A truck carrying sand arrived and we stopped it for a lift. The driver took us to Brits. We got off at the bus rank. He asked me to accompany him to the pass office for a reference book. At the pass office we saw convicts cutting grass and sweeping the pass office floors. He was given a duplicate and we departed.

I started to run through the town until I was outside Brits. The station of Wolhuterskop was very far and there were no short cuts so I used the main roads, like a car. I was tired and felt like a convict on the run. I could not imagine what was

---

1 *hemp* shirt

going to happen. My stomach was empty. As I was walking on the tar road I met two beautiful girls aged about eighteen to twenty. I am twenty-three. They were carrying boxes with dirty dust coats inside. I greeted them and asked for the Wolhuterskop station. One of the girls, speaking Pedi, told me that it was not so far away. The second girl asked where I was from. I told her that our factory van broke down near Brits, and I was reporting back to work. She asked where I worked and I told her at the United Tobacco Company in Rustenburg, about which I knew nothing really. We parted. Not far from the station I met a traffic inspector resting under the plantation trees. He greeted me nicely and I also accepted his greetings. I thought to myself that my road was now open because I had got a greeting from a White traffic inspector. That was nearly true and nearly false because I could never have imagined what was going to happen after my struggles. At the station there was a queue for tickets. My ticket cost 75 cents to Bleskop where Rustenburg Platinum Mine offices are, so I had 10 cents left. I bought myself a half brown bread costing 7 cents at the nearest café, and sat under the trees on the grass where I ate the bread alone. I drank some water and my stomach was full like a strong man. The train arrived, so I boarded it but my mind and future were still missing without hopes. My heart was very heavy as I got on to the train so I thought of my motto: 'If the Lord gives you a burden, he will also provide help to carry it, and in the whole world there are so many people who pray for a new life.'

When I arrived at Bleskop I wondered where I would sleep that night. I just took a stroll until 7.30 p.m., back to Bleskop station. There were a few people going home from the mines. And I started to breathe softly without fearing. There was a big waiting-room in which many people were asleep and I too slept there. People from the mines were playing records with their gumba-gumba.[2] Bleskop was very quiet but gumba-gumba men were blasting records the whole night until 2.30 in the morning, when they boarded the Pretoria train. I was left with the others who were going to the mines the next day.

---

2 *gumba-gumba* record-player

After the gumba-gumba men left, Bleskop station became quiet. When the sun rose over the mountains of Pretoria, we set off for the Rustenburg Platinum Mine, some wearing blankets. The mine was where we were going to buy our lives with blasted rocks.

We arrived at the offices which were still closed, and sat on the grass. Mine people were training on the sports ground. Some were jumping and singing in the mine hall in the mine language, 'sefanagalo'.[3] At 7.30 a.m. the ambulance arrived at high speed, its top lamp flashing. It stopped near the door of the mine hospital. Two people and the driver got out without speaking. Their faces were in sorrow. From the back came six people in mine clothes, with their head lamps still on. They off-loaded two coffins and carried them into the mine hospital. I shivered like the branches of a tree. My motto was still in my mind but I thought that I had seen Mabopane for the last time, and my parents, relatives and friends too.

At 8 a.m. the offices opened. We were called and our passes were taken from us. At 9 a.m. we collected our passes and the Black officer told us that there was work at Swartklip. They gave us tickets to Swartklip which cost R1.35, single.

When we arrived at Swartklip we were shown to empty rooms and given plates for food. Then we saw a film which ended at 10 p.m. Back in our rooms we slept well, with police guarding us with kieries.

On Friday morning the man known as Induna woke us at 5 a.m. He told us to report at the labour office as soon as possible. We did so. At the labour office our passes were taken. At about 9.30 a.m. a Black man in white clothes told us to follow him. We were led to a big house with many rooms and beds, which looked like a hospital. We were taken to a room where there was a chair, a desk and a scale ending in 200 kg. There we met another man, all in white, who had many files in his hands, where our names were already written. They told us to undress. We were checked from toes to head for wounds, then weighed. When the doctor pro-

---

3 *sefanagalo* pidgin

duced a big needle and injected us near the heart to kill shocks when we went underground, I felt I was fighting for my dear beautiful life. Late on Friday we returned to the labour offices. We were given three days' tickets for food at the compound and shown a film.

On Sunday at about 7.30 p.m., after my meal, I tried to find an empty tin and get a little chaechae, which is what mageu[4] is called on the mines. Joel! Joel Matlou! someone called out to me. I looked at the people sleeping on the grass, and saw a man with a tape recorder. 'Come here, come here,' he said. I moved slowly towards him. He stood up and said, 'Joel, what do you want here?' When I recognized him I was so happy that I kissed him. It was Joseph Masilo of Mabopane who was now living in Moruleng, Rustenburg. We were at school together at Ratshetlho Higher Primary in Mabopane seven years ago. We started questioning one another about our reasons for being on the mine. I told him I had taken the job because I needed money fast, to pay off a big instalment.

'How do you come here?' I asked him.

'Suffering brought me,' he said. 'In two weeks' time I complete my ticket and get paid.'

'Couldn't your people or relatives and friends help you settle your accounts?' I asked.

'It is difficult to reach relatives and friends. Are you married?'

'No,' I replied. 'I will think first before I marry. Mines do not have girls. Where and how often do you get to have a girl near you here at mines?'

'This place is a jail,' said Joseph. 'No girls around here and you must have respect for yourself until your sentence is finished. Stop asking me silly questions. All the people here have troubles.'

We parted and arranged to meet the following day.

I was so very happy to meet my best friend after seven years. My heart was open and all things were going well.

On Monday morning we went to the labour offices. There were three compounds, A, B and C. A compound is called

---

4 *mageu* (non-alcoholic) drink

Union Section. B is called Entabeni and C is called Hlatini. They are far away from each other. The officer told us we would be transferred to C compound, Hlatini. We fetched all our belongings and the mine bus took us to Hlatini compound. There were many people in Hlatini. Some were drinking beers, playing ball, running and playing tape recorders. A big man with a bald head took us to a room called 'School Mine'. In that room we found chairs and a big white board. We were told to sit down quietly and listen. Then all the windows and doors of the room were closed. We were shown a television film of a man teaching new labourers how to build and pack wood and another film on First Aid.

Then a Black man wearing a black dust coat, with a missing left eye, called us to the office. He gave us cards, then called us one by one to take boots, belts and iron (copper) hats. Then we were given numbers. A young man came running with a plastic bag containing small numbers. The numbers were on small pieces of iron 200 mm long and 100 mm wide. My number was 3281. That was on Tuesday.

There were twenty little windows, like those at which people buy tickets for buses or trains. There you got your lamp and battery for work when you produced your number. My number was 3281, and my window number was 8. We were told to report at the windows at 6 a.m. for work.

Back at the compound we enjoyed our mine meal, saw a film and went to sleep. At 5 a.m. we were woken by a loudspeaker. We got our lamp and battery and were taken to a big office where we were ordered to sit down on the floor. We were still to see and learn more.

A White man introduced himself as Mr Alfred Whitefield from Northam, Rustenburg. He spoke English, Tswana and Sefanagalo but not Afrikaans. He said: '*Umtheto wase* mine *uthi, aikhona wena sebenzisa umlilo lapha kalo* mine. *Aikhona wena hlala phanzi banye ba sebenza. Vuka umtheto wa* boss boy. *Sebenzisa a ma* toilets *a se* mine. *Aikhona choncha. Sebenzisa u*mine Bank *ku beka imali yakho.*' [The law of the mine says: Do not make fire here in the mine. Do not sit down while others are working. 'Wake up!' is the law of the boss-boy. Use the mine toilets. Do not steal. Use the mine bank to save your money.] Those were the words which I still remember from Mr A. Whitefield.

Before we went to work under the soil of Africa, we were given a hand belt with a number on it. It was a blue belt. My number was 2256731.

At 7.15 a.m. the boss boy took us to the lift. As it went down my ears went dead and I saw dark and light as we passed other levels. The levels go from 6 to 31. The lift stopped at 28 level. There I saw lights, small trains (*makalanyane*), a tool room, a work shop, toilets, a power station, big pipes, drinking water, a telephone and so on.

The boss boy gave us a small book which had twenty-four pages. Every day he tore out one page from it. When it was empty you get your pay and a new book.

We gave our tickets to the boss boy then walked for one hour to the end of the shaft. The mine shaft was very hot. I was wearing a shirt and trousers. The sweat ran off me like water. There were three tunnels. The small trains, the *makalanyana*, had red lights on the back and front indicating danger. Before the blasting, small holes were drilled in the walls and a man referred to as a chessa-boy put explosives into them. After the blasting we found broken pipes, the ventilator on the ground, bent rails, a cracked wall and other damage. The blast gave us heavy work. The *makalanyane* and its trucks were called to collect all stones. You can find a stone weighing 200 kg far from the blast.

A Zulu from King Williamstown was digging *mosele* (water concrete) when part of the ventilator fell on him and his left leg was trapped under it. The boss called us and we lifted the ventilator to take out the trapped man. His leg was broken and bloody. Four men carried him to the lift and an ambulance was called.

Water leaked from the top of the walls. Sometimes small stones fell on us. In another section of the tunnel were people called Loaders (*Malaisha*). My boots were full of water. The time for clocking out started to roll round, so we followed our boss boy to the station. We switched off our lamps while we waited in the queue because at the station there were electric lights. We were wet like fishes and ugly like hippos. Some were sitting and resting with empty stomachs. There were two lifts running up and down, taking people out of the shaft. When one was underground, the other was on the surface, off-loading. After twenty minutes, the lift arrived. The guard opened the door and we flowed in. The notice on the door said the lift took only twenty people. But we were packed like fishes in a small can. At level 6 the guard opened the door and we came out, one by one, as the door is very small. We gave our officer the lamps and he gave us back our numbers.

There was no time or chance to prove yourself: who you are and what you want. I did not wash my clothes or bath because I did not have soap and other clothes to put on. All I did was eat and sleep on the grass and listen to the music from the loudspeaker at the offices of Hlatini compound (C).

I had already lost hope of going back to Pretoria where I belonged. I could not even imagine that my girlfriend was thinking about me. Life was so bad; for me life was a little piece of stone. Washing, bathing, cutting nails, dressing in clean clothes and reading newspapers was far from me. It could be about 640,000 miles far from me.

The mine injection makes you forget about your parents, relatives and friends, even your girlfriend. The injection makes you think only about work underground. After three weeks underground I was part of that world.

In the yard of Hlatini compound there was coal and wood and in the rooms was only one stove. If it was cold you could make a fire or cook your own favourite food. The bar and shop were in the yard.

The days went on and on until my ticket said twenty-three days. Our month ends on day twenty-four. Then we'd get our money. When my ticket said twenty-four days, I was working underground for the last time. My last day underground went so fast. On the twenty-fifth day I went to the paymaster to get my money. I was told to come back after six days. This was bad news. Waiting for my six days to end, I slept in the bush every night because I did not want to go underground. My main wish was to escape. During my last six days in the lonely bush I came across many dead cattle killed by Pondos and Basothos because these nations like meat. I also saw old shafts and old machines, so I used to enjoy myself going underground using ropes and chains. The shafts were very dark. During my wanderings I saw people ploughing their lands and growing crops. I also came across a slum known as Mantserre near the big mountain, far from the Hlatini compound, where there were schools, shops and churches. In the bush I met some wild animals like spring-boks, hares and impalas, as well as partridges. I even met people riding bicycles from the mines to Mantserre slum on the narrow paths.

I wore my mine clothes during this time as I didn't want to show people that I wasn't working. When I returned to the mine I took off my mine clothes and wore my own dirty ones. I was so happy to know that tomorrow was pay day. I met young men at Hlatini playing records and singing. I joined in though I didn't know them. My meal was so good that I ate like a pig and drank chaechae like a drunkard. What I did not know was that I was on the verge of a complete mental breakdown. My last night at Hlatini was very long and ter-rible. It harboured demons, but it also symbolized escape from dangerous falling rocks to the gentle air of Pretoria City.

At 3.30 a.m. a loudspeaker woke up the people as usual. I was left alone in the room, waiting for 9 a.m., for my pay. I decided to steal clothes, tape recorders and radios but God refused to allow it. Music was playing on the loudspeakers. To me things seemed to be changing; even the birds were singing a chorus which I didn't understand. The hours went by and at 8.30 a.m. people started to queue for pay. I joined them. After an hour the paymaster arrived, police guarding him with revolvers. Each of us was asked for a number, and finger prints were taken. They gave me a pay slip which had two parts. At a second window they took one part and I was left with the pay slip with my thumb print on it. At the third window they took my pay slip and gave me the money which a policeman counted so that they would not rob me. The money was ninety-six Rand. It was for my own work. I risked my life and reason for it.

I went out of the main gates at Hlatini to escape to Northam station. I pretended to be counting my money at the gate so that the police guards would not realize that I was running away. I did not finish counting: I just thrust it into my empty pocket and walked out of the main gate towards the bush to free myself. That time life was not endless but everlasting.

The earth was once supposed to be flat. Well, so it is, from Hlatini to Northam. That fact does not prevent science from proving that the earth as a whole is spherical. We are still at the stage that life itself is flat - the distance from birth to death. Yet the probability is that life, too, is spherical and much more extensive and capacious than the hemisphere we know.

The black dots in my eyes turned brown, like a dagga[5] smoker or a dreamer. I felt like a political asylum-seeker, running to Tanzania. To get to Northam I had to cross two compounds. I ran like hell until I crossed A and B compounds. Then I ran to catch the 10.30 train from Northam to Rustenburg. Two Black men, and a White man on a tractor, looked at me, surprised. Far from the ploughing men I crossed a ditch in which a half-eaten impala lay. Birds were singing, animals roaring. At 8 p.m. cars passed me, one after another and I started to fear for my life. I hid under small bridges or in the long grass. At 9 p.m. I saw small yellow lights and I realized that it must be the station. My feet were aching and swollen and bloody.

At the station there was a café where I bought chips and a half brown and sat on the grass to eat it. After buying a ticket to Rustenburg, I found a small piece of paper on the grass. I took it to the toilets, wet it and washed my face with it. I even bought vaseline to smear on my dirty face. My face looked like that of a real man, but not my clothes.

The train arrived at 10.30 p.m. People looked at me. Some of them were laughing instead of crying blood. After I arrived in Rustenburg I went to the shops. People were laughing at my dirty clothes, even White people. The shopkeeper thought I was a robber, so I showed him my pay slip. I bought a three-piece suit, a blue shirt, black and red socks and a Scotch tie. It cost me seventy-one Rand and I was left with only twenty-two Rand. I couldn't arrive home with dirty clothes, so I decided to buy my pride with my suffering.

I changed my clothes at the Rustenburg station toilets and put the old ones in a paper bag. I was really a gentleman.

---

5 *dagga* marijuana

Man Against Himself

People, mostly girls, asked for the time when they saw me, just for pleasure. I had a *Rand Daily Mail* newspaper in my right hand, and walked like a president. I was smelling of new clothes.

Suffering taught me many things.

I recall a poem which is a plea for me:

I don't like being told
This is in my heart, thinking
That I shall be me
If I were you
I but not you
But you will not give me a chance
I am not you
Yet you will not let me be
You meddle, interfere in my affairs as if they were yours
And you were not me
You are unfair, unwise
That I can be you, talk act and think like you
God made me
For God's sake, let me be me
I see your eyes but you don't see your eyes
I cannot count your fingers because you see them all
Act yourself and I will act myself, not being told but doing it oneself.

Suffering takes a man from known places to unknown places. Without suffering you are not a man. You will never suffer for the second time because you have learned to suffer.

I am grateful to Mr Dlongolo who told me about mine work and that it was a fast way of making money.

It was Friday and most of the people on the train were students and mine workers going home to Pretoria and the Transkei. Everyone was happy. Even I was happy. If suffering means happiness I am happy. The 1.35 p.m. train pulled out and I sat reading the *Rand Daily Mail*. The train stopped at all stations: Colombia, Turfground, Maroelakop, Bleskop, Marikana, Wolhuterskop, Brits West, Beestekraal, Norite, Stephanus and Taljaardshoop, when it left the Republic of Bophuthatswana and crossed into South Africa. On the train people sold watches, apples, socks, liquor, shoe laces, lip ice and so on. When I saw the beautiful girls I thought of my own beautiful sweetheart, my bird of Africa, sea water, razor: green-coloured eyes like a snake, high wooden shoes like a cripple; with soft and beautiful skin, smelling of powder under her armpits like a small child, with black boots for winter like a soldier, and a beautiful figure like she does not eat, sleep, speak or become hungry. And she looks like an artificial girl or electric girl. But she was born of her parents, as I was. She is Miss Johanna Mapula Modise of Mabopane who was born during a rainy day. As I am Mr Joel Medupe Matlou of Mabopane and I was also born during a rainy day. Mapula and Medupe is our gift from God. So, we accepted these names by living together.

The train arrived in Ga-Rankuwa on time. I bought some groceries and took a taxi to Mabopane. From there I went straight home where I met my mother and young brothers. They were happy and I was happy with them. The following morning I visited my girlfriend.

She cried when she saw me, silently looking down on the soil of Africa. I did not tell her I had worked on the mine. I said I had got a job in Johannesburg.

'Why didn't you tell me that you were going to work in Johannesburg? You didn't even write to me. You just sat there and forgot me,' she said.

'One of my friends took me to Johannesburg where he found me work. So there was no chance, I just left,' I lied to her.

Back on Mabopane's dusty roads again I looked like a real gentleman. Many people were happy to visit me as they knew I was a peace lover and didn't drink or smoke. There was nothing which worried me. I had thought that getting back to Mabopane's dusty roads would lead me to suffer, but eating alone was almost more than I could bear. I learned to forget yesterdays and to think of tomorrows. Each morning in the township, I said to myself: 'Today is a new life.' I overcame my fear of loneliness and my fear of want. I am happy and fairly successful now and have a lot of enthusiasm and love for life. I know now that I shall never again be afraid of sleeping under a tree alone, regardless of what life hands me. I don't have to fear blasting. I know now that I can live one day at a time and that every day is a time for a wise man.

NADINE GORDIMER

from Burger's Daughter

She didn't live in an official township at all but in one of those undefined areas between Black men's hostels and the mine-dumps on the outskirts of the city. Small industries have taken over the property of worked-out gold mines, the hollows are mass graves for wrecked cars and machine parts, the old pepper trees are shade for shebeens, and prostitutes lie down for customers in the sand of the dumps. There were still hawkers' mules tethered in grazed circumferences of tin-littered veld; a tiny corrugated-iron church with broken windows, and a peach-tree half hacked-away for firewood; in abandoned cottages that had once belonged to White miners, and in the yards built up with shelters made of materials gathered from the bull-dozed mine compounds and the brick shells of concession stores, people were living in what had been condemned and abandoned by the White city. This was the 'place'; she assured me it would do to stop anywhere on the switchback I was driving between dongas and boulders of the tracks that bound bricks, tin and smoke. God would bless me: with this she went off with her stolid side-to-side gait through bicycles and listing taxis hooting at her. Perhaps she didn't really live there – she looked much too respectable for this sort of den existing on the sale of sex and drink to factory workers and railway-yard labourers. It's impossible to say . . . Probably the old mother thought she'd take advantage of the provision of a car and driver and go and visit an out-of-the-way friend – why not?

I was miles from where Marisa lived . . . I wasn't even sure how to get across to the township without going all the way back through town. There was a woman with a tin of live coal selling roast mealies and I got out of the car to go over and ask directions of her. She didn't know. Orlando might have been at the other end of the world. The ribbed papery husks stripped from cobs made a thick mat all round her, under the soles of my shoes as it was under bare feet when Tony, the other Marie and I pranced with Black farm kids around the thresher on Uncle Coen's farm. I made for a gang of Black children and youths now, the little ones dancing and jumping among excited dogs to touch a bike with ram's-horn racing handles, a young chap astride it in the centre of other adolescents sharing smokes and a half-jack of something wrapped in brown-paper. I called to them but they only catcalled and laughed back in wolf-whistle falsetto. I was approaching – smiling, no, be serious for a moment, tell me – I heard the hard ring of struck metal and saw the fall of a stone that had hit my old car. I drove away while they went on laughing and yelling as if I were at once prey and a girl for teasing. I took wheel-tracks deep enough to be well used that seemed to lead over the veld to a road away on the rise in the right direction. The hump of dead grass down the middle swished against the belly of the car and now and then the oil-sump scraped hard earth. The track went on and on. I was caught on the counter-system of communications that doesn't appear on the road-maps and provides access to 'places' that don't appear on any plan of city environs. I was obstinate, sure the track would be crossed by one that led to the main road somewhere; there was a cemetery half a kilometre across the veld with the hired buses as prominent as sudden buildings, and the mass of Black people and black umbrellas like the heap of some dark crop standing on the pale open veld, that mark a Saturday funeral. I gained a cambered dirt road without signposts just as one of those donkey-carts that survive on the routes between these places that don't exist was approaching along a track from the opposite side. Driver's reflex made me slow down in anticipation that the cart might turn in up ahead without calculating the speed of an oncoming car. But there was something strange about the outline of donkey, cart and driver; convulsed, yet the cart was not coming nearer. As I drew close I saw a woman and child bundled under sacks, their heads jerked rocking; a driver standing up on the cart in a wildly precarious spread of legs in torn pants. Suddenly his body arched back with one upflung arm against the sky and lurched over as if he had been shot and at that instant the donkey was bowed by a paroxysm that seemed to draw its four legs and head down towards the centre of its body in a noose, then fling head and extremities wide again; and again the man violently salaamed, and again the beast curved together and flew apart.

I didn't see the whip. I saw agony. Agony that came from some terrible centre seized within the group of donkey, cart, driver and people behind him. They made a single object that contracted against itself in the desperation of a hideous final energy. Not seeing the whip, I saw the infliction of pain broken away from the will that creates it; broken loose, a force existing of itself, ravishment without the ravisher, torture without the torturer, rampage, pure cruelty gone beyond control of the humans who have spent thousands of years devising it. The entire ingenuity from thumbscrew and rack to electric shock, the infinite variety and gradation of suffering, by lash, by fear, by hunger, by solitary confinement – the camps, concentration, labour, resettlement, the Siberias of snow or sun, the lives of Mandela, Sisulu, Mbeki, Kathrada, Kgosana, gull-picked on the Island, Lionel propped wasting to his skull between two warders, the deaths of questioning, bodies fallen from the height of John Vorster Square, deaths by dehydration, babies degutted by enteritis in 'places' of banishment, the lights beating all night on the faces of those in cells – Conrad – I conjure you up, I drag you back from wherever you are to listen to me – you don't know what I saw, what there is to see, you *won't* see, you are becalmed on an empty ocean.

Only when I was level with the cart, across the veld from me, did I make out the whip. The donkey didn't cry out. Why didn't the donkey give that bestial snort and squeal of excruciation I've heard donkeys give not in pain but in rut? It didn't cry out.

It had been beaten and beaten. Pain was no shock, there is no way out of the shafts. That rag of a Black man was old, from the stance of his legs, the scraggle of beard showing under an old hat in a shapeless cone over his face. I rolled to a stop beyond what I saw; the car simply fell away from the pressure of my foot and carried me no farther. I sat there with my head turned sharply and my shoulders hunched round my neck, huddled to my ears against the blows. And then I put my foot down and drove on wavering drunkenly about the road, pausing to gaze back while the beating still went on, the force there, cart, terrified woman and child, the donkey and man, bucked and bolted zigzag under the whip. I had only to turn the car in the empty road and drive up upon that mad frieze against the sunset putting out my eyes. When I looked over there all I could see was the writhing black shape through whose interstices poked searchlights of blinding bright dust. The thing was like an explosion. I had only to career down on that scene with my car and my White authority. I could have yelled before I even got out, yelled to stop! – and then there I would have been standing, inescapable, fury and right, might, before them, the frightened woman and child and the drunk, brutal man, with my knowledge of how to deliver them over to the police, to have him prosecuted as he deserved and should be, to take away from him the poor suffering possession he maltreated. I could formulate everything they were, as the act I had witnessed; they would have their lives summed up for them officially at last by me, the White woman – the final meaning of a day they had lived I had no knowledge of, a day of other appalling things, violence, disasters, urgencies, deprivations which suddenly would become, was nothing but what it had led up to: the man among them beating their donkey. I could have put a stop to it, the misery; at that point I witnessed. What more can one do? That sort of old man, those people, peasants existing the only way they know how, in the 'place' that isn't on the map, they would have been afraid of me. I could have put a stop to it, with them, at no risk to myself. No one would have taken up a stone. I was safe from the whip. I could have stood between them and suffering – the suffering of the donkey.

As soon as I planted myself in front of them it would have become again just that – the pain of a donkey.

I drove on. I don't know at what point to intercede makes sense, for me. Every week the woman who comes to clean my flat and wash my clothes brings a child whose make-believe is polishing floors and doing washing. I drove on because the horrible drunk was Black, poor and brutalized. If somebody's going to be brought to account, I am accountable for him, to him, as he is for the donkey. Yet the suffering – while I saw it it was the sum of suffering to me. I didn't do anything. I let him beat the donkey. The man was Black. So a kind of vanity counted for more than feeling; I couldn't bear to see myself – her – Rosa Burger – as one of those Whites who can care more for animals than people. Since I've been free, I'm free to become one.

MTUTUZELI MATSHOBA

Call Me Not a Man

For neither am I a man in the eyes of the law,
Nor am I a man in the eyes of my fellow man.

By dodging, lying, resisting where it is possible, bolting
when I'm already cornered, parting with invaluable money,
sometimes calling my sisters into the game to get amorous
with my captors, allowing myself to be slapped on the mouth
in front of my womenfolk and getting sworn at with my
mother's private parts, that component of me which is man
has died countless times in one lifetime. Only a shell of me
remains to tell you of the other man's plight, which is in fact
my own. For what is suffered by another man in view of my
eyes is suffered also by me. The grief he knows is a grief I
know. Out of the same bitter cup do we drink. To the same
chain-gang do we belong.

Friday has always been their chosen day to go plundering,
although nowadays they come only occasionally, maybe once
a month. Perhaps they have found better pastures elsewhere,
where their prey is more predictable than at Mzimhlope, the
place which has seen the tragic demise of three of their
accomplices who had taken the game a bit too far by entering
the hostel on the northern side of our location and fleecing
the people right in the midst of their disgusting labour
camps. Immediately after this there was a notable abatement
in the frequency of their visits to both the location and the
adjacent hostel. However the lull was short-lived, lasting
only until the storm had died down, because the memory
tarnishes quickly in the locations, especially the memory of
death. We were beginning to emit sighs of relief and to
mutter 'good riddance' when they suddenly reappeared and
made their presence in our lives felt once again. June

'seventy-six had put them out of the picture for the next year, during which they were scarcely seen. Like a recurring pestilence they refuse to vanish absolutely from the scene.

A person who has spent some time in Soweto will doubtless have guessed by now that the characters I am referring to are none other than some of the so-called police reservists who roam our dirty streets at weekends, robbing every timid, unsuspecting person, while masquerading as peace officers to maintain law and order in the community. There are no greater thieves than these men of the law, men of justice, peace officers and volunteer public protectors in the whole of the slum complex because, unlike others in the same trade of living off the sweat of their victims, they steal out in the open, in front of everybody's eyes. Of course nothing can be done about it because they go out on their pillaging exploits under the banners of the law, and to rise in protest against them is analogous to defiance of the powers that be.

So, on this Friday too we were standing on top of the station bridge at Mzimhlope. It was about five in the afternoon and the sun hung over the western horizon of spectacularly identical coalsmoke-puffing roof-tops like a gigantic, glowing red ball which dyed the foamy clouds with the crimson sheen of its rays. The commuter trains in from the city paused below us every two or three minutes to regurgitate their infinite human cargo, the greater part of whom were hostel-dwellers who hurried up Mohale Street to cook their meagre suppers on primus stoves. The last train we had seen would now be leaving Phefeni, the third station from Mzimhlope. The next train had just emerged from the bridge this side of New Canada, junction to East and West Soweto. The last group of the hostel people from the train now leaving Phefeni had just turned the bend at Mohale Street where it intersects with Elliot. The two hundred metre stretch to Elliott was therefore relatively empty, and people coming towards the station could be clearly made out.

As the wheels of the train from New Canada squealed on the iron tracks and it came to a jerking stop, four men, two in overalls and the others in dustcoats, materialized around the Mohale Street bend. There was no doubt who they were, from the way they filled the whole width of the street and walked as if they owned everything and everybody in their sight. When they came to the grannies selling vegetables, fruit and fried mealies along the ragged, unpaved sides of the street, they grabbed what they fancied and munched gluttonously the rest of the way towards us. Again nothing could be done about it, because the poverty-stricken vendors were not licensed to scrape together some crumbs to ease the gnawing stomachs of their fatherless grandchildren at home, which left them wide open for plunder by the indifferent 'reserves'.

'*Awu*! The Hellions,' remarked Mandla next to me. 'Let's get away from here, my friend.'

He was right. They reminded one of the old western film; but I was not moving from where I was simply because the reservists were coming down the street like a bunch of villains. One other thing I knew was that the railway constable who was on guard duty that Friday at the station did not allow the persecution of the people on his premises. I wanted to have my laugh when they were chased off the station.

'Don't worry about them. Just wait and see how they're going to be chased away by this copper. He won't allow them on the station,' I answered.

They split into twos when they arrived below us. Two of them, a tall chap with a face corroded by skin-lightening cream and wearing a yellow golf cap on his shaven head, and another stubby, shabbily dressed, middle-aged man with a bald frontal lobe and a drunk face, chewing at a cooked sheep's foot that he had taken from one of the grannies, climbed the stairs on our right-hand side. The younger man took the flight in fours. The other two chose to waylay their unsuspecting victims on the street corner at the base of the left-hand staircase. The first wave of the people who had alighted from the train was in the middle of the bridge when the second man reached the top of the stairs.

Maybe they knew the two reservists by sight, maybe they just smelt cop in the smoggy air, or it being a Friday, they were alert for such possibilities. Three to four of the approaching human wall turned suddenly in their tracks and ran for their dear freedom into the mass behind them. The others were caught unawares by this unexpected movement and they staggered in all directions trying to regain balance. In a split second there was commotion on the station, as if a wild cat had found its way into a fowl-run. Two of those who had not been quick enough were grabbed by their sleeves, and their passes demanded. While they were producing their books the wolves went over their pockets, supposedly feeling for dangerous weapons, dagga[1] and other illegal possessions that might be concealed in the clothes, but really to ascertain whether they had caught the right people for their iniquitous purposes. They were paging through the booklets when the Railway policeman appeared.

'Wha . . .? Don't you fools know that you're not supposed to do that shit here? Get off! Get off and do that away from Railway property. Fuck off!' He screamed at the two reservists so furiously that the veins threatened to burst in his neck.

'Arrest the dogs, *baba*! Give them a chance also to taste jail!' Mandla shouted.

'Ja,' I said to Mandla, 'you bet, they've never been where they are so prepared to send others.'

The other people joined in and we jeered the cowards off the station. They descended the stairs with their tails tucked between their legs and joined their companions below the station. Some of the commuters who had been alerted by the uproar returned to the platform to wait there until the reservists had gone before they would dare venture out of the station.

We remained where we had been and watched the persecution from above. I doubted if they even read the passes (if they could), or whether the victims knew if their books were right or out of order. Most likely the poor hunted men believed what they were told by the licensed thieves. The latter demanded the books, after first judging their prey to be weak propositions, flicked through the pages, put the passes into their own pockets, without which the owners could not continue on their way, and told the dumbfounded hostel men to stand aside while they accosted other victims. Within

---

1 *dagga* marijuana

a very short while there was a group of confused men to one side of the street, screaming at their hostel mates to go to room so and so and tell so and so that they had been arrested at the station, and to bring money quickly to release them. Few of those who were being sent heard the messages since they were only too eager to leave the danger zone. Those who had money shook hands with their captors, received their books back and ran up Mohale Street. If they were unlucky they came upon another 'roadblock' three hundred metres up the street where the process was repeated. Woe unto them who had paid their last money to the first extortionists, for this did not matter. The police station was their next stopover before the Bantu Commissioners, and thence their final destination, Modderbee Prison, where they provided the farmers with ready cheap labour until they had served their terms for breaking the law. The terms vary from a few days to two years for *loaferskap*,[2] which is in fact mere unemployment, for which the unfortunate men are not to blame. The whole arrangement stinks of forced labour.

The large *kwela-kwela*[3] swayed down Mohale Street at breakneck speed. The multitudes scattered out of its way and hung on to the sagging fences until it had passed. To be out of sight of the people on the station bridge, it skidded and swerved into the second side street from the station. More reservists poured out of it and went immediately to their dirty job with great zeal. The chain-gang which had been lined up along the fence of the house nearest the station was kicked and shoved to the *kwela-kwela* into which the victims were bundled under a rain of fists and boots, all of them scrambling to go in at the same time through the small door. The driver of the *kwela-kwela*, the only uniformed constable among the group, clanged the door shut and secured it with the locking lever. He went to stand authoritatively near one of the vendors, took a small avocado pear, peeled it and put it whole into a gargantuan mouth, spitting out the large stone later. He did not have to take the trouble of accosting anyone himself. His gangsters would all give him a lion's share of

---

2 *loaferskap* vagrancy   3 *kwela-kwela* police van

whatever they made, and moreover buy him some beers and brandy. He kept adjusting his polished belt over his potbelly as the .38 police special in its leather holster kept tugging it down. He probably preferred to wear his gun unconventionally, cowboy style.

A boy of about seventeen was caught with a knife in his pocket, a dangerous weapon. They slapped him a few times and let him stand handcuffed gainst the concrete wall of the station. Ten minutes later his well-rounded sister alighted from the train to find her younger brother among the prisoners. As she was inquiring from him why he had been arrested, and reprimanding him for carrying a knife, one of the younger reservists came to stand next to her and started pawing her. She let him carry on, and three minutes later her brother was free. The reservist was beaming all over his face, glad to have won himself a beautiful woman in the course of his duties and little knowing that he had been given the wrong address. Some of our Black sisters are at times compelled to go all the way to save their menfolk, and, as always, nothing can be done about it.

There was a man coming down Mohale Street, conspicuous amidst the crowd because of the bag and baggage that was loaded on his overall-clad frame. On his right shoulder was a large suitcase with a grey blanket strapped to it with flaxen strings. From his left hand hung a bulging cardboard box, only a few inches from the ground, and tilting him to that side. He walked with the bounce of someone used to walking in gumboots or on uneven ground. There was the urgency of someone who had a long way to travel in his gait. It was doubtless a *goduka* on his way home to his family after many months of work in the city. It might even have been years since he had visited the countryside.

He did not see the hidden *kwela-kwela*, which might have forewarned him of the danger that was lurking at the station. Only when he had stumbled into two reservists, who stepped into his way and ordered him to put down his baggage, did he perhaps remember that it was Friday and raid-day. A baffled expression sprang into his face as he realized what he had walked into. He frantically went

99

through the pockets of his overalls. The worried countenance deepened on his dark face. He tried again to make sure, but he did not find what he was looking for. The men who had stopped him pulled him to one side, each holding him tightly by the sleeve of his overall. He obeyed meekly like a tame animal. They let him lift his arms while they searched him all over the body. Finding nothing hidden on him, they demanded the inevitable book, although they had seen that he did not have it. He gesticulated with his hands as he explained what had caused him not to be carrying his pass with him. A few feet above them, I could hear what was said.

'Strue, *madoda*,'[4] he said imploringly, 'I made a mistake. I luggaged the pass with my trunk. It was a jacket that I forgot to search before I packed it into the trunk.'

'How do we know that you're not lying?' asked one of the reservists in a querulous voice.

'I'm not lying, *mfowethu*.[5] I swear by my mother, that's what happened,' explained the frightened man.

The second reservist had a more evil and uncompromising attitude. 'That was your own stupidity, mister. Because of it you're going to jail now; no more to your wife.'

'Oh, my brother. Put yourself in my shoes. I've not been home to my people for two years now. It's the first chance I have to go and see my twin daughters who were born while I've been here. Feel for another poor Black man, please, my good brother. Forgive me only for this once.'

'What? Forgive you? And don't give us that slush about your children. We've also got our own families, for whom we are at work right now, at this very moment,' the obstinate one replied roughly.

'But, *mfo*. Wouldn't you make a mistake too?'

That was a question the cornered man should not have asked. The reply this time was a resounding slap on the face. 'You think I'm stupid like you, huh? Bind this man, Mazibuko, put the bloody irons on the dog.'

'No, man. Let us talk to the poor bloke. Perhaps he can do something for us in exchange for the favour of letting him

---

4 *madola* 5 *mfowethu* terms of respect

proceed on his way home,' the less volatile man suggested, and pulled the hostel man away from the rest of the arrested people.

'*Ja*. Speak to him yourself, Mazibuko. I can't bear talking to rural fools like him. I'll kill him with my bare hands if he thinks that I've come to play here in Johannesburg!' The anger in the man's voice was faked, the fury of a coward trying to instil fear in a person who happened to be at his mercy. I doubted if he could face up to a mouse. He accosted two boys and ran his hands over their sides, but he did not ask for their passes.

'You see, my friend, you're really in trouble. I'm the only one who can help you. This man who arrested you is not in his best mood today. How much have you got on you? Maybe if you give something he'll let you go. You know what wonders money can do for you. I'll plead for you; but only if I show him something can he understand.' The reservist explained the only way out of the predicament for the trapped man, in a smooth voice that sounded rotten through and through with corruption, the sole purpose for which he had joined the 'force'.

'I haven't got a cent in my pocket. I bought provisions, presents for the people at home and the ticket with all the money they gave me at work. Look, *nkosi*,[6] I have only the ticket and the papers with which I'm going to draw my money when I arrive at home.' He took out his papers, pulled the overall off his shoulders and lowered it to his thighs so that the brown trousers he wore underneath were out in the open. He turned the dirty pockets inside out. 'There's nothing else in my pockets except these, mister, honestly.'

'Man!'

'Yessir?'

'You want to go home to your wife and children?'

'Yes, *please*, good man of my people. Give me a break.'

'Then why do you show me these damn papers? They will feed your own children, but not mine. When you get to your home you're going to draw money and your kids will be

---

6 *nkosi* term of respect

scratching their tummies and dozing after a hectic meal, while I lose my job for letting you go and my own children join the dogs to scavenge the trashbins. You're mad, *mos.*' He turned to his mate. 'Hey, Baloyi. Your man says he hasn't got anything, but he's going to his family which he hasn't seen for two years.'

'I told you to put the irons on him. He's probably carrying a little fortune in his underpants. Maybe he's shy to take it out in front of the people. It'll come out at the police station, either at the charge office or in the cells when the small boys shake him down.'

'Come on, you. Your hands, maan!'

The other man pulled his arms away from the manacles. His voice rose desperately, *'Awu* my people. You mean you're really arresting me? Forgive me! I pray do.'

A struggle ensued between the two men.

'You're resisting arrest? You – ' and a stream of foul vitriolic words concerning the anatomy of the hostel man's mother gushed out of the reservist's mouth.

'I'm not, I'm not! But please listen!' The hostel man heaved and broke loose from the reservist's grip. The latter was only a lump of fat with nothing underneath. He staggered three steps back and flopped on his rump. When he bounced back to his feet, unexpectedly fast for his bulk, his eyes were blazing murder. His companions came running from their own posts and swarmed upon the defenceless man like a pack of hyenas upon a carcase. The other people who had been marooned on the bridge saw a chance to go past while the wolves were still preoccupied. They ran down the stairs and up Mohale like racehorses. Two other young men who were handcuffed together took advantage of the diversion and bolted down the first street in tandem, taking their bracelets with them. They ran awkwardly with their arms bound together, but both were young and fit and they did their best in the circumstances.

We could not stand the sickening beating that the other man was receiving any more.

'Hey! Hey. *Sies,* maan. Stop beating the man like that. Arrest him if you want to arrest him. You're killing him, dogs!' we protested loudly from the station. An angry crowd was gathering.

'Stop it or we'll stop you from doing anything else forever!' someone shouted.

The psychopaths broke their rugger scrum and allowed us to see their gruesome handiwork. The man was groaning at the base of the fence, across the street where the dirt had gathered. He twisted painfully to a sitting position. His face was covered with dirt and blood from where the manacles that were slipped over the knuckles had found their marks, and his features were grotesquely distorted. In spite of that, the fat man was not satisfied. He bent and gathered the whimpering man's wrists with the intention of fastening them to the fence with the handcuffs.

'Hey, hey, hey, Satan! Let him go. Can't you see that you've hurt that man enough?'

The tension was building up to explosion point and the uniformed policeman sensed it.

'Let him go, boys. Forgive him. Let him go,' he said, shooting nervous glances in all directions.

Then the beaten-up man did the most unexpected and heart-rending thing. He knelt before the one ordering his release and held his dust-covered hands with the palms together in the prayer position, and still kneeling he said, 'Thank you very much, my lord. God bless you. Now I can go and see my twins and my people at home.'

He would have done it. Only it never occurred in his mind at that moment of thanksgiving to kiss the red gleaming boots of the policeman.

The miserable man beat the dust off his clothes as best he could, gathered his two parcels and clambered up the stairs, trying to grin his thanks to the crowd that had raised its voice of protest on his behalf. The policeman decided to call it a day. The other unfortunates were shepherded to the waiting *kwela-kwela*.

I tried to imagine how the man would explain his lumps to his wife. In the eye of my mind I saw him throwing his twins into the air and gathering them again and again as he played with them.

'There's still a long way to cover, my friend,' I heard Mandla saying into my ear.

'Before?' I asked.

'Before we reach hell. Ha, ha, ha! Maybe there we'll be men.'

'Ha, we've long been there. We've long been in hell.'

'Before we get out, then.'

SHEILA ROBERTS

from The Weekenders

I used to be a nurse but I didn't finish my training. It's not nice work, you know. Man, you're on your feet the whole day and the pay's not good. And after a while people get you down, always wanting attention for the slightest thing. You don't get used to pain and blood and all the mess, people wetting themselves, old people who can't wait for the bedpan, the enemas, the bedsores, the catheters, and having to wash the dead. A lot of girls think they'll end up marrying doctors, but I can tell you, the students'll screw and drink with you but they mostly end up marrying their senior partners' daughters once they've finished with their internship. Some of the younger doctors are already caught: they married so that their wives could work and help put them through med school. And the older doctors usually have a lot of bloody kids. They're not even worth having affairs with. The Afrikaners are building up the South African nation, the Catholics won't use birth control, and the Jews don't believe in abortion. Another thing, if a doctor can stick up a family photo with a ton of kids on it, his female patients think he's a nice guy and they don't mind stripping.

Nursing's no life, man. They say you get hardened to all the cruelty and misery in life, but I don't know. Maybe I didn't stay long enough to test the truth of that. I just gave it up after two years. I think my talent is for getting on with people. I like people, especially men.

So when I saw that job advertised by Champagne Inns, I said to myself, now honestly, Annette, what training do you need to be a hostess and chauffeur? None at all, just a pleasant personality, the ability to keep smiling, and a driver's licence. I applied, and they seemed to be impressed with my nursing experience. Also, I'm not bad looking and I look nice in tailored skirts and blazers, especially in shades of blue.

They first put me to work at the small inn at Umhlanga Rocks and then offered me the job in the new inn out here. I was tired of the heat and humidity of Natal, so I said yes. I was one of the first women they sent out and I really enjoyed myself. There was the construction team and all the contractors all over the bloody place. I was the driver they used to send out to the airport to fetch Venner and Robinson and the others whenever they flew in. We all used to have a lot of fun at night, especially when they started installing the roulette tables. We gambled for small amounts just for fun and, God, we used to drink!

Once they tried to start training Black staff things weren't so good. I was telling the others this when we were going to drive those people to that stupid picnic. I can't associate with a Black on equal terms. I don't know why, I'm just uneasy. As soon as they talk right and smarten up they seem to be thinking themselves great, and it gets my back up. I hate it when Tshithaban men make passes at me in the street, I could kill them. I'll soon be transferring to Milner Park, I hope.

At first I fancied that Arthur Robinson, I can tell you. He's a damn good-looker, with those big shoulders and straight back, and, man, I like the way he walks. But he kept to himself, didn't seem to want to know me. And then I noticed him with that snob-face, Gretchen. She was among the first of the croupiers to be sent out. I'm bloody glad now I didn't let that Arthur put his shoes under *my* bed. My conscience would worry me something awful now. His poor wife so badly hurt by those terrorists. Not that I liked her much when I did meet her. One of those people who look as if they've got the whole bloody world on their shoulders. Concerned about the Blacks all the time, and talking about this being right and that being right and the next thing being wrong. It gets you down. And the men she was with, the skinny *ou*[1] and the American, on that picnic, just went to show what her taste was like. No wonder her husband was screwing around. Though, actually, I always feel sympathetic to the woman. Men mess around whether they've got reason to or not.

I hope the police round those crooks up. Then they can turn

1 *ou* guy

them over to me, one by one. I could think of some tortures for them. First I'd cut off their pricks with a blunt scissors.

On the one hand my nursing experience was a good thing: it got me this job. But, on the other, it's been a damn nuisance. Every time somebody cuts himself, the cry goes up, Annette, Annette, where are you? Once one of the Blacks got his finger cut off in a saw. What did he do? He put the damn thing in a match-box and brought it to me! What must I do? Stitch it on again? And every time one of the girls gets a period pain, she'll come and tell me all about it. If people only knew how boring they are. But I have been of help occasion-ally, like that time when Yvette fainted and when Marcia decided to take an overdose of sleeping pills, stupid thing.

So naturally when that bearded American found the sack in front of the hotel and realized there was a body in it, every-body started screaming for Annette. Thank goodness there was a doctor in the hotel, poor devil, trying to have a bit of a holiday. They got him up right away, feeling it was only right that he should cut open the sack. And people were pushing me forward to help. God's truth! I'd never seen anything like it!

The smell was terrible! Down her mouth and all over her chin and breasts was this drying mixture of vomit and semen, you could just smell it! Those bladdy Black bastards. Honestly, if a Black came in my mouth I'd just die. Her crotch and backside and thighs and everything were sticky with blood and shit. It was to be expected. Her body was stiff, her knees clenched to her chest, but she was conscious. Every now and then her body would tremble and then be still.

'God, who *did* this to you?' I asked her as we lifted her on to a stretcher.

Doctor Steinberg told me to shut up.

She didn't answer but her eyes looked. Twice in my life I've seen that look. It frightens you. At school back in Daspoort there was this kid with very dark skin and krissy[2] hair. We all knew he had the tarbrush, and some of the boys used to beat him up bad. I remember once when Hansi Schoen beat him

---

2 *krissy* kinky

so badly that his collar bone was broken, he got this look in his eyes. Kind of hard, but faraway, and very steady. I've seen it in a woman before too. There was this woman in the General with cancer, they told her she had about two years to live. Her kids were tiny and apparently she'd had great trouble conceiving them. I came to straighten her bed and she looked at me and said, out of the blue like that, I am certainly not going to die yet. And Arthur Robinson's wife too. It's hard to explain. It's as if the person's soul has changed shape. I don't know whether people have souls. I read in a book once that somebody was weighing souls. Weigh the body before death and weigh it immediately after death. The human soul weighs twenty-one grams. What do you know? Anyway, Robinson's wife had this look in her eyes. A devilish look, as if nothing can ever really move her again, you know, to pity or tears. Something that says, forget it man, I am going to survive even if it means hating God.

But, man, she wouldn't talk. Not at all, for nobody. Doctor Steinberg wanted to put her out altogether, but there was no anaesthetist to be had or anything. He got supplies of local anaesthetic from the nearby clinic and he gave her a couple of shots so that he could do some stitching. Myself and Gretchen (it serves her right) we had to put on overalls and help wash her down, very carefully of course, while Doctor Steinberg treated the burns and cuts and bruises. He himself washed her head and put antiseptic on it and bandaged it, telling us he didn't need us. Man, he had tears in his eyes, which is a very rare thing for a doctor. Meanwhile, Gretchen was throwing up in the bucket, things had finally got to her. Then the South African police arrived from the border post. The Tshithaba police had already put in an appearance, looked around, and taken themselves off.

But she wouldn't talk, not at all. The officer tried very gently to ask her questions. But her mouth was closed. Just her eyes stared at nobody.

'I honestly don't think Mrs Robinson is in any condition to answer questions,' said Doctor Steinberg.

'We understand, Doctor,' said the lieutenant. 'But we'd like to apprehend the people who did this to her . . . as soon as possible.'

'I know,' said the doctor. 'But I am seriously worried about her . . . her mental condition . . . as well as her physical . . . I think you will simply have to make do with questioning the other people . . . involved.'

'Yes, we will have to do that.'

So the police left.

She turned her head away when her husband came tiptoeing in. She would not look at him even when he whispered her name. He stood there, stiff as a post, white in the face. He really didn't persist. Had I been her and if I had a husband, I would have expected him to fling himself across my bed and howl like a lost soul. But men these days . . . Anyway, he just stood there, looking down at her as if it all was her own fault. And she just looked at the wall.

Let me tell you my own theory about why those bastards did this: they were surprised, you see, when the White people came riding up – they thought the game was up. So they nabbed them and threw them into that hut. But something, there must have been something about Joanne Robinson that caught their attention. Something unusual. So they took her and raped her. But to their surprise, she didn't scream or cry or anything. So they lit cigarettes and burnt her. But she still didn't cry. Maybe she didn't want to frighten the others by letting them hear her screams. Stupid woman! Anyway, then they raped her up her arse and her flesh tore. I've seen it happen in childbirth. But by that stage the tissue can be numb, I hope it was in her case. But she still keeps quiet, and they can't understand it. It makes them mad, crazy, so they take out knives and make little cuts on her, but she remains dumb. They are infuriated, but they're also a little bit scared. But what really grips them is her unnatural silence. Why won't she scream? At last they get a fine idea. A white woman's hair. Madam at the hairdressers. Cut it off. But they don't have a scissors, so they use their knives and they hack the stuff off her head.

I think if Blacks admire *anything*, it's strength. Why do you think Idi Amin stayed in power that long hey? They see her silence as enormous strength, and probably it is. So they decide not to kill her. But, she is a terrible sight, so they get a mealie sack and pull it over her and tie it closed. They want to show the White people a thing or three. And they want the money and the political prisoners or whoever to be released. So they dump it in front of the hotel.

Man, the truth is, Joanne Robinson should have screamed and screamed like hell to begin with and she would have got off with just being raped.

Things have at least cleared up, or should I say settled themselves. Joanne has left me and is living with her sister. I knew the break was coming even before she left the hospital and so had taken the time to discuss with Advocate du Toit my chances of gaining custody of the children. He thought they were good, particularly in view of Joanne's obviously disturbed mental state. But, believe it or not, she didn't even ask to take the children with her. She told me she wanted to leave and when I said it would be very sensible if I instituted divorce proceedings, she agreed without a fuss. I then said very reasonably, I thought, touching her on the shoulder, that I felt it would be best if the children stayed with me, and again she agreed, just nodding her head silently. You know, the more I see of female behaviour, the more I am convinced that men are more deeply parental than they are. Anyway, Laurie and Ronald seem to be doing perfectly all right, what with my mother's constant visits, Gretchen's kindness in coming over each night to cook for them and me, and the Black servants' truly indulgent attention. I feel an immense relief being able to come home at night to smiling faces and not having to anticipate solemn discussion about poverty and misery and the political cock-up when all I want to do is relax with my family. Gretchen is also a fine woman to have in bed. She rouses easily, expresses her enjoyment, and comes without any difficulty. I've never understood why so many women turn sex into a complicated business when it's essentially a very simple human activity.

The trial is over too, thank goodness. I was bloody glad that Black swine got life, and glad that the judge agreed to Joanne's testimony being brief. It was hard for me to believe that the person standing in the witness box was my wife. She didn't look like the woman I'd married. The loss of her hair has certainly changed her appearance, not only in that it somehow alters the shape of her head, I mean the very short curly hair-style she wears, but also in that it distorts her facial expression. Of course, some of the facial scars are still there and have an effect, but all the same there is now an intangible unfamiliarity about her and I am certainly glad she decided to leave. I mean, after *that* experience I could not have asked her to leave and have retained my image with the Company. People, not understanding, would have been disgusted with me. And I don't think I would have liked my face in the mirror when I shaved in the morning. It's all so very complex.

She doesn't wear the same pretty clothes either any more. The outfit she wore in court was not old but it looked dowdy and mannish, and the other day when she came to get the children for an afternoon she wore old jeans, tennis shoes and a loose tee-shirt. Nor had she tried to disguise the remaining scars with make-up. She looked like a released convict. Actually, she looks now, frankly, more like the class to which she belongs. Let's face the fact, Joanne married *up*. Certainly, she put herself through university and easily learned to copy the manners and ways of the upper middle class, but there remained something ineradicably working class about her. She never learnt to avoid unpleasant subjects of conversation (I always felt uneasy when I took her to Company functions), her sense of humour was at times bawdy and dull, and she never even tried to hide her origins. I persisted in referring in public to her parents' little plot of ground near Vanderbijl as 'the farm', but she would not play along with me, telling several people the truth, that her father was a retired NCO from the Permanent Force! Why could she not have transformed him into a farmer for my sake?

Things are going well with me at Champagne Inns. Venner has taken me off the Kwa' Metse job and sent me to start the ball rolling with the Lichtenburg Inn. He thinks I don't know why, but I do. Ever since all the newspapers splashed the story of Joanne's kidnapping and rape and the way the other three hotel guests were kept locked up in a hut, the Inn has been doing brisk business. The horse-riding guide now takes all riders along the very path Joanne and Stella and McLaren and Bob took and shows them where the incident occurred.

Venner also had the Board of Directors vote to pay me a most acceptable compensation for my embarrassment and, since Joanne and I separated, my relationships with other women have become easy and flattering. I was discussing this with Freddie Mostert the other day and he said that in his opinion Joanne was the kind of woman that made other women uneasy about getting off with me, something to do with her sincerity, he said. But then Freddie always did like Joanne a lot. I always thought he was in love with her hair. To tell the truth that's what I fell in love with myself.

At first I wasn't very happy about the magistrate's ruling that I pay Joanne a monthly sum for two years to enable her to improve her qualifications, but I must say when I see how she lives I don't feel so bad. She doesn't waste a penny on herself. She is continuing her studies with an obvious compulsion, never goes out, buys very few clothes, and seems to see no one but her sister and, twice a week, the children. I thought it would be worth my while to have her watched: I mean R260 a month for two years adds up to R6,240: a down-payment on a new car. But the detective confirmed what her sister had told me – Joanne is becoming a studious recluse. Fine. I also have outstanding bills to submit to my medical insurance fund for her and more will be coming because she has to have another stint of plastic surgery to her face and more patching up to the lower bowel. But after that the accounts should stop coming in.

Gretchen has marvellous taste and is full of great ideas of how we could renovate the house. I really admire a woman who can transform a home into a work of art. I love beautiful furniture and hangings and don't mind at this time spending some money on a few objets d'art and a statuette or two. It always used to annoy me that Joanne was indifferent to whatever shade of carpet or curtain we put in the rooms of that house. I remember how, when it was first built, she left the choice of colours and designs to me. She wasn't very good at entertaining more than about six guests either. Bron-wen Mostert could set out a delicious spread to feed twenty, while poor Joanne would make the sea-food sauce too thin, the French fries too dry, the steak too rare, and the salad dressing too sour. She just could not cook well. She did nothing well, really. She didn't have first-class dress-sense; she didn't run the house meticulously; she didn't organize the servants efficiently (Gretchen has remarked how very easy both Nimrod and Nomhla take things. 'If you don't watch it, this house'll turn into the Robinson Hotel,' she said half-jokingly the other day); she was never quite sexy enough for me; she was obsessed by but badly informed on politics – an annoying combination. She had no awareness of how her behaviour could affect my position – she never tried to influence the right people, and Goddammit, she *would* buy me things I didn't like. It took her so long to learn that I don't like others buying me clothes. I never wore the clothes my mother bought me as surprises, and I couldn't stand the pullovers and shirts and ties that Joanne would bring home for me. I like things to be perfect, exact, and totally appropriate. I'm not one of those easy mix-and-matchers when it comes to clothing. Things must fit properly and the colours must blend superbly or I'm just not interested!

The latest in-thing for men is coarse-lace shirts. The guys are wearing them unbuttoned to below the sternum with no undershirts but with chains or pendants round their necks. Last Saturday I wore mine with the fine gold chain Lillian bought me and my black Calvin Kleins. Gretchen told me on the way home that she had overheard one woman say to the other, 'Who is that gorgeous creature in the black pants?' I had a good laugh.

In a couple of years Joanne should qualify herself to get a decent job, say, with a law firm or even with the legislature. I foresee her taking to tweedy skirts and flat shoes, but also becoming a pillar of strength when it comes to the matter of organizing Laurie and Ronald's education. I am very thankful that freedom from marital duties hasn't turned her into a gad-about: that would have been so bad for my position. If there is one thing that does bother me, though, it's the curious detachment in her manner. I am friendly, even jovial with her when she comes to see the children, and I have even recently offered her more money if she needs it for necessities. I tell her of things that have happened in the office, and show her the improvements I've made to the house and the things I've bought, but she just listens politely while giving the impression that she hasn't heard a word I'm saying.

I must admit this too. Sometimes I am sad. She used to be a beautiful woman and she did love me. Honestly, sometimes it just seems to me that this country screws up everything. Luckily I have Gretchen and my job is doing well. But, this country . . . really you know, sometimes I wonder.

Look at the urban terrorist situation. Not good, man, not good. We've had trains derailed, bombs in shopping centres, shootings out in banks. The government and the police should be doing their job better. We all should be better informed, I say.

Those Blacks easily take over the police station at Mazelspoort. They kill a Black constable and they hold three Whites, including a lieutenant, hostage. They want money and the release of Mtlatla and Sigwili. They know, man, they *know*, the S.A.P. don't negotiate. Again, there's a shoot-out. Three of the Blacks are killed, the White sergeant wounded and the White lieutenant dies in hospital. It turns out that the poor bloody lieutenant has five kids, one of whom has had polio, and the man has been supporting a sickly mother. The result? A big fright for us all in the papers, and there's Joanne lying in hospital refusing to speak while they're stitching her up all over. What a wholesale bloody disaster!

At least the fourth criminal stood trial and got life. I'm sure he would have got the death sentence had it not been for Joanne's vague and sometimes incomprehensible testimony.

'Is this one of the men who raped you, Mrs Robinson?'

'I think so.'

'But you are not sure?'

'No.'

'Do you not recognize him?'

'I'm not sure.'

'Is he one of those who inflicted other injuries on you?'

'No.'

'Did he help to cut at your hair?'

'No.'

'Were you able to identify among the corpses which man it was who inflicted those multiple injuries on you?'

'No.'

'Thank you, Mrs Robinson.'

Oh well. I know the best thing for me is not to look back, but to look forward to a better, more comfortable life with Gretchen and the children.

CHRISTOPHER HOPE

The Flight of the White South Africans

(In 1856, a young Xosa woman, named Nongquase, preach-
ed that the day was approaching when Europeans in their
country would be driven into the sea — ENCYCLOPAEDIA
OF SOUTHERN AFRICA)

1

Kinshasa, we feel, is not the place to reach
At noon and leave the plane to endure inspection
By a hostile ground-hostess, observing the bleach
On her face, her cap tacked with leopard skin,
Faked, and far too tired for the erection
A good bristle requires. We make no fuss,
However, knowing why she snarls at us;
But proffer our transit cards, and march in

To stand at the urinal complaining aloud
Of filth, flies and spit, amazed that this
Is it, an Africa the white man bowed
Before, growling outside the walls of the Gents:
We fumble uncomfortably, unable to piss
Till a soldier, bursting from a booth, clodhops
Past, still buckling up, and the talking stops.
Steady yellow stains white marble in silence.

2

Perhaps, Nongquase, you have your revenge. Tell me
Why, when surf rides like skirts up a thigh, we bare
Ourselves, blind behind black glass, bellies
Up, navels gaping at the sun? We lie
Near ice-cream boys, purveyors of canvas chairs:
While they and the fisherman who stand

The Flight of the White South Africans

116

Off-shore, shooting seine, busily cram
Their granaries: we gasp, straining to fly:

While in the upstairs lounge, our waiting wives
Caress expensive ivory souvenirs;
By rights, white hunters' spoil; and home-made knives.
We flounder about, flying fish that fail,
Staring with the glazed eyes of seers
At our plane, hauled from the sky, lying like dead
Silver on the tarmac, feeling hooks bed
Deep in our mouths, sand heavy in our scales.

3

Our sojourn: what might dear Milne have made of it
Or Crompton, Farnol, even the later James,
Who promised homely endings, magi who lit
The lamp we wished to read by, gave us The Queen,
A Nanny we almost kissed, our English names?
We blink and are blinded by the Congo sun
Overhead, as flagrant as a raped nun.
Such light embarrasses too late. We've seen

So little in the little time spent coming
To choke on this beach of unbreathable air
Beyond the guns' safety, the good plumbing;
Prey of gulls and gaffs. We go to the wall
But Mowgli, Biggles and Alice are not there:
Nongquase, heaven unhoods its bloodshot eye
Above a displaced people; our demise
Is near, and we'll be gutted where we fall.

MIKE NICOL

Choosing a Cottage

Choose well your cottage you who come
To this cold country from angry cities.
It must keep you dry in wet months
When cloud closes in and the constant rain
Repeats that this may be home to some
While to you the hedgerows, gaunt trees
And black soil divide north from south:
Separate these hills from arid plains.

Peer through leaded windows on a country lane:
A marble face shifting from room to room
Unable to name the birds at the berries,
Unable to quiet those helpless screams
That torture the night. Wipe the pane,
Misted from close breath, assume
That elsewhere all is as usual; carries
On in the interrogator's white dream.

When your cottage, sited near a stream,
Built from local stone, the roof thatched,
A straight path to the door through
Thyme and other herbs, is touched pinkly
By a late winter sun it may seem
Pastoral – an ideal picture postcard:
But think of those remaining few
Behind high walls, surrounded by sea.

Mark this, no Cotswold cottage can free
You from the past. The death on the border,
The death in the Square still hold us
Who, wrapped against the cold, brave wet days
To exercise the dog. Even warmed with tea
We should not forget either him or her.
Choose well you who settle in cottages:
Betray no one, adopt the colour grey.

STEPHEN WATSON

Freedom

The almost naked man is running through the surf,
in a summer warm and weightless as the blood now in his
    veins.
He's running in the sun, in the daylight newly come,
racing the green breakers along a glassy morning shore,
veering to the sea that's skating white and beige,
half-floundering through thick water, through swirls of cold
    like smoke . . .
He is alive again, the light evaporating round his body,
his every stride igniting the metal, mineral brine
sluicing down his chest and legs, and rinsing out his clotted
    mouth.

In the distance the dunes are white as salt-mounds; the pine-
    mountains cones of green.
In the distance, two women, young like him, stark-naked,
lie facing the land, face down upon the hot, packed sand.
They don't see him approach and pass, don't see him seeing
    them
and increase his speed, the down-drive of his arms,
and fix his eyes to five more miles of waves that pucker,
heave, and skid across the flats of water-hardened strand.
They don't see him, that he's almost sprinting now,
puncturing the skin of water, fracturing its skin of light –
running in the only freedom he knows, the freedom of the
    body when it's alone;
in this lovely suppleness of lungs, flex of tendons, muscle,
reliving the light, thin limbs, the boy that he once was,
reliving the time before he became this body half-
    disembodied by its need of another body.

But now the women are behind; now there's no desire.
Here, in this vertigo of light, there's no need of any other.

With the beach disintegrating beneath a backwash,
in the glaze of water on his thighs and breasts,
with this coral roar of waves landsliding in his ears,
he wants only to run, to run on like this forever, through the
    summer,
in the water made sun, the light made water, the water salt as
    blood,
with his own sweat no different from the sea's,
his mind no different from those scoured shells the tide
    shovels back and forth like grain.
He wants only to run, faster, far beyond his own exhaustion –
always deeper in this freedom whose futility he'll know long
    before the summer's over.

OUPA THANDO MTHIMKULU

Like a Wheel

This thing is like a wheel
It turns
Today it's me
Tomorrow it's you

Today I'm hungry
Tomorrow it's you

Today I'm hungry
Tomorrow it's you
Today I'm homeless
Tomorrow it's you

Today I'm in prison
Tomorrow it's you

This thing is like a wheel

PART TWO

E. KOTZÉ

Day of Blood

Lya Solms shook out the last of the laundry with a hearty slap and pegged the trouser legs to the line. Then she tipped the bath of blued water on to the grass, scraped steel wool over the cake of soap and fell to scouring the buckets and basins with short fast strokes.

She kept an eye on the shadows, lengthening at the corner of the water tank. Early this morning, before she came to the farmhouse, she'd put her own washing in to soak and mixed the yeast and flour, rolling it into a ball. It was still to be kneaded.

'White and coloured on the line,' she said to herself. Then, in anticipation, 'And tough and tender in the pot.' A sheep was to be slaughtered later today. In her imagination, she was already stripping the fat from the wether's offal. She could almost smell the roasted crackling of the tail fat.

The sun blazed down on her shoulders. It was a sweltering hot day. The turn of the season sometimes brought such heat that a sulphurous smell rose from the rocks – as if the devil was hauling you once more over the coals for old time's sake before autumn's gold flamed in the trees. Not a good day for slaughter. On days like this the mugginess collected in the thatch and came down on you at night. The meat could go off too. But there were workers in the orchards who had to have rations.

Lya rinsed the clean buckets in the overflow trough, turned them over to drip on the washing stone and stuck the laundry blue, tied in its cloth, up out of reach. Then she swallowed the last drops of her cold midday coffee, rinsed out the mug and gathered her things together.

Her children were lying in the sun: the small one sleeping under a nappy, and the lame one with his grubby face. He watched her with clear bright eyes and tried to raise himself up when he realized it was time to go. She tied the baby on to her back, swung the lame one up on to her arm, and went to take her leave of the farmer's wife.

At the back door she was given her laundry money, a paper bag of coffee and sugar, and a pilchard sandwich. She was told she could keep the sliver of left-over soap for her own washing.

'And don't forget we're slaughtering. Come up when you see the shepherd's brought the sheep into the farmyard,' said the farmer's wife.

She followed the well-trodden path down to the river, over the dam wall, up the slope opposite and past the row of identical squat thatched cottages. The Solms family lived in the last cottage, a little way from the others, near the spinney of wild olives. One room and a kitchen, with a window, a door, and a chimney. And a worn verandah that was raised just enough to keep the pig from the back door.

School must be out because the chimney was smoking and the top half of the door was open.

An aproned Mimi had already done the kneading: a double loaf waited in the paraffin-tin pan.

'Mother,' she said to Lya as the woman stooped under the low lintel and put the lame child down on the threshold, 'Lewis and the others have got potatoes in the coals again.'

Lya snatched the rod from behind the door and whacked it down on the table. The two brats dashed past her and she swung in the air missing them. 'Why are you so disobedient? You can go to bed hungry tonight.' The farmer was getting very strict about the potato harvest and he checked personally that not too many went astray. You couldn't just go and help yourself any more.

It was getting more and more difficult to fill the children's stomachs every night. Yellow marrows and damaged potatoes weren't enough.

At least tonight she could count on the pluck. They didn't eat lung in the farmhouse, and if she cleaned the head, she'd probably also get the nose. She totted it up while she took the baby off her back and suckled it.

'You must run to the shop,' she told Mimi, 'and then help me to fetch water. I don't know if there's time to wash before they slaughter.'

The coins she'd earned with the laundry that day lay on her palm and she flicked them apart with a thumb, thoughtful then practical: two candles, a bottle of lamp oil, a box of matches, a packet of tobacco, a packet of curry powder. Sugar? No, then there wouldn't be enough for coffee, and the pinch from the farmhouse kitchen was already sweetened. But suddenly she longed for something tasty. After a brief tussle she gave way to the desire: 'And a packet of crisps.'

'And a jelly mouse for me? For the trip?'

'Mouse!' The lame one raised his torso. He paddled himself forward with his elbows and hung halfway up the table leg.

'All right, bring two mice. But you'd better make it snappy. Jackie, let go of the table-cloth, if you pull my crockery off . . .! Lewis, come and take the child.' But Lewis was out of earshot so she put Jackie outside with the hens. She couldn't risk leaving him in the house alone, he turned everything upside down.

Everything she had was hard-earned and there was no money for replacements. And there never would be. They were poor. Jan Solms's clothes were patched all over. Mimi's dresses were too tight, the younger children's hand-me-downs were worn thin. These days they were short of everything – bedding and warm clothes – and they were behind with their payments. It was bad if you fell behind and couldn't afford to bury your dead. There was nothing else for it: she'd have to take the children to pick rushes this weekend. They said six cents for a decent bundle and Mimi was already quite handy at it. She could look for more laundry work and Mrs Radyn from the brown people's school sometimes had darning and mending to be done.

She'd also get paid for cleaning the offal.

There was a threatening closeness in the air and the clouds banked up like great cauliflowers over the mountain.

Lya stood at her washing bath with her burden of guilt.

It was she who had brought ill-fortune upon their household while Jackie was still a baby. She had contracted milk fever and had to bottle feed him. Jan Solms had exchanged a sow and piglets for a nanny goat in milk so they had enough milk for the baby and themselves. Jackie was as fat as butter and right through the winter they'd eaten curds sweetened

127

with cinnamon sugar. Those were the good old days.

Then one afternoon when the baby had reached the crawling stage, she was standing at the stove stirring a pot of food, when she heard something behind her. At first she thought it was the child under the table, but when she looked round, she saw it was a woman, and then she looked again, she saw the woman's eyes. They were two flames. She got such a fright, she shouted a terrible curse at the woman. With that, the milk boiled over behind her and when she looked round again, the woman had disappeared.

It was the fire witch, Aunty Katy told her, and she'll be angry because you cursed her.

One afternoon when the men were busy among the peach trees and she was down at the spring with her washing, a black storm brewed. The wind howled and a great bolt of lightning shot down into the gum tree where their cow was tethered. Just one streak of fire, the smell of sulphur and the tree was shrivelled black and their cow lay under it, burnt through.

That was the beginning of their troubles.

She had to go out looking for a little skim milk for Jackie. He suffered. One day he got a fever and she and Aunt Katy did all they could but he didn't improve so they took him to the doctor and he was sent to hospital. When he came back he looked like he did now – his little legs so crooked he could only drag himself along.

Indeed, she suffered for that curse.

Lya kept an eye on the farmyard while she did her washing. She had only to rinse the clothes by the time they started slaughtering. 'We won't get it up tonight,' she told Mimi, 'so take it in otherwise the hens will sleep on it.'

'Lewis,' she shouted as she went down to the river, 'when I call you, come and get the pluck. And see that you fetch some water and look after the children.'

She was a very deft assistant at the slaughter. She made a fire under the black three-legged pot full of water and took the carcase from the men.

The farmer's wife brought a dish for the liver and kidneys. 'You take the heart and that fat and roast it for yourselves.' And the delicious sweetbreads.

Lewis came to collect the newspaper-wrapped parcel. 'Give

it to Mimi so she can get on with cooking it,' Lya told him.

In no time, the sheep was hanging. Then she tackled the offal. There was no one on the farm better than Lya with offal. But today it seemed more difficult than usual.

'I must get another blade,' she apologized, embarrassed about the delay. 'This one isn't scraping so well.'

The weather was closing in and the wind gusted against the fire. She pushed the burning logs in further and moved the blue bath that held the clean stomach and feet.

Lightning flashed now and then. But a long way away. The labourers, who'd knocked off, stood waiting at the cellar door for their ration of wine.

The farmer's wife came to see how she was getting on. 'If you've finished with the head, leave the chopping and the rest of the cleaning until tomorrow morning.'

But tomorrow she wanted to rinse her washing and then take the children up the valley to look for casual work – cleaning onions or hanging tobacco . . . Without stopping or even looking up, she said: 'It's all right, I'll soon be finished. I fed the baby before I came up.' She battled a bit with the tuft of wool between the sheep's ears, then at last the head lay in the basin with the rest of the offal.

She tipped the pot of water off the fire and collected the knives together. Just as she picked up the basin to take it to the chopping block, a clap of thunder set the earth trembling. The wind ripped the paper on the block to shreds. Lya chopped with short deft strokes, each one falling exactly where she meant it to. She chopped the nose off and clove the skull open, then she trimmed it here and there, fast and efficiently.

A few loose sheets of iron clattered somewhere.

Someone screamed and all hell broke loose. 'The lightning has set fire to Jan Solms's house!' someone yelled. 'Run, Jan!'

'Lya!' the people cried. 'Your house!'

Standing with the basin of offal in her hands, she watched the black smoke shot through with tongues of flame rising from her house. Then the wind whipped the flames up to consume the roof.

'My house is burning!' Lya took a few steps forward, then

froze. She turned with the basin of offal in her hands. The flames leaped up, livid against the black thunder clouds. 'My children, where are they?'

Jan Solms took a short cut through the mandarin trees.

The farm truck revved, loaded with workers and their spades.

'Put the basin down and go to see what's happened to your children. Run, Lya!' someone yelled.

She hardly felt the bramble thorns that scratched her as she rushed down to the river and up the other side. She'd once seen a child who'd fallen into a coal fire. And the charred cow lying under the gum tree.

One of the women had her baby. The lame one was hanging on to Mimi. He collapsed against her and she grabbed hold of him. His bottom was bare and he was shaking, but not from cold because even from a distance the fire was blazing hot.

'Ma,' he howled. 'Ma!' and clung to her neck with his strong sticky little hands. As she comforted him she could smell his singed hair. The fire crackled in the roof. Everything in the house was old and tinder dry and it burnt like petrol. The men flattened the grass all round to stop the fire from spreading.

Little by little the roof caved in. When the wind caught them, the rafters glowed in the darkness and sparks leapt out like fireworks. Quite beautiful.

Grandma Ruth said: 'Mimi was still out getting water with the two cans. Next thing I knew, she was screaming and when I looked, she'd thrown the cans down and she was running and then I realized everything was covered with smoke. I shouted to her: "Get the children." With Jackie it was touch and go – he was in the bed. He wouldn't have stood a chance if Mimi hadn't got him out because the fire was already at the door.'

Mimi was sobbing uncontrollably.

'Bring some sugar water, she's had a terrible shock.'

'They could both have been burnt to death.'

In the glow of the fire, they saw the skeleton of their lantern standing on the low wall between the bedroom and the kitchen.

Of all that had been in the house, it was the only thing she could still recognize. Everything else was burnt. Lya stood mute.

Her children were safe but they had nothing to sleep on tonight, no mug to drink from, no candle, not a pinch of coffee, or a single cent. The fire had taken everything: her table and the crockery, the portraits on the wall, the scrap of carpet on the bedroom floor, the clothes chest behind the bed with her good dress and Jan's black suit.

Lya covered her face with her hands. Twenty rand at the farm store, a rand a week, but the rand hadn't been there for more than one week . . . almost a year before she was square. How would she ever get it together again?

'Even the stove,' said Grandma Ruth.

'With the bread in the oven. And the offal and fat.' The pots and pans, the water scoop, chairs, the footbath, the sleeping mats . . . Lya Solms stood with wet cheeks and before the ruins of her house. It creaked and collapsed. The end had come.

Smoked curled up from the rubble.

Her guilt had been expurgated, Lya thought, turning away.

She was surrounded by the people she knew. They all chipped in. Everyone was good to her. The farmer instructed someone to clean out the unoccupied house next to Annie and George's. Lya's family were taken back to the farmhouse in the pick-up. There they were given an evening meal and a bit of everything to take away with them – maize meal, coffee, candles, and blankets from the bed in the outside room. Food and shelter for the night.

As it always is with a fire, the news spread quickly up the valley. And everyone who knew Lya came up with something. They were given food. Cheese, butter, jam, tea, canned milk and rice. They were given clothes. By the boxful. Summer clothes and winter clothes – all wearable. A kettle, a bucket and some crockery. The old man at the shop sent two flowery enamel plates with matching mugs. One woman sent tea-towels and a basin. Someone brought a table that only needed a little attention from Jan.

When the farmer's wife came down in the late afternoon with a pail of milk to see how they were doing, the house was filled with the fragrance of cabbage, stewing slowly on the open hearth. The crooked table stood securely against the wall, draped with a checked cloth that reached the floor.

And Lya was glowing. Yesterday she had been stripped to the bone, naked as the day she was born. For one moment she'd even wished the fire would take her too and make an end to it all. Now she had everything and more. Even a bed with an inner-spring mattress. She'd been down and out on a pallet of straw and now she had a soft bed and an almost-new wool blanket.

She had flour in the house and milk and she was going to make some curds with stick cinnamon and plenty of sugar. 'Mickey, bring in some wood and get Jackie out from under the table. He's in the sugar again. I'll smack you!' Jackie was suddenly still as a mouse under the long table-cloth.

Lya sang as she rolled her dough out, sprinkled it with flour and then folded it over again. 'Dear Lord, draw near for our feast, fill our hearts with gladness and your Holy Spirit . . .'

And she tried to work out what she'd heat the milk in – she was still short of pots.

Then, over the sharp aroma of the summer cabbage, she recognized an unmistakable smell. She glanced anxiously up to the roof, sniffed, then looked down at the floor. A piece of kindling had fallen from the fire and set fire to the sweepings she's pushed into a small pile. The flames were licking at the green and red checked table-cloth.

Lya stared at the fast-growing hole in the cloth. Fire, she thought, glancing quickly over her shoulder. Then hot rage overwhelmed her. She had paid. Her debt of guilt had been wiped out. What did the fire want with her now? She picked up the basin of sweetened milk and flung it in an arc under the table, over the burning cloth and the glowing kindling.

Jackie gave a horrified shriek and scrambled out between her legs, dripping wet. Breathing heavily, she stared at the wet patch her milk left as it sank into the floor.

She put the basin down and bent to pick up the child tenderly. Then she went outside into the cool breeze of evening that steamed up the valley.

Translated by Catherine Knox

JAN VAN TONDER

Dube Knew

It was Dube who had smuggled out the information. That was what the chief of the prison believed. And if it hadn't been Dube himself, then at least he should have known who it was.

'I know a prisoner,' the chief always said.

There had been an escape from the magistrate's court. One of the men from this prison had been up for a new case the police had brought against him. Daniel Banana, a blue-jacket who'd barely begun doing his stretch for his latest misdemeanour. Somebody outside had known that Daniel would be appearing on that day and had arranged for a man to throw him the loaf of bread in the dock.

The chief wanted to know how and through whom the information had reached the outside world, for I believe escapes count against a prison chief. This chief was still a young man but he'd already been made a major on account of the small number of escapes from our prison.

We'd heard about what had happened in court. When it wasn't Coffeeman who brought news it was one of our wardens. Sometimes these young White wardens shoot off readily when they get bored in their sections. So we find out about what is going on. When we heard about the loaf we didn't need anyone to tell us about the knife inside.

Banana was a dangerous man. The chief would have to explain how he managed to get away, even if it was in the courtroom.

Dube was called in for questioning. That's Richard Dube, not the fat Dube who never moved a finger except to smuggle or to carry tales to the chief. And so Dube was taken to the office. Coffeeman told me.

You see, Coffeeman always does the rounds with his little kettle. Walking slowly whenever there is something to listen to, and sharp of hearing in spite of his age. He said he could hear Dube telling them no, he didn't know anything about it.

'You don't want to go to the quad so we can ask you again, do you, Dube?' the chief apparently asked. We all knew about going to the quad. Who among us old hands will ever forget the time they rounded up the gang?

'It won't be necessary to go there, will it?'

''s true, Nkosi. I already told you the truth, Makosi.'

Who brought him the loaf, was what the chief wanted to know, and how he'd known that Daniel would be there.

It's a real madhouse at the courtroom sometimes with all the cases to be heard. One after the other our cases are taken. An endless number of accused coming to court. The prosecutors have a hard time keeping track of them all.

The regional court is also housed in the magistrate's office building. That's where Daniel appeared. F Court, I was told, and I know F Court well. The box is right next to the door, and once you're out there, it's just down the passage and into the street. The policeman and one or two warders usually sit beside the door. Behind the box is the public gallery.

I know F Court well.

And I know Daniel when he's got a knife in his hand; then only bullets can stop him. He flicks the knife in front of him in such a way that you never know when he's going to strike. He was doing his second stretch in the blue jacket because of that blade he loved so much. I know Daniel. We're buddies, he and I.

Daniel knew there would be somebody before him. He was just waiting until after lunch when everybody would be waiting for the magistrate to enter. The prosecutor was fiddling with his papers and more people came into the courtroom and the policeman was stacking the money they'd found in Daniel's vegetable garden. Daniel kept on looking round, and then he nodded.

The chief wanted to know.

'You're lying to me, Dube. You're lying!' He was shouting, and Coffeeman got too scared to go on listening. He went to the kitchen with his kettle.

The moment Daniel nodded, that loaf came flying towards him from the public gallery. It was too late for the warders or the police to do anything. Daniel caught the bread and twisted it. The knife was inside. He didn't even have to attack anybody.

Dube knew how it happened, said the chief. It's still Richard Dube I'm talking about. The other Dube is a good-for-nothing. What he needs is a spoon handle, that fattie, I often urged the gang leaders (that was before they got betrayed under the batons in the quad, I mean). The leaders used to listen to me because people call me Boss, but Fat Dube had too much money and grass. And wisdom is a whisper compared to the voice of smuggled wares.

So Richard Dube was taken to the quad with four warders. The steel door was locked after them.

I told a cleaner to keep the two warders of our section occupied, so I could look through the peephole in the door in the direction of the quad.

The six of them were close to the door and I had a clear view. A circle right round Dube, four warders with batons and the chief a bit to one side, just to check that the questioning didn't get out of hand.

'Right, now you can come out with it, Dube,' said the chief. Wanting to know who'd thrown the loaf and where Daniel had escaped to and how the information had got past the walls.

Dube shook his head and told them no, he really didn't know.

Holding up one hand to ward them off he kept the other one clutched in front of his belt like a man wearing leg-irons. I was some distance away when they brought him through the section so I couldn't see the way he walked, but I'm sure I heard the chains. I was upstairs in one of the cells when I heard the chains. If I could have seen him I would have been sure, because a man in foot-irons has a peculiar way of giving one small step at a time and he holds the ring to which the chains are fastened up in front of his belt.

I was keeping out of the way when I heard them bringing Dube past, for one never knows – the chief might get it into his head that you also know something and then it's off to the quad with you too. After all, Daniel and I were such close buddies.

Well, truth is a thing with many colours.

I saw Dube running from one warder to the other. And when I chose to close my eyes, I could hear him running. Warding them off with one hand, until the chief had him handcuffed. Then it was easier for the warders to get on with their questioning.

Dube didn't shout.

A few times he fell on his knees, but the chief is a man of mercy and then he would hold them back so he could get up again.

'Have you thought it over properly now, Dube?'

But Dube couldn't think properly any more. He didn't try to ward them off any more either. There was blood on the concrete, from his nose and mouth and head – from the few times he stumbled, I suppose.

I'm no longer sure how long the questioning went on. Later Coffeeman brought the chief some tea and the warders took a break. Until he put down his cup again.

I felt sorry for him. For Richard Dube. But how could I go and tell the chief that Dube didn't know anything about Daniel Banana's business? You can't expect me to tell them about Daniel being my friend and all. They'd have taken *me* out into that quad and then it would all have been in vain.

That evening Dube couldn't stand in the queue for his food and I personally took him his plate, with a bit of my own food besides. He didn't want it.

He just looked at me the way he'd looked at the chief when it was all over. The same eyes. And I could see that Dube knew.

Translated by André Brink

JEANETTE FERREIRA

The Lover

Crazy girl. I loved her. She laughed at me when like a bloody fool I told her one evening. On her birthday too, birthdays were always important to her. Old-fashioned, candle-light and a basket of flowers. She tugged at my tie and gazed at me with those two wonderful eyes: 'Hell, one can only love until one's thirty. After that you only start reliving all your old loves.'

Then two weeks ago she quite callously came to ask me if I didn't know a quiet seaside place where she could meet a lover. God, did she think a man had no feelings? It was like squashing one's heart under her heel, the way she stood there, wind in her black hair, white face demure. Shit. Probably a married man too. Her lover. OK, I know I'm no one to talk, I was also married. But I was prepared to get divorced. She was the one who didn't want to. Said it wasn't necessary. Jesus, one can't just go on fooling around like that, I wanted to be good to her. This kind of thing happens all the time. It's she who had all these strange ideas. After that you only start reliving your old loves. And now this other bloke.

'Who?'

She was blithely happy, goddamit, as if there'd never been a thing between us. If only I could get his name from her.

'Whitest of white hair,' she stood dreaming, remote from me, 'and these tiny freckles on his hands. . .'

'Oh fuck it. I'm asking you who he is?' Then she just walked away, that everlasting hurt like a hole in her eyes. If only I'd used my head. But one could never hold her, never contain her in your hands, she was always dancing on the tips of one's fingers. She was still laughing at you when her eyes would suddenly be crying, she would be standing there with her trim hips between your hands, then make the tiniest shrug. Gone. No way of getting to know her.

137

She'd been born alone.

I knew her body. Long ago. She could destroy a man. When she woke up in the morning you couldn't believe it was last night's randy little bitch lying so sweetly at your side, the two pillows like children in her arms, the mouth trembling, what hell she could condemn one to with that mouth.

She never wanted to love me with words. Always entangled in a web of theories and shit philosophies, especially Nietzsche. 'We're a civilization enamoured of death,' was her personal insignificant contribution.

Friday evening, when I went to her, she was still sitting peacefully at her desk, reading. I'd kept on visiting her, even after that night when I'd blurted out my whining love to her. I could still go to her, she knew of no finalities. Yesterday's unfinishedness could be fine again tomorrow, no problem. I went on Friday night because it was the next day she was going to meet her clandestine lover. Perhaps because I was jealous as hell, perhaps because I thought I'd find him with her. Why should she meet him clandestinely, with how much irritating smoothness could she withdraw herself from the opinions of others. She would receive him in her flat in full view of the whole damned world if she felt like it.

But she was sitting all on her own reading beside the lamp, her face on her knuckles. Quiet tears on her cheeks. She had such a peculiar way of crying, without contorting her face. The way she made love. With her total lovely body, abundantly filling my hands, but it irritated me and unsettled me, I always felt she wasn't really giving, she was keeping the heart out of her body. God knows.

We still had a talk that Friday night. The tears didn't amount to much, she often cried, nothing serious. 'Tears and orgasms are the same,' she shrugged off my question, 'both are over very quickly.'

Actually she was looking quite happy, she brought tea and from the small lounge came Haydn's Surprise Symphony. Surprise, like hell. All my questions about the so-called lover were in vain. The gentleman. She refused to mention a name, just tortured me with intimate details. 'His eyes are so gentle, and he can touch me so softly that I'm not sure whether I should fall asleep or wake up.' My God, what do I care about the bedroom techniques of some lecherous swine? I wanted to kill her. I wanted to protect her.

In the small kitchen the picnic basket was already packed. A blanket and her guitar. The prospect of a voluptuous day at the sea, and there she was chatting to me as if nothing was wrong. She was mine, I tell you, she should have been mine, I would have been good to her.

If she had been mine I wouldn't have been sitting here on this Sunday morning with her clothes in my dumb hands. One white skirt, broderie anglaise, size 34, made in Germany (stained), one pair of white panties of oriental silk, medium (stained), the blouse of broderie anglaise no longer white, she never bothered about a bra, one leather sandal missing. The clothes are torn, they had to cut them from her, they only found her late on Saturday. The sweet smell is not her perfume. Private Collection from the house of Estée Lauder has an exclusive, dry scent.

I want to see – a quiet seaside place, just like she'd asked. Why the sea? It could just as well have been done right here. If I hadn't been such a fool, she'd never before taken the pistol with her when she went to the beach, not even when she was alone.

I don't know whether she'd lied about the other man. Now they're all trying to prod me for the questions. There was no sign that she'd been waiting for somebody. There was only one wine glass and one piece of bread in the basket. But the wind could have blown their tracks away. How can one tell? And they could have drunk from one glass. How does one know? If only I'd known who the bastard was, because there was someone, I'd been suspecting it ever since her birthday. Perhaps he'd always been there, she said I knew him, everybody knows him. One doesn't know.

The blanket and the guitar were still there, everything.

On the blanket there was a damn crow, pecking away, before it calmly spread its wings and flew away as I approached. As if he'd been there first.

Translated by André Brink

GEORGE WEIDEMAN

The Afterthought

The Mirjam business happened just when serious trouble was starting once again. There were pictures on front pages: bus skeletons, people in camouflage gear, corpses. Stout headlines, however, reassured: 'Government Checks Rioting.' 'Minister Calls For Restraint.'

Then came the news about Mirjam, which was more distressing than the shocking headlines. And she thinks about it this way and that, and in her perplexity she does not dare cry on anyone's shoulder. And she rings Mirjam every second day because she does not want to believe it and she weeps and demands: why? why? until Mirjam, crying, slams down the receiver. And she reproaches herself, and thinks and thinks until a bizarre plan takes shape in her head.

She can visualize the astonishment on their faces when she, greying already from the temples backward, announces: 'Theunis and I are going to have a baby . . . an afterthought.'[1] She practises a few half-smiles in front of the mirror and tries to rouge over the resentful pallor of her cheeks. What she needs now is composure. The bitterness of the past weeks! So much discord her home has never yet known; it was as if an old abscess had started festering anew.

'The disgrace of it! Oh, Mirjam, how *could* you?'

'Talk is cheap, Mamma. You should rather have told me in time what is the best, the pill, or . . .'

'Mirjam!'

'Well, anyway, I'm going to have a baby, whether you want to know it or not. And then I'm going back to 'varsity and finish my studies. And I'll pay back every cent!'

---

1 *Afterthought* In Eastern Cape slang it refers to a child born many years after its siblings.

The Afterthought

For a moment there, one moment amongst days of cast-down eyes, she recognizes her own fierce pride in the firm line of Mirjam's lower jaw.

Then Mirjam cries.

Theunis holds her against him, and, past Mirjam's shock of dark hair, motions Martie to keep quiet.

Tempestuously she slams down the bottle of nail varnish on the marble surface. So angry is she that the stopper jumps off and the lacquer splashes like blood right over the dressing-table, across her hands, up against the mirror and into the cheeky mug of the golliwog, lolling there on its patchwork haunches. God have mercy . . ., she whispers to the mirror, throws herself upon the bed and wails until Theunis gently clasps her shuddering shoulders with both hands.

'We shouldn't blame her,' he says, after a while.

'How are you going to face your colleagues?' she asks between sobs. 'And what about Denyssen's post, when he retires later in the year?' He does not answer, but she can feel the stiffening of his hands.

Then she sits upright.

'I've thought of something,' she declares. While she utters the words, they sound so implausible that she nearly loses the thread of what she has been planning to say. Joltingly she then presents the scheme to Theunis, while all the while taking off and putting on her wedding ring: she is only just past forty – surely not too old to find herself with child . . . Mirjam could be sent away – the remaining seven, eight months she could stay with Sylvia in the Cape; Sylvia can be relied upon to be discreet. 'In the meanwhile I'll be buying maternity wear and putting together the layette . . .'

After a few long moments of awkward silence he asks: 'What about her studies?'

'Why, you've got influence, man. Write to the Rector and tell him that Mirjam wishes to study elsewhere; that she wants to change courses, or whatever . . .'

'And what if it doesn't suit her wishes in the matter?'

'She *must*. She has got no choice. After all, it's all her fault: it is she who is bringing disgrace upon us!' She wonders at the strangeness in her voice, and shivers.

'And when it comes to term . . .?'

'You're a doctor: it's easy.'

'It's not *that* easy.'

'Then what else? Can you think up something better?'

'There are places . . .'

'Never! My child is not going to share the same roof with a pack of hustlers. If you can't think of something better . . .'

'I don't know. I'm at my wit's end, I tell you. All we can do is to face facts . . .'

'What about your position – our reputation? You know perfectly neighbours will go to town on this. Remember the Olckers' daughter . . .?'

'I remember. I was against the ostracism; I still oppose it.'

She knows only too well; that is why he resigned as a church elder.

'And now it's *your* child.'

His meek eyes suggest: she is yours, too. She tosses her head.

'Of course there is *one* other possibility,' she says.

'Never,' he replies firmly. 'I'll never act in a way that's not ethical.'

'But you must know of someone . . . it could so easily be kept quiet.'

'It could equally well become common knowledge. And where would we be then? What would *that* do to my practice?'

For a long while they just sit like this, huddled close, but with the chill of the room between them. He looks at the mirror, at the rag-doll. 'No,' he finally says, 'I will not have my grandchild's blood on my hands.'

'But you don't care that we will become the laughing-stock of the town.'

Theunis sits with his head in his hands. When Martie has set her mind on something . . .

'I do care. I suppose we'll have to do as you suggest. And yet it's madness . . .' He falls silent.

Later he raises his head. 'Are you sure you want it that way?'

'Yes,' she replies. It's the only way.'

142

'And what if there's something wrong with the child? Suppose . . .'

'I've been thinking about that. If anything is wrong, we'll have to live with it, that's all.'

Then he remembers Sylvia: '*Will* she be able to keep it secret?'

'She'll be as silent as the grave.'

'I'll consult Ernst then. He is efficient . . .'

'Ernst Strassberger? But of course. Best of all, his practice is in Cape Town.'

'But then you'll have to go there yourself, later.'

'Of course. You'll just have to hint somewhere that complications have set in, that I therefore had to . . .'

'At your age there could easily be complications.'

'Must you always rake up my age? At all events: what do we do when the Women's League and other organizations send flowers – they would, wouldn't they . . .?'

'You're very sure of your popularity.'

'Be serious, Theunis. Don't you see that our whole future in this town depends on it?'

'I certainly realize that. Well, don't worry about it any more. I know Bailey of the Sunflower Maternity Hospital. I'll write to him; or no – better still: I'll speak to him when I see him at the Congress . . . It'll be easy to arrange that visitors be kept away from you; afterwards you'll just have to embroider on the complications.'

He stands up, his shoulders slightly stooped. But to her it feels as if they hadn't yet talked it over enough; as if he, as so often before, had passively accepted *her* plans.

The solitude of the house with its cold stone floors closes in on them, and when the street lights come on, Theunis switches on the lamp beside the bed.

On the table beneath it stands the framed photograph of an impish curly-haired little girl, in a red bonnet, parading a doll in a pram.

'Little Red Riding Hood,' he mutters roughly, and hastily turns towards the door.

That evening, like the previous fourteen evenings, he retreats, already dressed in his night-clothes, into his study, to be surrounded by heavy medical books, framed university photographs and certificates. When, for the umpteenth time, he hears Martie's heavy sigh, he swallows the last mouthful of wine, firmly shuts the door and lies down on the divan, his head resting on his crossed arms. He gazes at the ceiling, pondering mock pregnancies which he has encountered. But his thoughts whirl dizzily, like the black moth circling the neon bulb.

How can the child have changed so much? Or has he – they – never really known her? Rebellious she had been, always, and that he had spoiled her he must admit; even concede that he had favoured her above the boys. But hadn't they brought her up fairly conservatively? Martie? There was no emotional contact between Martie and her; as if they rejected one another. But that alone . . .

It had to be the university then. The peer group. Oh, but he'd been there himself, didn't he know how imperceptibly it overtakes you? There had been signs: the fuss about the multiracial hop. It had been kept out of the newspapers, but only just; and he had actually pleaded with the Rector: Mirjam had been innocently involved . . .

But *her* reaction had disturbed him even then: Very well, she had said, but you're not going to tell me whom I choose as friends! About a month and a half after that he had seen front page pictures of two students; clandestine presses, leaflet bombs, dynamite sticks. One name had sounded vaguely familiar: Gregory. And that weekend, when Mirjam arrived home, he could see the strain in her eyes. He would not question her about Gregory, for he feared that Martie would then upset her even more.

Martie tosses about: it seems as if the objects in the room are coming to life, as if they encroach on her with their peculiar and grotesque shapes. The golliwog looks at her with bloodshot eyes; the large brown *chaise-longue* thrusts its shining round thighs against the bedside; the abstract figures on the lampshade resemble fertility symbols. The wind bulges the curtains to the outside; across the street the mayor laughingly takes leave of the headmaster and his spouse. She pulls the pillow over her ears. If only she could open the

The Afterthought

Bible now; how readily she has performed that act in front of the prayer group! But for some weeks now, it has felt as if that Christ to whom she refers so readily has never been resurrected – as if He was still lying behind chill stone.

News is that the town is going to be incorporated into a neighbouring independent homeland. For two days the townspeople have been talking of nothing else. They are divided by speculations – into those who think that it is the most satisfactory move for the Government in its present dilemma, and those who fear that a new dilemma is being created and that the authorities are bending over backwards to appease pressure groups. Still others are convinced that the forthcoming election will prevent the Government from yielding to further demands. Some fatalists regard everything as happening too late in any case.

Martie is rather grateful: now she has the opportunity to announce her tidings more confidently.

Naturally, Theunis is in the thick of things: he serves on the Board and will probably be the next mayor. Last night he has had to explain to two unruly farmers that he would oppose incorporation with every means at his disposal.

'Otherwise it will be war, it is as simple as that: a frontier war just like before – we have been too indulgent,' threatens one man, a pig farmer, thickset with a ruddy complexion.

She pours coffee and, although she is repelled by the yellowish sweat stains around his socks just above the shoes, enthusiastically assents, for she has been brought up that way: to yield too much means in the end to lose everything that has been yours.

'They take everything that we have won with blood and sweat . . .' puts in the other farmer, a stringy man with double bags under his eyes; and he knocks out his pipe so vehemently that half the ash spills in a black rain all over the small yellow-wood table.

'It is like a sow: if the litter is too large, they'll guzzle her to death,' the red-faced farmer adds. 'The whole country is being swilled, and we can do nothing about it. The Government is paralysed . . . What will happen to our children?'

Martie, tensely alert for an opportunity to break her news, breaks in: 'True, Mr Lubbe, and our people hesitate to have

more children. It seems a disgrace to have more than . . .' –
she thinks of her own boys and Mirjam – 'three children.
Why, the last census shows that . . .' She ignores the warning
in Theunis's lowering eyes.

'Precisely!' agrees the lean farmer, 'that hits the mark,
Madam. Look at those farmhands of mine . . . they breed like
flies. And it's no use talking to them, trying to make them see
sense. They'll blandly let you know children are God's gifts.
The Lord knows, I don't know what will come of it all.'

'That's why Theunis and I' – she pats her husband on his
knee and smiles archly – 'decided to make a contribution . . .'

The ruddy-faced farmer looks up, uncomprehending. Then
a smile breaks over his face and his eyes subside into his
plum cheeks. 'You're not saying, Madam . . .!' A chuckle rises
low in his throat. He rises and heartily hits Theunis between
the shoulder-blades. 'Well I never, Doc – and you seemed all
dried up!'

Martie can see how irritated Theunis is under the looming
farmer, but she feels distinctly relieved now that the ice has
been broken. Van Aswegen's wife, that much she knows, has
got a party-line phone right in the kitchen. So it won't be long
now before the whole district knows that Doctor Koorts's
wife is expecting again, after eighteen years. An *afterthought*,
as they say in these parts. A last lamb.

'Congratulations, Madam,' the stringy farmer now drawls,
'we have to start somewhere or we'll completely vanish from
Africa.'

These last words of the farmer echo in her mind in the days
to follow: the possibility of vanishing has not occurred to her
before. *Because of all the obvious things that were being done.* With
so many charitable good works and rescue actions in which
she is involved continually, which link up so beautifully with
the Government policy of rapprochement . . . There just isn't
chance to think of such possibilities.

'Good luck with the breeding!' One farmer finally rises,
heavily nudging his neighbour. She does not immediately
grasp the ambiguity of his words. But when she sees how
familiarly he scans her body, she stiffens, then consciously
relaxes, ready for her new role.

Night after night she suffers from insomnia. Even the sedatives given to her by Theunis are of no use. And when she finally falls asleep, she is overwhelmed by torments past and present. Hannie Beukes from down by the river, with whom the Church Sisters have had so much trouble because of her boarders' libertine habits, that same Hannie is now pressing herself voluptuously against the bed, her hair bound preposterously into a kind of high pony-tail: Well, well, Martie; serves you right! Now you'll have to swallow your own medicine. And she gulps down a disgusting mixture, a witches' brew of redbush tea and gouts of rag-doll's blood, so that she starts from sleep with a shriek, her stomach heaving.

From the study she can hear Theunis's calm breathing. She senses the heavy presence of the small hours of the night.

With precision she and Theunis make their arrangements. There ensue drawn-out telephone (hush! is there no one on the verandah? has Emily gone home?) conversations with an evasive Mirjam and a motherly Sylvia: as many as three calls a day.

Until everything has virtually been programmed.

A few things give her quiet pleasure though: she can wholeheartedly tuck into all that is sweet and rich now; the tedious penance of a doctor's wife's thin waist can, at least temporarily, be put aside. And the stuffing leads to indulgent reminiscences of past primary-school stage appearances: she had always been cast in the role of the heavy, blackened maidservant saying yes-madam and no-madam, much to the pleasure of the Strandveld farmers whose paunches heaved as they laughed, filling the school hall with tobacco smoke and braces.

The knitting of the baby's clothes brings pangs of regret mixed with pleasure. After all, it *is* going to be the first grandchild . . .

Hoodwinking Emily is the real test. Strangely enough, Martie has always been just a little in awe of the tall woman with the stoical expression. Now she surprises herself by chattering in and out of season to Emily about her pregnancy. And goes to bed at night with the knowledge that Emily didn't say a word. Almost like the time of the first riots: Emily, she had said, you should take your two sons away from the city; they'll only bring home trouble in the end.

But Emily hadn't said a word.

Mirjam, alone with her swelling stomach and her morning sickness, feeling lost without Gregory, looks from the dusky room towards the window, sees confused patterns of rain-drops thrust against the window pane, so that the landscape behind the glass seems strangely in motion. She leans for-ward and pulls the lace curtain to one side. In the drenching rain outside there *is* movement: a person, someone, a dark stooped figure at the waterside. In the semi-dark of the early morning someone is out there on the bank of the Liesbeek. A fisherman? But now it resembles a woman, moving to and fro through the coarse growth on the river bank, to and fro, and the movements of the upper part of her body make it seem as if she is nursing or hushing an infant. A woman and baby out in this driving rain!

Mirjam shivers, and reaches for the warmth of the room around her; and towards the unmistakable stirring in her belly.

She leans even closer to the pane. But the rain is pouring down more heavily than before, and she is no longer sure whether the woman is still there.

Where have they taken Gregory? She wonders if he can see the rain. It must be cold there, where he is. Oh, if only she could press his face against the warmth of her body!

The day just before they came to take Gregory and Essop away, she told him about the child. 'Ah,' he had said, 'per-haps it is his destiny to redeem our people from the slavery of the mind.'

At touchdown Cape Town is windy: one corner of Table Mountain's cloud cap is fraying down a kloof behind Devil's Peak. Everything is bulging in the wind: newspaper pages against fences, tarpaulins on lorries, curtains in high-rise windows, the shirt of a news-vendor. Posters are flapping out the latest news: 'Bomb Blasts in Durban . . .' 'Students on the march . . .'

The Afterthought

She cannot decide whether she should be upset by them, or be grateful that they divert unwelcome attention. She felt silly when Theunis parked the hired car in a cul-de-sac and helped her to dispose of the sponge from underneath her dress.

Theunis parks the car behind Sylvia's cottage, removes his sunglasses and nearly forgets to help the struggling Martie out of the car.

'You are forgetting your part,' Martie tries to tease, but in her eyes he can see dread of what lies ahead.

'And you must learn not to walk awkwardly any more, or to sit with spread legs,' he jokes back. 'The balloon is pricked now.'

It is true, she thinks. Now for the final two months; and then the week or so of waiting for Mirjam to recover.

From behind the lace curtains Mirjam sees the car being parked; as if in a film of which the sound has suddenly stopped, and for a few moments she is overcome with giddiness. Week after week she has been bracing herself for this: the bitterest of three bitter things.

That Gregory is not with her to support her (but would he? would he? the uncertainty!) is now almost a comfort. (But where can he be? What are they doing to him?)

The confinement here in Sylvia's house – however dear the old family friend may be ... Everyday's newspaper headlines, *ad nauseam*: Look, my dear Mirjam, they've caught some more subverters ... And why do they burn down their own class rooms? What is the matter with them? (What is the matter with you people, Gregory? You wouldn't understand, he said. How can you?)

The confrontation: come it *must*. Together with the growing unease day after day, her ambivalent feelings towards the little kicking being inside her, the fear of pain (nightmares of them cutting her open and sewing her up again, and then throwing her into the river, baby and all!). The truth simply *must* come out. (Gregory: we are the cutting edge ... He caressed her belly. Who knows, he said, who knows ...?)

She can hear them talking to Sylvia, in muffled voices they

149

speak, and with honeyed cadences, and she locks herself into the bathroom and vomits so that she can no longer hear them.

That evening she admits only her father to her room. He enters hesitantly. Are those lines of care around his eyes? Around his mouth? But his eyes are laughing.

'Granny, why do you have such a big tummy?' he laughs, and takes her hands in his.

'And how is my old wood-cutter pa,' she says and starts to cry.

He sits down heavily on the bed.

For a long time they sit like this, wordless, but he is clasping her hands in his. She still jerks and trembles, then finally becomes still.

If it wasn't for the lump underneath the blanket, she could still be six years old and very afraid of the dark, he thinks.

'You have always lied to me, Pappa,' she suddenly says, and giggles. 'Little Red Riding Hood was swallowed by the wolf, and she *did* die.'

'Why?' he asks, dumbly.

'I found out,' she says, proud in her privacy. 'I found out that one must die before one can live.'

That discomfits him, and he presses her hands even more firmly.

'You've grown up, Little Red Riding Hood.'

'In many ways, Pa, yes. But deep inside I am still very small.' Her voice threatens to wobble. 'And I fear for the little world which is forming itself in here. Just as I fear for the large world outside there.'

He dabs at the tears forming quietly beneath her eyes, but the conversation halts. It is as if both of them are wary of what must be asked and declared.

He wants to question her, about Gregory, but the words elude him.

Then he talks about politics. The election. The incorporation of the town. The spectacular concessions by the Government. Mistakes and wrongs of the past now being redressed.

With a shock Theunis realizes how wide the gap is between them: 'I do not say it to reproach you, Pappa, for I know that you will not blame me for this,' and she strokes the bulging blanket, 'but these things are coming too late.'

He cannot immediately reply.

Then she tells him about Gregory and Gregory's father, the haulier, and of Gregory's childhood days on the Cape Flats.

He listens, deep creases between his eyes.

'You see, Pappa, it's one thing to tell fairy-tales. It's something quite different to live them, and to survive them. The day comes when reality sets fire to those fairy-tales.'

In the heavy silences between them the years which part them shrink. Suddenly Theunis realizes that he no longer has an answer for tomorrow; that there no longer is a programme. He only knows that there will be a morning when he will have to take her to the labour ward.

Martie is knocking on the door: 'Now, now, what secrets do you have that we are not allowed to hear?'

Mirjam clutches his hands with both of hers. Helplessly he looks down at her.

'And then they filled the Wolf's tummy with stones,' she says.

'Then they filled the Wolf's tummy with stones,' he slowly repeats.

Theunis suggests that he and Martie shall stay in Dr Strassberger's holiday cottage until just before the baby is due. At first she protests, but is finally persuaded by Sylvia.

It is a difficult time. Theunis uses the dragging days to prepare Martie for the truth.

'The child will be different,' he says.

'Different?' She grasps his hands. 'What do you know? Do not hide things from me! Will it be disabled? Deformed? A mongol? But that can't be!'

'No, it's something else. But remember what you said: we'll have to live with it.'

'I remember,' she says grudgingly, after a while. There is something trapped in her eyes.

She sighs. 'If that must be our punishment, so be it. God knows why . . .'

'It's not a question of deformity, or physical disability,' he says at last. 'It has to do with genes . . .'

He tells her, saying that these are only suppositions.

Never has he seen Martie like she is now. His own perplexity can find no answer to her despair.

Then her anger flares in virulent eruptions that leave him speechless. She cries until there are no tears left. She pulls him towards her by the hair above his temples and shouts in his face: 'How dare you say it so complacently? We must do something! We can give it away . . . there will be some . . . an organization . . . you'll arrange something . . .'

'That's not Mirjam's wish.'

'But it's mine! Are my wishes of no account? We must go to Mirjam, immediately.'

He stops her. 'I will not permit it,' he says.

She is speechless before his resolution. She threatens, she pleads. Later she collapses, and he supports her. She hardly sleeps, and when she does drop off at last, she finds herself wrestling against awesome images from the past: Emily standing at the back door, her twin babies strapped to her back; the two little boys with dust from the yard like flour on their round little faces; the wolf-dog standing, froth at its mouth, over one of the boys; Emily crying hysterically; herself seizing the bleeding child and rushing into the house . . .

It turns out to be a difficult delivery. Although Martie is much calmer, Theunis doesn't leave her for a moment. When she speaks, she repeats certain phrases over and over again, as if they were all she had to cling to.

'What am I going to say when I go back?' she asks. 'What am I going to say?'

Outside, midwinter dreariness of a July day, a woman sings and sermonizes.

When the nurse beckons them from the corridor, he thinks: Yes, the preaching woman outside is right: when the Truth comes, no Lie will be big enough.

And pale, as if she herself has just come out of the labour ward after an exhausting delivery, Martie rises from the protective softness of the waiting-room chair, and as she stands next to Theunis, awaiting the small, cocooned bundle, she is looking at least ten years older.

And she cannot raise her arms from her sides, so that

Theunis has to prompt her at the elbows. But for the first time in days her lips soften when she sees the crumpled little face, the flatness of the nose.

'Little golliwog,' she falters. 'Little golliwog.'

Then she helplessly looks Theunis in the face. 'I cannot go back,' she says.

'No,' he says, 'no – we cannot go back.'

Translated by the author

HENNIE AUCAMP

For Four Voices

A JOKES'S A JOKE

The whole business began as a joke (Oom Toon Lourens said); a practical joke. Without jokes life in Die Hoek would get one down. It was a time of drought and depression and we bachelors – Beimen Botes, together with the little Scot who had taken over the store and post office a short while before, and myself – couldn't go on the tiles every weekend. It was a question of money and transport. Besides, you needed to be on your farm to save what could be saved. Saturday evenings were a killer for everybody. Before you knew it, you were on your way to Oom Frik's place. He was better off than we were, but that wasn't the thing. He was a cheerful person and so was his fat wife, Tant Das. At their place you could forget your sorrows for an evening, laugh and eat *vetkoek*, drink coffee or orange syrup, and sometimes dance, for Oom Frik had a gramophone – and a daughter. Nobody had ever thought of his daughter, Let, as a life's companion: she didn't either, I guess, because of the disfiguring birthmark that covered half her face like a purple rag. But even she was jolly and was fun to dance with. Often particularly in winter, we also played cards – nap and whist and *klabberjas*.

Freddy, the little Scotsman, must also have felt the loneliness in that world so full of sorrow, for every so often he would join us – although he could cope better than most, for he was a bookworm. He read big fat books, sometimes right through the night.

Good old Beimen, on the other hand, had probably never looked at a book since his catechism, except for the Bible – and even that, between friends, I doubt if he ever read. Not that he was stupid. He just wasn't that sort of person. He was

154

a man for deeds, of action. Hunting, swimming and breaking in horses. He was also the keenest on girls. He was bored after work. It was that keenness that made Oom Frik think of the plan. We were all gathered in the *voorhuis*, Freddy too, only Beimen hadn't yet arrived.

'Freddy,' said Oom Frik,' you're almost too good-looking for a man. Let's pull Beimen's leg tonight and dress you up as a girl.' 'Go on, go on,' we all shouted, the women first. I've often noticed that women are mad about games and seldom think of the consequences. Freddy tried to resist us. 'What about my moustache,' he pleaded. 'You can grow another,' said Oom Frik, 'and next time fertilize it from the beginning to show the mangy bits what's what.'

The moustache was shaved and the women took Freddy off to the bedroom. In the meantime Oom Frik and I kept cavey to see when Beimen was coming; we were as excited as schoolboys.

When Oom Frik's cousin from Kimberley made her appearance, both Oom Frik and I caught our breath, for the picture was perfect. Years ago Tant Das had had a switch made of the long hair she had worn as a young girl, and she had worn it until her own hair had begun to go grey. The switch was exactly the same colour as Freddy's hair, straw blond, and almost golden when the sun shone on it. With that he wore an old dress of Let's which Beimen wouldn't recognize since nobody ever paid attention to what Let wore, lots of powder and scent, a blood-red mouth and earrings. Then Tant Das and Let coached him with a vengeance on how a woman walks and sits to be ladylike.

Never will I forget Beimen's face when he saw Freddy for the first time: wonderment and joy, as if his prayers were being answered. He could not keep away from Fifi, as the niece from Kimberley was called for short.

Every so often Oom Frik had to go outside to laugh. So did I. The old chap was doubled up with laughter, and to recover from our fits of laughter and coughing we had a quick nip behind the quince hedge.

Our long absence suited Beimen. When we returned, still flushed from laughing, he and Fifi were in each other's arms, dancing to *The Young Bullock Waltz*, and Beimen, gazing pop-eyed over Fifi's shoulder, was singing.

> 'My ma's milk is sent to the farmer's table,
> what's left I drink as fast as I am able.'

Tant Das and Let nudged each other in the corner. They so enjoyed the joke that they pretended not to notice the smell of brandy on our breath.

We danced until three o'clock that night. Oom Frik and I pretended to cut in for a dance with Fifi, but Beimen said flatly, 'Sorry, chaps, you dance with Let and Tant Das, this girl is booked by me.'

How Beimen could have been so easily deceived remains a riddle. Freddy spoke in his own voice, a tenor. (I can still hear him singing *Bonnie Prince Charlie*.) Perhaps he was taken in because Freddy acted so well. The way he looked up at Beimen and then batted his eyes and rested his head on Beimen's shoulder.

Beimen was persistent. He must have a date on the very next day, and when could he come and visit her in Kimberley?

Tant Das and Oom Frik had to make up excuses on the spot. They said that Genevieve was leaving the next morning at the crack of dawn.

Beimen's disappointment made one feel really weird. It wasn't just disappointment, it was as if he was afraid that he was being robbed of something precious. It was then that I thought: a joke's a joke. Oom Frik didn't feel that. Not yet. 'Write to her,' he urged.

'Naturally,' said Beimen, even though it wasn't at all natural for him who never read and hated to write even a short note.

Those letters must have taken him hours. Two letters a week, we learned in a round-about way. Freddy never said anything about them until he came self-consciously to borrow the whole get-up, switch and all, to have a photograph taken. Then he mentioned the letters, in fact he had to. 'Beimen insists on a photo,' he said.

Freddy could control the letter business easily since he was both shopkeeper and postmaster. What he did about the postmark I don't know. Perhaps he had a Kimberley stamp.

As regularly as clockwork Beimen got his two letters a week and then waited, sick with anticipation, for the next.

Oom Frik went to talk it out with Freddy, and I, as an accomplice, went along as a witness.

'This nonsense must stop now, Freddy. I began it and I'm sorry I did now. We must call Beimen in and explain it all.'

Freddy didn't want to know. 'He'll kill you, he'll kill me.' (Did Freddy think then about that farewell kiss? That passionate kiss that Oom Frik and I had spied on from behind the lace curtain?)

'Beimen is a real brick and man enough to know when he's been made an ass of. He'll pay us back in his own way.' Freddy gave a strange laugh. 'I don't want to be around when it happens.' He stroked his upper lip, which was paler than the rest of his face. Suddenly I realized that he had not grown his moustache again.

'We dare not insult him. He must never know what happened. It would break him.' Freddy's voice got shriller.

Oom Frik and I looked at each other.

Freddy continued, growing more agitated.

'The niece must die. I'll see to it in a telegram.'

The niece did die. She killed herself.

That Saturday afternoon a young labourer walking past the post office saw something red seeping out from under the door. He thought it was paint, a pot of paint that had spilled. he walked nearer. Smelled the red. Tasted it. Then ran away to find help: blood.

Oh God, why did Freddy put on that bun and that dress before he ... I mean it was terrible enough, so unnecessary ... Why, why, why? Perhaps one of you educated people can explain to me. Sometimes after hunting we swam together, and I can assure you there was nothing wrong with Freddy. To be quite honest ...

EVERYTHING HATH AN END

Shortly after coming to Die Hoek Freddy McTavish wrote to a close friend in Cape Town: 'The landscape is quite Brontëesque, stark and desolate, but breathtakingly beautiful towards the evening, and the mountain air is invigorating, as Dr Sim promised me it would be. That, of course, is the whole purpose of my exile, for the mountain air is supposed to cure my asthma. But will I survive the Afrikaners? There is not a single English-speaking person in the whole of Die Hoek. Luckily for me I learnt the *Taal* at a very early stage, when my dear Mother, an Afrikaner by birth, was still alive. I can therefore converse with ease. But the Boers have so little to talk about, except the drought, which, by the way, *is* very severe. Basically they are kind, but naïve, the whole style of living nineteenth-centuryish. There is one character though who is fun, called Oom Frik. His wife, Tant Das, is rather corpulent; the daughter Let has no choice but to be virtuous, on account of a birthmark that disfigures her completely . . .'

His letters remained in that strain: something about the landscape, the weather and something about the people. Sometimes he wrote a long letter about a jackal hunt or an open-air communion service. There were regular references to individuals: Oom Frik and his family; a local philosopher called Toon Lourens; and increasingly to a young Samson, Beimen Botes, who could carry a sack of corn as easily as if it was a paper bag, but who shook like a leaf whenever he had to fill in a form.

Once Freddy sent a few snaps, but all were black and white and showed nothing of the soft sandy colour that can make the Stormberg seem so huge and desolate. They were depressing little snaps: one of the brick house in which he lived and worked (post office and shop) with two tamarisk trees in a bare yard. One was of himself, but out of focus, because Beimen, who took the photograph, shook. The friend in Cape Town never came to visit as he once or twice promised to do and later he stopped writing.

But that didn't bother Freddy. In fact it suited him, because he began to feel as if his letters had been treacherous. One doesn't gossip about one's friends. He had also discovered that the farmers did have something to say once you got past the façade of drought and Calvinism. They know the veld and the name of every indigenous plant and animal, from the resurrection bush to the river cat, and they tell wonderful stories set in the natural world, some of the stories chilling testimony of shadows that lurk in man. Of a boy of nineteen who fathered a child on his sister of thirteen, and, in despair, murdered her and hanged himself from the giant blue gum next to the toll-house. Oh yes, it is the selfsame tree that stands there at the entrance to Die Hoek, although of the toll-house no more than the foundations survive.

Freddy began drawing again, small precise drawings of plants and animals. He also kept a diary of the stories and sayings of the farmers. In the evenings he read Dickens, for he had promised himself that he would read the complete works during his exile. He spent his time in Die Hoek profitably, as it is called. But there were evenings, particularly over weekends, when they could not contain him, evenings when his emotions needed some focus other than books; evenings when he was desolate and needed people or, to put it better, a particular person. But that he only realized too late.

One Saturday afternoon when there was only an hour or two of the day left, driven by an indefinable restlessness, he climbed on his bicycle. First he rode in the direction of the town, that lay twenty-five miles away, but after a quarter of an hour he turned around and rode instead to Oom Frik's place, as he had often done recently.

In front of Oom Frik's house, with its high stoep decorated with the horns of buck, grew a hedge of sage bush, the kind with the red flowers that have sugar-sweet nectar. This was the only evidence of garden in all that drought.

Freddy sucked one flower after another of its juice, just as children always do. The sweet taste and the heat intoxicated him. Then Tant Das's voice broke the spell. She leaned over the half-door and beckoned him to her.

'Come in, Freddy, you'll get sunstroke – and be careful of those flowers, they are fading.

Tank Das served orange syrup on the stoep. Toon Lourens had also arrived and came to the House with Oom Frik from the stable. Freddy could swear that he smelt drink, but Oom Frik and Toon were both decorous. Too decorous, according to Freddy; this was usually the prelude to banter and rowdiness. And when they wouldn't stop, not even when what had been funny was no longer funny.

'I wonder if Beimen will come over tonight. Old Streepsak tells me he's having trouble with his windmill,' said Oom Frik and squinted up at the sparse clouds as if there was a direct link between the arid heavens and the problem of the windmill's pump.

'Oh, he'll come,' chuckled Toon Lourens. 'He's more scared of being alone than of buckshot. But only when the pump is fixed.'

A light breeze lifted on the stoep, but Tant Das from habit fanned herself with a handkerchief wet with sweat and eau-de-cologne. Let came out on to the stoep with a jug of orange squash. 'Shoo!' she said. 'It's hot.'

'Give Freddy some more,' said Tant Das in a motherly way, he's looking very down-at-mouth. How are your family, my boy?' Let nudged her mother, who had once again forgotten that Freddy's mother had died very recently.

'Well,' said Freddy, smiling absently. Why was he so disappointed when Oom Frik speculated about Beimen? Beimen contributed nothing to conversation; he just laughed at everything and got in everybody's way with his great big body.

Later, when the breeze became a south wind, they all moved indoors to the living-room, where the gramophone stood on its own table and the family Bible lay on another table made of yellow-wood that was inlaid with bone and stinkwood.

Once more Beimen was the topic of conversation.

'Poor devil,' laughed Tant Das, 'he needs someone to look after him, what with his only sister away in Tzaneen.'

Oom Frik interrupted, somewhat abruptly, as it seemed. 'Let's lead the old boy a dance this evening,' he said mischievously and looked at Freddy expectantly. 'Will you play along with us, Freddy?'

Freddy felt threatened, but vaguely excited. 'It depends, Oom Frik.'

'Look,' said Oom Frik, 'you're almost too good-looking for a man, Freddy. If we were to make you up . . .'

'Go on,' shouted Toon Lourens, 'it'll be sports. We can forget for a while about our mortgages with the Land Bank and the drought.'

'Yes, go on, Freddy,' begged Let.

'I've still got my switch,' said Das. 'We can use one of Let's old dresses. Come on, man, a good laugh never hurt anyone.'

Freddy tried to fight his growing excitement. 'My moustache . . .' he hedged.

'Grow a new one. And this time make a good job of it. Every morning and evening spread a layer of chicken shit on it.' Oom Frik laughed uproariously at his own joke, and Toon Lourens joined in and they both neighed until they were thoroughly boring.

'OK,' said Freddy quietly.

Then and there Let shaved off Freddy's moustache, after she had fetched soap, water, a razor and a strop. Then the women took him off to the bedroom, where they worked on him for a full half-hour. He came out of the room nicely rounded out, with red lips and cheeks and his straw-coloured hair caught up in a bun; a slightly vulgar-looking woman, perhaps, but with a certain undeniable plus quality.

'Hot stuff! If only Beimen would come . . .' Oom Frik looked out of the window and then went out on to the stoep. Hurriedly he came back. 'He's on his way, chaps; now we must get our story straight. Look here, Freddy, you're my niece from Kimberley. We'll call you Genevieve.'

'That's too long,' said Tant Das. 'We'll call him Fifi.'

Let and Toon Lourens laughed fit to bust.

'Just don't stand and laugh like that in front of Beimen,' Oom Frik warned them. 'Go outside if you can't hold it in.'

Beimen's shirt was open across the chest. (No shirt ever remained fastened across his broad and muscular chest.) He seemed to grow even larger when he saw the almost fragile Genevieve standing before him. He crushed her hand too hard and held it too long. Welcome, he rejoiced, looking deep into her eyes and meaning: welcome into my life. And she signalled the same message to him.

Never had an evening passed so quickly in Die Hoek. After supper – whole-wheat bread, dripping and golden syrup – the gramophone was wound up. *Old Hessie's Tipple* and *The Young Bullock Waltz*. Sometimes Tant Das and sometimes Let disappeared to laugh helplessly in the kitchen or bedroom.

Oom Frik and Toon Lourens celebrated the joke behind the quince hedge.

Coming back, they spied on Beimen and the niece through the window. Viewed from outside the dancing seemed more intimate, and on entering Oom Frik said, 'Ach no, Beimen, half-time, change partners.' But Beimen was adamant: 'Oom Frik has Tant Das and Toon can dance with Let, but this lady is booked by me.'

The later it grew, the more unreal it became for Freddy: was he playing a part or was he finally at home with himself? He took fright at his thoughts and tried literally to distance himself from Beimen, but Beimen, perspiring and jolly, quickly re-captured him. (Does he suspect nothing? thought Freddy. What about my hands and my skin? And what about the others giggling and suddenly disappearing?)

After one dance he excused himself and went and smoked a cigarette in the bedroom. Oom Frik peered through the doorway. 'You 're sitting with your legs too far apart, Fifi,' he bellowed with laughter.

'How long are you going to keep it up, Oom Frik?' Freddy asked. 'I'm beginning to pity Beimen.'

'No, you mustn't spoil the sport, man! We must start up a correspondence. Think of the letters and all the trouble Beimen will have getting his words in order.'

But the letters weren't Beimen's cause for sorrowing. They were Freddy's. Beimen came to him at the post office, big and clumsy and lost, just as he had been on that Saturday night.

'It was love at first sight, Freddy,' he confessed. 'My letters must bring her back here, but I can't find the words. You must help me, old man . . .'

Twice a week Beimen received letters from Kimberley, and twice a week Beimen rode over to dictate his passion.

'Freddy,' he asked one day in the middle of a sentence, 'what is it? You seem different.'

'I've shaved off my moustache.'

'Is that what it is? I could have sworn . . .'

But what he could have sworn to even Beimen didn't rightly know. He felt restless when he was with Freddy. Freddy strengthened his yearning for Fifi, for there was something in Freddy's gestures, his appearance that for one tormenting moment brought Fifi back to him, and he knew he must have her with him, at any cost.

'A photograph,' he said, 'ask for a photo. I want a photo of her.'

After a long debate with himself, Freddy rode over to Oom Frik's to collect the get-up of the big night.

'Do you mean you're bloody well writing letters and have said nothing to us?' demanded Oom Frik angrily. 'After all, the whole plan was mine!'

And when Freddy rode away with a cardboard box full of clothes fastened to his carrier, Oom Frik was still offended and decided to tell Toon Lourens all about it.

The following day Oom Frik and Toon pitched up at the post office.

'Look here, Freddy, this nonsense has gone on long enough. I don't like to see two grown-up young fellows making a spectacle of themselves.'

'But it's precisely what Oom Frik wanted.'

'Yes – then, but not now. A joke's a joke, but everything has an end. We must tell Benjamin.' (It was only when he was serious about Beimen that Oom Frik called him Benjamin.)

Freddy went white. 'It will humiliate him terribly. He'll kill me. No no, it's better he should know nothing. The niece from Kimberley must vanish – have an accident, marry, or go abroad. Please leave it to me.'

Oom Frik walked off morosely. Toon looked as if he wanted to stay, his long face suddenly serious, but Oom Frik shouted: 'Well, come on, what are you waiting for?'

Freddy stared after them. The afternoon was not yet beautiful. It was too early. Later the mountains would turn purple and the bare ridges would be clothed in final light. But now it was still dry and everything was desolate and empty.

He walked up and down in his room, confused and tormented. Occasionally he looked out at the yard, but never registered the two tamarisk trees. He had left three choices to the cousin from Kimberley, each as impossible as the other. He recalled Beimen's rough kiss, his china-blue eyes that were clear even after a day in the dust and heat, and he knew that he was lost.

Perhaps he had one chance. One chance in a thousand.

Carefully, as if for a wedding, he put on Let's old dress. A bluish dress with delicate flowers. He struggled with his hair, but managed to pin the switch after a fashion. He collected cosmetics from the shop that led off from his room, powder and lipstick. His hands trembled so much that he smeared the lip line, so that his mouth looked wounded, smeared with blood.

Hours later Beimen found him. He was sitting, legs spread wide, his head between his knees as if he were vomiting. When he finally looked up his eyes were empty, without hope or recognition or love.

AND HATH LOVE 1

On the road home Beimen Botes thought with a rising sense of shame: I went too far. I should not have done it. I must turn back and see.

He allowed his horse to carry him deeper and deeper into the afternoon. For he did not want to see the smeared mouth, the crumpled flowered frock, the bun crooked across the neck. The drought-stricken sunlight pressed like hands against his shoulders, pressing him forward against the horse, that smelt of saltpetre. He pulled himself upright: the last gate before his house. The gate glittered and faded, glittered and faded. Beimen shook his big head violently: was this what sunstroke felt like? He dismounted, opened the gate, and let his horse into the yard.

In the bitter cool of the pepper trees he found respite. He let the horse drink at the trough and walked him until he was cold, but did not unsaddle him: who knew, perhaps later. He went indoors and fell into a heavy sleep on his double bed. A troubled sleep. He saw Genevieve before him, sitting in a garden or in the veld. He walked closer to her, but when he placed his hands on her shoulders it was Let who looked up at him with red eyes in her purple, disfigured face, an ugly laugh on her lips.

Toward milking-time he woke, soaked through with sweat and with a violent headache. Perhaps it would help if he bathed. So, taking a towel, he walked down to the stone dam. It was too narrow for swimming and in any case had too little water in it, but he could at least cool his feverish body. He let himself sink through the shreds of duckweed, pushing the slime away in disgust. He began to wash himself passionately, particularly his genitals. Briefly he lay flat on the dam floor, the water and slime a roof over him.

His bath refreshed him, but it did not resolve the anxieties in him. The pain and anger that fought for precedence; the emotions that were foreign to his nature and for which he had no counsel. Self-loathing, hate for his fellow man and for God, regret, compassion. Someone, he felt in desperation, someone must accept responsibility; the practical jokers, not himself or Genevieve. Even though she had played along. (The body had not resisted, but the eyes were empty, the smeared mouth open but without sound.)

Beimen looked in at the kraal and once again mounted Poon. He leaned down to the pricked ear: 'I'm sorry, Poon'; and rode toward the Van Onselens. Toward Oom Frik, Tant Das and Let with her purple face. If they were not responsible, who was? God? And if it was God, what was to be done? Live resignedly with your sin and your anguish? Fix your windmill and pray for rain?

The Van Onselen homestead was deserted; curtains drawn and doors locked. None the less he continued to knock, walking from window to window. The panes on the western side were tepid beneath his fingers and suddenly he began to weep; he wanted people because he felt hopelessly lost.

Streepsak found him on the stoep bench. Legs apart he sat, head bowed, his huge body wracked with sobs.

'The master knows?'

'What should I know?'

'About the other little master, master Freddy.' Streepsak opened his mouth, showing the rotten stumps, opened it wide and slowly raised his hand and slowly crooked a finger.

'Huh?' Beimen asked stupidly.

And Streepsak repeated the slow gesture more with lasciviousness than with sympathy. Beimen stared with

165

revulsion at the finger that was both finger and trigger. '*Kapukile!*' Streepsak cried at the end of his mime. 'He killed himself, blew his head off.'

'My God, my God,' moaned Beimen, but he did not cry. His earlier tears had dried on his cheeks in the south wind that had risen.

'And everyone has gone there?'

'The police he was here and the doctor. The old madam has gone to help . . .'

Streepsak couldn't remember the word and Beimen was grateful, he did not want to hear it. But on the road to the post-office-and-store where Freddy had worked he muttered continually: lay out the body, lay out, lay out. Only a few hours earlier, that body, the same body had lain under him, the flowered dress pushed up above the white buttocks, and he had emptied his rage and disappointment into that body.

Two weeks ago he had met Genevieve, Oom Frik's so-called niece from Kimberley. He had lost his heart to her. Everyone was giggling that night, but he had thought: It's because I am so much in love. Let them laugh: I have the feeling and they don't, and it is a good way to feel, for someone wants me. Someone who is beautiful as well. There were no lamps in the room that Saturday night, only candles. And not many of those. 'A lamp makes the room so warm,' was Tant Das's excuse, and he had accepted it because in that soft light he could come closer to Genevieve. But they were already close from the moment that Oom Frik had said: 'May I introduce you to my niece Fifi.' At that moment Toon Lourens with the long face had started giggling and Tant Das had said angrily: 'Behave yourself, Toon! Why are you being so silly!'

Later it had been ugly Let who had laughed in his face when she had come butting in with her everlasting orange syrup. He had been on the point of saying: 'Here is my heart. Take it. Trample on it, do what you will with it, for it will never again be mine.' That was just how he would have said it, but Let had buggered it up by coming in with her damned orange squash. There is a time and place to say something, and the time was that precise moment, and the place was the settee in old Frik van Onselen's front room. He had tried to say it later, with a kiss, when they said goodbye. And she had answered back as no woman had ever done with a mere kiss, saying clearly and without false modesty: 'Take my heart and do what you will.'

The following day he had even tried to write a letter, but the words became unwieldy when he tried to marshal them. On the Monday he was at Freddy's at the crack of dawn. In the little store, between the chintz and pungent tobacco, blue soap and coffee, he explained the love he felt and Freddy expressed it in beautiful, learned words. 'That's not what I said,' he taxed Freddy. 'But it's precisely what you think and feel, isn't it?' Freddy had replied teasingly. 'Write it down nicely while I go and make tea for us and call me if someone comes to collect post.'

It was wonderful to talk to Freddy about Genevieve. Freddy understood everything. He almost stopped longing for her when Freddy was with him; suddenly she seemed so close.

Poon stumbled and with a curse Beimen reined him in. It was now twilight and the light was false. A measureless sorrow possessed Beimen Botes. Why had he done that to Freddy? Because he wanted Genevieve back? To punish Freddy? But to punish him like that? With violence and humiliation?

He had ridden to Freddy's early that afternoon. Hoping that there would be an extra letter from Genevieve, one with a photo enclosed. But it was Genevieve herself who awaited him in Freddy's room. She was different in the daylight from what she had been by candlelight. Her mouth was messy, her bun crooked, her hands were male and her naked feet were big, with corns on them. He wanted to revenge himself on her: he wanted to take her.

Beimen spurred on his horse. It was the hour when bats flit and owls hoot. It was only when he came over the rise and saw the lights in the post office that he became calm.

He wanted to see Genevieve again before they fastened the lid over his face, to see her face, clean, without make-up and false hair. Then he recalled what Streepsak had said and halted his horse. Afraid of the house of the dead, even more afraid of the dead in his own house, he sat and felt the night sink into him like dew.

Hennie Aucamp

AND HATH LOVE 2

The Van Onselens drink their coffee at four o'clock on the stoep because it is cool there and there is a breeze. They sit next to one another, upright, on the bench: Oom Frik, skeletal and mischievous with a drooping moustache, next to him his corpulent wife, Tant Das, then their unmarried daughter, Let, who – although mature – has been passed by because of the birthmark that mars her face. She has inherited something of her father's sense of humour, but in her it has darkened into irony that from time to time sours into cynicism. About herself she often says: 'I should sell myself to a circus as a clown, I'm already made up.' And recently, when she repeated the observation again, it was touch-and-go whether Oom Frik said: 'Yes, by all means, it will bring in a little extra money.' The times were bad for the farmers at Die Hoek: the drought and depression. For Oom Frik it was better than for many others, especially beginners such as Beimen Botes and Toon Lourens – they were thoroughly choked in those days. For that reason he entertained them willingly, but he would not offer even one bale of lucerne from his stone barn, no matter what they were willing to pay.

The Van Onselens sat as if for their portrait, dead still as if they had forgotten about the cups in their hands. Above them hung a set of horns which Oom Frik's brother-in-law had brought from South West: kudu, gemsbok, eland.

They sat frozen, as if they were afraid the horns would fall on them.

It was Let who finally broke the silence. 'Shoo, but it's hot.'

Tant Das, annoyed, pulled her handkerchief out from between her breasts. It was damp with sweat and eau-de-cologne. Let was young and thin and knew nothing yet about hot flushes.

'I wonder whether the fellows will come visiting again tonight. Old Streepsak says Beimen is having trouble with his windmill's pump.'

'What, again?' asked Let.

'Yes,' sighed Oom Frik, 'mark my words, always in a drought when you need your hands for other problems.'

'Poor Beimen,' began Tant Das.

'He'll be all right,' Oom Frik cut her short, 'he's got character.'

Let took the cups away. 'He won't be all right,' she said loudly in the kitchen, 'because he hasn't got character.' Angrily she began to wash up.

For two years she had been darning and mending for him, without payment. Why did she do it? He never even looked at her. He couldn't look at her because of the stain on her face. He liked things to be whole and complete. He retreated from deformity or deviation. An animal had to be well-formed for him. Yet she continued to darn for him, to repair the holes and tears in his trousers and shirts that happened whenever he thoughtlessly stretched or bent too quickly. When nobody was near, she buried her face in his clothes, smelling them to seek out whether some trace of him lingered, sweat or the smell of tobacco, or something private, sweet or stinking, close, like the smell of old toadstools.

Let began drying the cups. One slipped from her hand, but she caught it in time. Let it break. Let something or somebody be broken. Beimen had no character and no money either. What did character matter if you had money? Her father had money, more than he cared to admit. They could go and farm Wolfiespoort, take over the mortgage from her father. Because Beimen was a hard worker. He had huge hands. And at night in the dark, when all cats are grey (even the piebald ones), he would not need to wince.

'Let, Le-e-t!' her father called from the stoep. 'Toon's coming. Bring something to drink.'

'Something' wasn't going to be coffee, Let decided angrily. It would be orange syrup. And if the water in the water-bag wasn't cold enough, her father and Toon could make some other arrangement. That they would do in any case, but later; Toon always brought something with him for her pa. They drank it secretly, in the stable or behind the quince hedge, and in their simplicity they thought that if they chewed peppermints neither she nor her mother would twig. Oh, they were a pair, her father and Toon Lourens; they laughed at each other's jokes over and over and over again and boasted about their knowledge of the world.

If anybody had knowledge about the world in that district,

then it was Freddy McTavish, even if his sort of knowledge had no meaning in a godforsaken hole. He had taken over the post office and store, but only temporarily, everyone said; he was in the Stormberg for his health. He was from Cape Town and had travelled abroad, he understood people. Also women, although he wasn't really interested in them. He was like a brother to her. They talked about everything under the sun, the depression and poultry diseases. She showed him her embroidery and he advised her on the colours she should use. Sometimes he brought English books for her to read, but they were too full of difficult words and the print was too small. Now they lay on her bedside table on top of her hymn book.

'Let! Are you saddling horse?' Oom Frik yelled from the stoep.

'I'm coming!'

So Let played the role of Martha who served, a role that made her acceptable to everybody – even, from time to time, to Beimen Botes. She loaded her gaudy tray with multi-coloured glasses and a glass jug with pale orange syrup and a jug of water. As she walked, the beads on the doilies covering the jugs clinked against them; delicate music, like that from a music box.

She shook Toon Lourens's hand and said, 'Shoo, it's hot!'

'I wonder if Beimen will come tonight,' her father said. 'I understand he's having trouble with that windmill pump.'

'Oh, he'll come,' chuckled Toon Lourens. 'Because he's dying for company. He even rides over in the middle of the week to the post office just to talk to Freddy.'

'What could they have to talk about?' laughed Tant Das.

'Oh, lots of things,' said Toon. 'Freddy is writing down his stories.'

'What does Beimen know of stories?'

'Not those sort of stories, Oom Frik. Anecdotes about Die Hoek,' explained Toon.

'But I know those better than he does, and I can tell them better. Old Beimen is heavy of tongue.'

'So are you, sometimes,' Tant Das landed a blow below the belt. She nudged Let, who giggled behind her handkerchief.

'Come on, Toon,' said Oom Frik, taking offence, 'these women have nothing to say.'

Let took the glasses and jugs to the kitchen. She didn't feel like washing up yet and fetched her bonnet and apron.

'What? In this heat?' asked Tant Das in amazement.

'I'm going to look for eggs,' said Let stubbornly. 'There are some hideaway hens that have strayed away to lay under the karree bushes.'

'In this heat? What about the snakes?'

'Precisely because of the snakes. I don't want them eating up my profits. I'm not scared of snakes, I'll take a kierie with me.'

It was much too hot to collect eggs and Let knew it. The heat struck from all directions, from above as well as beating up from the earth. She could feel it through the soles of her shoes. But she needed to think, and for that she had to be alone.

Let took a round-about way to the stables; she held a few eggs cradled in her apron. She caught her father and Toon in the act, just as she knew she would. Hurriedly they tried to stash away the half-jack behind a tin of dubbin in the cupboard. But they were too late.

'Let, if you tell your mother . . .' said Oom Frik, half angrily as well as ashamed.

Let laughed. 'Pa knows that I'm a good sport, but then Pa must help me tonight. I have a plan for some fun. That's if Beimen and Freddy come over tonight, because I need them both.'

'Oh, they'll come,' said Toon with a spiteful laugh.

'Freddy as well?'

'Yes, because "Jonathan delighted much in David". Read your Bible.'

Let didn't actually like Toon Lourens, but for tonight he would be an ideal ally. He also had it in for Beimen for he and Beimen had been inseparable before Freddy came.

'I want us to make Freddy up like a girl. Then we'll introduce him to Beimen as Pa's niece from Kimberley. We'll call her Genevieve.'

'I don't know about that,' said Oom Frik. 'It's crazy, and Beimen would surely know at once.'

'Oh no, he won't! Not when I've finished with Freddy.'

'All right, then,' sighed Oom Frik.

'But Pa must suggest it to Freddy. He has a great deal of respect for Pa.'

'And what if he won't?'

'Oh, he will,' Let laughed with deadly certainty. 'Oh yes, he will.'

And she was right, for finally Freddy only had one reservation: his moustache.

'That's nothing,' said Oom Frik, who was beginning to enjoy the game. 'We'll shave it off and you can start growing it again from the beginning. But this time treat it with chicken shit.'

Let fetched the razor, the strop, the soap and water.

There was something deliberate in her movements; something masculine about the way she stropped the razor that surprised Oom Frik. He looked at Toon, but Toon simply sat smiling.

Freddy didn't seem too willing to allow Let to shave him, but Oom Frik reassured him: 'She shaves me regularly.'

It was soon apparent that Let knew what she was doing. There were no cuts, not a drop of blood. She shaved off Freddy's moustache and then she began shaving his cheeks. 'But I shaved this morning,' he protested through the mounds of foam, but Let went calmly ahead. 'I want your face to be as smooth as a baby's bottom,' she said.

After that she took him to the room, where she had laid out a dress, a blue one with daisies printed on it. Tant Das sat watching, bemused by Freddy's transformation. Her switch, from the days of her youth, blended well with his long blond hair, while Let's red earrings made his cherry lips look even more red. Even shoes weren't a problem, for Let had particularly large feet for a girl. Something strange happened in the process: Freddy was transformed from within. He laughed flirtatiously, his voice became slightly higher than usual, from sheer excitement. His gestures became feminine.

Let van Onselen had never laughed as she did that night, intensely and often. Sometimes she went to her room to smother her fits of laughter in her pillow; sometimes she went behind the *bakoond* to catch her breath.

With the prescience of an experienced woman she knew when Beimen would ask the fatal question. She saw it in his eyes when he danced so closely with Genevieve – pressing himself against her thighs – and he sang raucously:

'When I was a little calf
I didn't get no milk.'

'Well, drink then!' Let thought with contempt. 'Drink until you shit.'

She waited in the passage with a tray and with perfect timing she intercepted his proposal. 'Here, you must be thirsty,' she giggled and offered orange syrup.

The Van Onselens knew nothing of the exchange of letters between Genevieve and Beimen. They first got to know about it when Freddy came one afternoon on his bicycle with his crazy request to borrow the Genevieve get-up. Of course they were furious. The whole scheme had been theirs, and now they were pushed aside and didn't have a share in the sports. But still they lent him the clothes.

As they watched Freddy ride away, Oom Frik said: 'I wonder if that boy is all right, he looks so pale.'

'It's because he's shaved off his moustache,' explained Tant Das. 'It makes him look pale.'

'There is something else,' Let agreed with her father, 'a restlessness.'

'Yes, that's it, yes,' agreed Oom Frik, 'a restlessness.'

'Now that you mention it,' said Tant Das, 'he trembled when he took the box from me. Yes, I remember it quite well, he trembled.'

Even years later the Van Onselens would recall this short exchange in the finest detail. People simply like to be considered prophetic.

The accident happened the following week. Sergeant Zietsman brought the tidings and Doctor Rowland was with him in the side-car. Both men, strong and hardened, looked ready to break.

'He did it with a revolver, Oom Frik, which he put into his mouth. His brains spilled out like kapok from a cushion. The worst is that he was wearing women's clothing. That's why we are here.'

Doctor Rowland took over from the sergeant. 'Would Tant Das please come and lay him out, please. It is tragic enough and one doesn't want gossip. He was such a dear boy.'

'I will go with you,' said Let. 'I can help.'

Doctor Rowland hesitated. 'Oom Frik . . .'

'Oh, Let is strong, doctor. And she and Freddy were like brother and sister.'

It was Let who took control. Tant Das was overcome by the shock. It was Let who gathered towels and soap and gauze and asked in a practical way, 'Shouldn't he have a shroud?' Without waiting for an answer she went to the camphor kist and fetched her father's.

Let looked stark, something to which the dark half of her face contributed greatly, but inwardly she was seething. While she worked her hands now here and now here, she thought constantly: If only it was Beimen. If only it was Beimen Botes's body.

Translated by Ian Ferguson

LETTIE VILJOEN

Lament for Koos – *Fragment*

Süsses Kind, dein braunes Haar ist wunderbar
Nina Hagen

I am a diffident, timid woman. Your values and judgements I made mine. (Mine, all mine). And now you are gone. The world outside is threatening. I dream that the millions of mites to which the human body plays host become visible on my skin like small, pale eggs; they sit tightly packed between my breasts.

The day after the woman with the burnt child knocked on my front door, I stand in the kitchen at lunch time, in front of the window. (Does everybody on the fringes, the meths drinkers and the homeless, know that I live, a woman alone in this house, and that I am manipulable? The word is possibly spreading.) I become conscious of a woman waving her arms and gesticulating outside, on the other side of the hedge. I recognize the woman from last night. The same boots, the same *kopdoek*[1] (where is the double head-dress?), the same old, adolescent face. A (young) man hangs back slightly to her left. Open the window, I eventually understand her gesticulation. (Am I not safe in the isolation of my house? Can I not stand in front of my own window without being seen, and addressed, no, much more than that?!) I open the window. I was here this morning, the woman shouts, I rang the doorbell and there was nobody. *Kleinnooi*[2] said last night I must come back this morning. I did not, I

---

1 *Kopdoek* a piece of material wound round the head of (usually) Black women, like a turban.
2 *Kleinnooi* literally 'little miss', form of address used by (Black) servants for young White women.

shout back. She cannot hear me, behind her on the national road lorries are driving past at thunderous speed. I stick my head further out the window. I didn't say last night that you should come back here this morning, I shout again. I was here this morning, because my house burnt down yesterday, she shouts back. Did the child then burn down with the house, I wonder, and did she in her devastation (she is still gesticulating) omit to mention that the house had also burnt down? She goes on shouting. What? I ask. Remember, she shouts, my name is Sylvia and I will come again! I'll remember, I shout, come back in a week's time, I'm keeping the dresses for you! I close the window. She is still indicating something in the direction of the man, who has straightened up from behind the hedge. I nod mechanically, wave, and turn round. Farewell Sylvia, on your delirious journey. Maybe all she had had indeed burnt down, gone up in flames: her house, her (three) pieces of furniture, her little girl; maybe this had set her free from the bondage of worldly goods or material ownership, and maybe she could now live from day to day, teetering and untrammelled, from hand to mouth, on grace and from grace. I hope I never see her again.

An increasing number of our former friends seem to be getting disillusioned with our (lovely) town. As you my husband experienced the town as unbearable and a dangerous dead-end. They move to the city or to the North, or withdraw in isolation, but no one so far has had your courage to move completely outside the catchment of the hated system. I do not know what happens behind the screens. I suspect that there is no lack of theory or analysis, I suspect an assortment of private solutions for private hangups, for those who no longer experience a sense of communion with the community. All behind the screens, or in the presence of a few trusted friends, confidantes, or behind closed eyelids at night, like a rearing horse.

But I am losing perspective, I am seeing too much of those who move on the borders of my property. Silver (fucked) Sylvie, spaced-out Frans and Betty, the hungry children, the older poor. And the constant memories of my husband, who could see through it all and decide: life does not amount to much, or rather, life in this town and in this political set-up. I think of the breadth and resonance of his insight. And where did he end? Where? I am going mad with not knowing.

In my doubt and despair I phone the welfare worker, late-ish one evening. She sounds slightly irritated (or am I imagining that?) (have I perhaps interrupted love-making?) Open your hand, she says, let your husband go, you are undermining your own chances of happiness.

Happiness! She may be right. Happiness may still be possible in some other context.

The need to be anaesthetized remains, in fact, increases. I feel the need to transfer to a deeper level of consciousness (if such a thing were possible), maybe by means of long and uninterrupted dancing, a transcendent dance, a dance of healing, during which the hands of the healers of the community would be laid on me (God knows, I very much doubt if such exist in *this* community): a subliminal cure effected. I feel the need for such an activity. But all I can do in my present circumstances is organize a party and dance cheek to (Afrikaner) cheek with the glistening young men. Except that I have long ago lost contact with young and nubile men: I had no taste for them within the protection of my marriage. My desire was for my husband and when he left me (undoubtedly to fight also for the expansion of the restrictive limits of the nuclear family), I lay with you in a state of shock and deprivation, as substitute, as protector of my interests; a surrogate ritual domain. The country forms a basis for identity and an analogy with emotional states; in the absence of both of you I fantasize about the affiliation of each of the dramatis personae with the (tragic) destiny of the country.

The polished floors, the ironed curtains, the washed walls reflect the light. The reflected order is like death, I want to escape it. I long for a Black woman (my domestic help would do) to take my head in her hands and sing to me:

177

Lettie Viljoen

Oa lema oa lema oa lema mosadi
oa lema mosadi
o fokotsa mathata
basadi basadi basadi ba thabile
basadi ba thabile
ba ja merongo

But nobody, nothing, my domestic help is unreachable.
She keeps her eyes downcast. She moves aside for me to
pass. She is Black, but she speaks Afrikaans to her children.
(She comes to work this week with a black shadow on her
upper lip, I do not enquire.)

I walk in the garden, this morning. The domestic help/
servant is hanging out the washing. The weather is mild
these days, but not warm yet, although the rains have ceased
for the time being. In front of me on the ground I see a
grasshopper. Well camouflaged. I squat. The grasshopper
does not move. Then I see: she has made a little hole, in
which she has lowered her ovipositor. She is laying eggs – the
little pocket of seeds in the ground! But she has chosen a bad
place: right in the path between the washing line and the
kitchen door. I call my child. We both squat and watch. I am a
little apprehensive, but especially scared that the servant will
(accidentally) step on the (defenceless) insect on her way back
from the washing line. Does the grasshopper cover her eggs,
for them to hatch? The little pocket of seeds in the ground.
(The weapons found at Hammanskraal). I tell the woman, the
servant, watch out for the grasshopper, she is laying her
eggs. The woman/servant says yes, she hadn't noticed her.

I go back into the house, with the child, and prepare the
food. That day I do not go and check up on the grasshopper
again. And that evening I dance (alone) to my tapes in my
sacred, abandoned house, immaculate as the desert.

Translated by Ingrid Scholtz

M. C. BOTHA

The Fisherwoman

As far back as any of those who regularly saw her on the rocks could remember, she had always been there. To the other anglers her thin, slightly bent figure was part of the coastal landscape.

Although they knew where she lived the people of the town did not know her personally. She never received anyone in her cottage and no one knew what it was like inside. They knew her as Miss Mary and that was about all they knew of her.

The women of the town were consumed with curiosity and would sometimes gather in little groups just to talk about Miss Mary. It was all gossip, of course, since no one knew anything about her life. And the thing that intrigued them most and was the subject of most of their gossip was her age. The younger ones guessed her to be a little older than they were, between fifty and sixty, say, while those who were between fifty and sixty felt she must be over seventy. That was how the women were: the last thing they wanted was to establish any kind of relation between Miss Mary and themselves, and the easiest way of ensuring this was to imagine her to be older. Miss Mary did not display a woman's usual signs of neatness and physical care, and that was why they looked down on her. To them she was the opposite of what a woman should be, for she lacked the good taste they were so sure of in themselves. She never wore anything but a pair of tan-coloured corduroy slacks and a white shirt, with a grey pullover that hung on her like a sack. And if this shocked their sophistication, they were even more shocked by the rest of her clothing: cream-coloured highish-heeled shoes, and a red hat which she tied down around her chin with a white silk scarf. She never wore anything else, and it was thus that she stood on the rocks with her old brown wooden fishing-rod in her hands, day after day.

To the men of the town Miss Mary was merely a very fine

angler. Her personal appearance made no impression on them and it is improbable that any one of them would have noticed if one day she had stood on the rocks dressed in anything else. No, they were only interested in studying her skill as an angler. When they saw her using red-bait, they knew that they would catch nothing that day with any other bait. On the other hand, if she fished from the rocks at Kreefpunt, they knew that if one wanted fish that day, Kreefpunt was the place to go.

She knew the sea and the habits of fish better than any other angler. She knew that if the north-west wind was blowing, the galjoen would take pudding-worm at Rooigat; that when the sea was churned up after a few days of south-easter, one would catch red steenbras with crab at Sandwalletjies. And the men followed her. Even the seasoned anglers watched her, following very conspicuously at a distance, the more so because they tried so hard to be unobtrusive. Then they would stand fairly close together, fishing at more or less the same spot as Miss Mary. They seldom spoke to her and when they did, it was a monosyllabic and inconsequential remark like 'the tide is slow today', or 'the fish won't shoal in the reefs today'. And when they went home, Miss Mary would still be sitting there. They would know that while they themselves were returning with perhaps a single fish in their baskets, there would be several in hers.

Even on the days when the big ones did not bite, and that was often, there would be a few 'twakkies' or 'mooinooientjies' in her basket, while they had to return home empty handed. They did not always know how she did it – after all, they used the same bait, caught in the same sloops; how was it that she made a catch and not they. They would speculate among themselves and say: 'Perhaps she uses a different size hook, or perhaps she fishes with a thinner line; or is it the longer trace she uses?' There were so many possibilities.

But what did Miss Mary think of herself? She was lonely. Her memories of the past faded more and more as the years went by and she had already forgotten how, very long ago, she had been sitting on these rocks, dreaming of the husband she would have one day. That day never came, perhaps because of her father, and so the sun also set on her need to have children.

She had been able to buy the cottage for one thousand pounds out of the money her father had left her after his death. She had never really been able to get over his death, and had come to live alone in the cottage to think about him. Several times a day she would remind herself that she was living in a place bought with his money. She never went out and felt no need for conversation. Her father had been everything to her. She had been the only child and her mother had died giving birth to her. In everything she did while her father was still alive, she was more concerned with what he would think about it than with her own feelings. She had wanted to get married, but he had thought her too young and she accepted that; she wanted to study, to become a teacher, but he said that college was a waste of time and money, and she believed him.

And when he died, the shock was so great that she had to convert it into a kind of unreality. She moved into the cottage and tried to extend her life with him. His face was in her dreams and beside her fishing-rod on the rocks.

But she had grown old, and her images of her father had become the lines upon her face. She suffered hardship and had to live frugally to come out on her pension. Sometimes, for a little extra cash, she did sell fish to the fish-shop in town.

Her cottage was not exactly neat inside. She seldom swept and dusted and there were always flies in the kitchen. Because of her poverty she hardly ever discarded anything. She would keep empty margarine containers, tins and boxes and in the living-room, beside the dinner table, there was a large heap of plastic bags. Her bedroom was the neatest room in the house. A fairly large, heavy wooden bed stood in the middle of the little room. She made it every morning, drawing over it the brightly coloured patchwork quilt, covering the pillows. On one side of the bed stood a wardrobe and on the other side, a little table with a reading lamp and a Bible. On the floor, next to the table, was her dog's bed. It was a black sheepdog, her sole companion.

She washed the fish she caught in the cement sink outside the kitchen. This chore she always found somewhat unpleasant, although she had been doing it for so long that it had become almost a mechanical action. When cleaning a fish and taking out the gut she disliked coming upon layers and layers of unhatched fish-roe, and tape-worm in a fish's stomach made her shudder. When cleaning a freshly caught fish, she always took out the heart next to the gills and placed it on the cold cement slab. In wonder she would see the contraction of the tiny red organ and would stand watching it as it lay beating.

It was spring-tide and the tide was high and she was sitting on a high rock between Saliesklip and Soetsee. The dog was lying on a strip of sand beside a large shallow pool on the landward side of the rock. With pricked ears he was watching the water with concentration. Years ago the ebb-tide had trapped a few mullet in the pool and, pouncing wildly in the water, he had caught them one by one. He had not forgotten it and each time he saw the pool, he expected to find mullet in it.

Miss Mary baited her hook. It was mussel-worm which she had just extricated from under the black mussels. The worm in her hand had a silvery gleam to it as the sun's rays caught it. It was too big for her hook and carefully she nipped it right through in the middle with the nails of her right thumb and forefinger. Then, cautiously, she took hold of the front part behind the head, feeling the worm moving backwards to escape from her grip, and swiftly slid it on to the hook before it had a chance to get at her with its two hidden black pincers. The back part she pressed over the barb at the tip of the hook. She saw the other part of the worm writhing on the rock, picked it up and put it in her tin with the few black mussels and seaweed. She stood up to cast her bait and sat down again.

The sun was shining and the water was very clear. A light breeze was stirring from the south-east. She knew her chance of a catch was slim. She hauled in her line. On her hook was a small snail with a pointed shell. That means the holes around here are silted up, she thought instinctively.

She sat down again holding the fishing-rod slanted over her knees. Lost in thought she gazed at the water. Miss Mary was not happy. She felt old and tired. Day by day she moved over the rocks more slowly and wearily. It worried her that she might fall seriously ill with no one to care for her. She had

182

no friends, only the dog. She thought of her life and a frown came to her brow. There was a pain in her breast and a great sadness clamped on to her heart like a black mussel. She did not understand this. Vaguely her eyes stared out over the water before her. If a little fish-woman should weep in the sea, she thought, no one would see the tears.

Translated by Anna de Wit and Peter Lilienfield

ABRAHAM H. de VRIES

Tin Soldiers Don't Bleed

Everything was just as he'd expected it, yet the little chapel was also different: more bare, more stark, even chillier. The wooden benches had been scrubbed clean. Behind the altar was a crucifix, the only one. Except for the stained-glass windows and the strange light it might well have been the chapel of the English undertaker in their village.

The friendly nun crossed herself, from forehead to chest, and then from shoulder to shoulder, a slow, relaxed gesture, before she continued in her usual voice:

'This is ours. I thought I should let you see it. Of course we allow every child to attend its own church. For the bigger churches there's a bus, the other children are taken by car. There are many children here whose parents do not belong to the Catholic Church.'

'The *dominee*[1] in our town came to see us,' the woman remarked, speaking for the first time in what seemed like ages. She had simply been nodding her head from time to time as if the explanations and all the pointing and showing did not really concern her. 'It was he who recommended your school – as my husband told you. And he assured us that Boetie could go to our church. Dutch Reformed.'

'We trust we shall always be worthy of the trust people have in us.'

What else can we do but trust? the man thought.

'Now I'm going to show you the dormitories. Just let me jot down something, before I forget. This window should have been repaired during the holidays.' From the folds of her surplice she took a notebook with a golden cross on the cover. The ballpoint with which she wrote was suspended

---

1 *Dominee*: Minister of the Dutch Reformed Church

from a chain next to the rosary and the small crucifix.

Through the broken window he could look outside. He felt caged in, and not just because of the strangeness of the place. He always felt like this if he couldn't see the world outside. On some Sundays it got warm very early in their town, then the church windows were open. From the pew where they usually sat he could see the blue gum trees. Here the trees were far in the distance – must be the playground hedge running behind them.

Below the window were pleasant lawns. No drought here. There were several children already, some of them were standing with Denise and Boetie. Different ones from the two who'd come to escort them from the office. How easy it was for children to make friends.

'Shall we go?'

They went down the long, new corridor. His wife was between him and the nun, the latter went on chattering as if suspicious of silence.

He heard his wife reply: 'Sister, we had many, many arguments about a boarding school. My husband always wanted the children to move out as soon as they were old enough. But you know what a mother is like.'

'I've seen enough to make up for my lack of experience,' smiled the nun, turning a door handle with her white hand.

'This will be his room. As you can see, there are three beds, he's with two other boys. They're both older than him. We've found that it works quite well. You'll meet the two other boys tomorrow, they're from up country.'

There was no crucifix in this room. It struck him immediately, perhaps because it left the walls so bare. The window sill was quite high, but fortunately there was a big tree right outside.

'You now, we're really so fortunate to have such a peaceful place. There's not even traffic to disturb the children. Oh, there's a car coming now, but it must be one of the other families . . . Anyway, the children can play around and attend to their studies without any distraction. Sometimes it makes me long for Ballyshannon. You must have noticed my Irish accent.' She smiled again, shaking her hood back evenly over her shoulders.

'But you don't know our Boetie yet, Sister. He can't sit still for two minutes. At home he always had the radio on.'

Perhaps the children preferred not to hear, the man thought.

'You've seen the dining-hall and the kitchen – I still think the microwave oven doesn't belong in such an old building, but it was a gift. So now you've seen the lot . . .'

'Thank you very much, Sister.'

He became conscious of the hat clutched in his sticky hand. 'It's the best we could do . . .'

'Shall we go back to my office? Sister Glöckner will bring us some tea in a minute. She's spending some time with us. The German community is also planning to start a school like ours. Perhaps you still have a few questions? You look like easy parents to me. If you could hear the questions I've had to contend with in the past! But that's exactly why . . . come on.'

He looked at his wife. She at him. Was there something they should still have asked? Something other parents asked?

'You said we could bring him tomorrow?' he asked.

'That we leave entirely to the parents. If you still want to visit relatives here in Cape Town, bring him in tomorrow. Otherwise he's quite welcome to stay here. We think it's better for the kids to get used to their new home as soon as possible. And it's a good thing if parents don't let on that they are the ones who try to postpone the goodbyes.'

When she spoke about relatives they glanced at each other again, and the nun noticed.

'He seems to make friends very easily.' She stood looking through her study window. Sister Glöckner came in with the tea.

'Yes, he does. But we're so scared, Sister, that he may miss our daughter Denise terribly. They grew up together on the farm, you see. There are no other children. But then, I don't know. I suppose he's got used to being on his own, hasn't he, Pa? She's been at school for a whole year now . . .'

'She's been very quiet lately,' he answered and sat down on the chair in front of the desk. But the nun invited them to easy chairs and a tea table. Leaving the tea for a while she sat looking at the woman. There was no smile on her face now.

'It's always the best for all concerned not to evade the issue. I don't find it surprising at all that she's become quiet.'

She looked at the man. 'And I presume you also know why. We can look after Boetie, there's no need to worry about that any longer. But I'd like to give you some advice and I hope you don't mind my doing so.'

'Of course not, Sister. We're at such a loss, really.'

'Look after her. This may sound strange, but it's going to be harder for her than for him. She needs your love and your attention. All the brothers and sisters of the little ones we have here. It's the same for all of them. Remember, our kids are quite well protected here. They don't have much contact with other children. But the others . . .'

'That's so true, Pa. We've almost forgotten.'

'You've had many worries. But it will be better from now on. Black, or with milk?'

'I take black, but my husband likes milk.' Had he heard what the sister had said? She couldn't read anything in his face. Previously she could. But she no longer knew how.

He had such a peculiar way of staring and seeing nothing.

The woman put down her tea. She took out her handkerchief but she did not cry. Her husband stared at the table in front of him.

'If you want my advice I'd say you should leave the little chap here tonight. However, it's for you to decide. He knows he'll be seeing you again tomorrow at our opening,' said the sister. 'Wouldn't you like to bring in his suitcase?'

But the question was unnecessary, for the suitcase was already beside the door.

The man tapped his hat on his knee. Replacing her handkerchief in her handbag, the woman got up.

'I'll have the two of them brought in,' said the sister.

This is a new kind of ache, the man thought as they drove in to Cape Town. Are there more kinds? It is hard to think it possible for any more to exist. But that was what he'd thought every time, and every time he had been wrong.

'Look at the mountain, Sis. Isn't it beautiful? Dad must really take us up in the cable car, don't you think? Look at it – you see?'

In the back of the car the child pressed her face against the window, but she gave no answer.

187

Sometimes my wife changes so rapidly that I hardly know her any more, thought the man. She took it very much to heart, what the sister said about Denise. I too. We've been like two leaves in a whirlpool in the river lately. Every gush of wind, every stick undermines our certainty.

'Did you enjoy talking to the others? They look like very nice kids, don't they?'

Denise still gave no answer. Turning back towards her, the mother stroked the child's striking blonde hair. 'Where did you get that thing you have in your hand?'

'Picked it up over there.'

'What is it? Let me see . . .'

'Just a tin soldier. I forgot, I wanted to give it to Boetie. But Boetie didn't cry,' said the child.

'He's big enough now. You really won't recognize him when he comes home for the holidays.'

'They speak English, those children,' said the child.

'I know, but not all of them.'

'Almost all of them. Some can speak Afrikaans, but even they speak English.'

The man took a cigarette from the cubby-hole and lit it with the car lighter.

'Then he can pick it up too. It's a good thing if he learns to speak English,' he said, and he heard the raucous tone of his voice, for it was the first time he spoke since they'd left the convent.

'Boetie's school always opens before yours. That's good. Then we can all take him there together.' The woman regretted having mentioned both schools. She'd been avoiding it so far. She didn't know why. She could hear herself speaking even before she'd thought about what she would say. In the principal's study she'd become aware of it too.

Then they fell silent and the silence in the car became oppressive, as if caused by the humid wind blowing in through the window. On either side of the road the trees were bent and listless. Ahead of them was the tall mountain with wisps of cloud round the highest peaks. Even the people on the summit at this moment wouldn't be able to see a thing, she thought.

'Why couldn't Boetie go to Aunt Susan with us?' Denise asked suddenly.

'It's better for him . . .,' the mother began, then realized that she didn't know how to go on.

'Why must he come to school here in Cape Town? Why can't he go to our school?'

It was the first time the child had put the question so bluntly. They had both assumed that she knew. There had been so much talk about it in their home lately. They had never tried to hide anything from her. But they hadn't discussed it directly with her either. And now that she had put the question, neither of them knew what to answer.

'It's better for him. . .,' the mother began again, looking round. Denise was very pale. Her jaws were tightly clenched.

'Daddy, stop!'

Her mother helped her out of the car. She kept her hand on the child's back, looking at her husband in sudden helplessness as the girl went on retching and retching.

'There's a cooler-bag in the back of the car. Please give it to us. Is it something you've eaten my child?'

Denise shook her head, trying bravely to swallow. But she could no longer restrain her tears. Her mother held her head, pressing her against her body.

'Why,' sobbed the child, 'why don't they want Boetie in our school? Why must he go away from us?'

'It's better . . .'

A Coloured man approached on his bicycle, looking at them as he rode more slowly, then seemed to change his mind and went on. Denise stopped sobbing, took a few gulps of water from the bag and looked at her father who was standing behind the car, his eyes averted. Her mother wiped her face with a wet handkerchief.

'That's all right, you'll be feeling better soon. Must have eaten something. Perhaps the pies we had in Worcester this morning,' she said, looking at her husband.

She'll come back to this, he thought. She was expecting me to help. But what can I do? Still. The slightest hint sets her off. We seem to be drifting apart, he discovered, for the first time. But his thoughts were too much of a barren wasteland to dwell upon. The child came towards him. He opened the door, stroked her hair, but she pulled away her head, as if she too were accusing him. Of what?

He could feel himself perspiring more and more. During the last few years one door after another had been closed to him. Some slammed in his face, others – and that had been worse – shut with warmth and understanding, like when their *dominee* came to see him. Now his wife and Denise seemed to be turning against him too.

A hard anger rose up in him, but ebbed away as he looked at the child.

'Feeling better?' his wife asked through the window.

'I don't want to go to Aunt Susan, Daddy,' said the child. She laid her head on the seat-rest against her father's shoulder. He turned round and put his arm round her body. She grew tense and wrenched herself away and returned to her place on the seat.

'Well, let's go to a hotel then,' he suggested. 'I don't feel in a mood for company either.'

He shifted the gears.

Denise began to sob again.

'All those children in that place,' she said, 'they're even darker than he is. And you, you're both glad that he's there now.'

Translated by André Brink

DALENE MATTHEE

The Animal Tamer

Now that it's obvious I'm pregnant, I can feel the shock waves reverberating around town. I've had four months to come to terms with the fact that's only hit them now. Four months to prepare myself to meet their eyes. Four months to make so many resolutions!

As a nursing sister, I understand the clinical implications of a first pregnancy for a thirty-six-year-old woman. I could have procured a safe abortion, but I passed that turning-point six weeks ago. I am healthy and fit; I come from a line of good breeders. My pedigree is excellent.

Leave town?

No. I was born here, I have a right to be here, and in the long run, it will be better for the child too, if I stay here.

I am not as naïve as I may appear to be. I suspect the question, 'Do you think she knows who the father is?' has already been asked a hundred times. And it hurts more than I thought it would.

I do know who the father is. But no one else will ever know. Not even the father himself.

In any case, I no longer entertain men.

It's funny, sometimes these days I feel a strange joy welling up in me and I want to hug my bulging stomach and laugh. Then the guilt returns.

Matron summoned me to her office yesterday. I had anticipated this for a long time. She asked me point blank about the rumours she'd heard and, just as directly, I confirmed they were true. I was certain that my post would be secure for at least another three months: she'd go a long way to find a theatre sister better than I was. For the same reason, I knew that once I was ready to come back to work, they'd readmit me to the service. But when Matron tried to draw me out with false sympathy I had to disappoint her. I had no intention of confessing merely to satisfy her appetite for gossip. Like everyone else, she'd just have to go on guessing her guesses.

Up until then, I had only been pressed into confession once before in my life. It was on the evening before I was due to go on holiday. I had heard about the firebrand who had been sent as a second minister to our parish and when I opened my door that night I knew instinctively that this must be he. I also knew that the visit meant trouble and I was going to have to curb my temper.

It was very clear that he was not a conventional type who would hide behind his cassock if he was challenged by a recalcitrant sinner.

'Do sit down, father.'

'Thank you. I understand you are the social whore of the town, Miss Vine.'

Hell! I had underestimated him. This was the shortest short cut I'd ever seen anyone take, and it left me stunned. What could I say? It was the truth, paradoxically bundled in with a gross lie.

'You haven't answered me.'

'I have nothing to say.'

'Do you deny it?'

'Well, I feel somewhat taken aback. If these are your normal tactics, I congratulate you on their success.'

'As a minister of this parish it is my duty to help stamp out promiscuity. I will not hesitate to bring ecclesiastical discipline against you if you are guilty. I am not issuing this as an idle threat, as you'll soon learn if you wish to take the trouble.'

My mind had started to function again. 'Has someone complained about me?'

'Yes.'

'Who?'

'A woman.'

'What is the charge against me?'

'That you lead other women's husbands astray.'

'But that isn't true!'

'I am prepared to listen to your side of the story.' He might just as well have said: *I'll listen, but I won't believe.*

'I have never solicited a man. It's up to you to believe that or not.'

'But have you not intentionally encouraged them?'

'Where else can they get it? Must they go to the Cape? Or to the location?'

'I understand.' He spoke with biting sarcasm. 'You see yourself as a do-gooder, providing sex for other women's husbands.'

My control was beginning to slip. 'No, but I repeat the question: where else can they get it?'

'Listen to me, young woman, no married man needs to "get it" elsewhere, as you suggest. Domestic problems are not solved that way – they are aggravated by people like you.'

'More domestic problems have been solved in my bed than you could ever imagine.'

'Indeed? You believe that?'

'Yes. I believe it because I am a woman and I know what a fool a man is in bed. You think you're clever, but in carnal knowledge you haven't advanced much above the level of an animal. Throw in an equally stupid woman and you have four-legged coupling *par excellence*. With the marriage certificate under the pillow, they fornicate like dogs, then trot off to report me to the minister.' I saw it all too clearly. 'And here's another home truth: no man with a clever wife ever landed up in my bed. The cleverness I'm talking about has nothing to do with intellect.'

'Well what has it to do with?'

'Are you asking me?'

'Yes. I'm sure you've had all the answers ready for a long time ago.'

'Kindly reserve your judgement. A clever woman can draw the beast out of a man – slowly, subtly, slyly. Once she's done that he'll never stray again and even the bluest of blue movies won't lure him back into bestiality.'

'And you regard yourself as one of these clever women?'

'Yes.'

'What is your success rate?'

'At the moment I am handling six.' I had thrown caution to the wind. I had only one desire: to shock him to the soul. 'One of whom is chronically impotent.'

'I beg your pardon?'

I knew that would hit home. 'Yes. Probably a Vitamin E

deficiency. If the male body runs out of Vitamin E completely, it loses the ability to absorb it. So see that you top up
your reserves regularly.'

'But what does the man come to you for?'

'We talk, play cards, simply keep each other company. I am
very fond of him.'

'And the others?'

'I am fond of each of them in a different way – and I pity
them all their stupid wives.'

'If we were to assume that some of your theories were
valid, wouldn't it be better to devote yourself to enlightening
these so-called stupid women? It would be compatible with
your kind of work.'

Was I dreaming? Was that cassock soiled?

'A stupid woman is the most intractable creature on earth,
father. Because she is so clever.'

'That sounds like nonsense to me.'

Should I risk it?

No.

Yes.

'Do you have a clever or a stupid wife, father?'

In the long silence I stripped his cassock off with my eyes –
slowly, mercilessly. Mankind.

Could a man really be so stupid? Even one of the strong
ones? Was Freud right? I wanted to snatch the question back
out of the air; I wanted to draw the turmoil from his body
with my hands . . .

Then he spoke the lie. 'Clever. She is very clever.'

It was the eve of my holiday. Stupidly I took the chance . . .
and lost.

Translated by Catherine Knox

PIROW BEKKER

Under a Shepherd's Tree

'We got him! In the bag!'

The two brothers grabbed each other and danced a clumsy jig on the dry karoo earth.

By the time they'd calmed down again, the creature wasn't jerking so desperately on the chain.

'Is it a black-back?'

'Looks like it.'

Thanks to the earth in its fur.

They'd tried for so long to catch him. To catch one of them.

Two or three lambs every night. As many as five a night during the last two weeks. The first time they went home and announced that five had been taken the night before Jack Wiseman had said nothing. But the pupils of his eyes had dilated. He came back to them carrying a razor strop.

'Fetch two milking-riems from the kraal wall,' he thundered.

He tied them spread-eagled against the back wheels of the wagon and he beat them until there was no feeling left in their backs and thighs.

He sent them back to the veld without food. 'Just you dare to come back here again with news of such a slaughter,' he threatened.

That night four lambs were taken. They were too frightened to go home. When darkness fell, they slept only in short snatches. Then they tried resting in shifts but most of the time they were both awake. Listening without a word as the jackals' laughter echoed in the low hills round them. Suddenly it was quiet. The silence that falls when fear is on the prowl, and death is ready to strike. Where, oh heavens, moon and stars, stunted karoo scrub, where? *Where*!

'And there were shepherds out in the fields, watching over their flocks by night . . .'

Where was the clatter of cloven hooves coming from?

Where were the fleecy bodies so restless? Where was that lamb bleating?

Waiting for dawn, the moon was as pale as a sliver of soap, here a scrap of white, there another. It looked as though this one was just sleeping but why was he alone and that tongue that any minute could suck on your finger so cold and already dry! No breath lifted the tight little curls and then you noticed the chunk the jackal had ripped out of the belly. Tasted and then abandoned to lie grotesquely quiet because although the leg was dislocated like the one behind the shale bank, this one's hide had remained intact.

Murders!. . . It echoed in the hills and the jackals quivered with anticipation in the twilight.

Day crept out, yellow as a crab, into a fresh and innocent world. But beyond the day were the rumbling of their bodies and the silence.

The younger brother spent the whole day walking to a neighbouring farm to borrow a jaw-trap. The spring wasn't very strong, but it was better than nothing.

They built an enclosure from thorn tree branches round the lamb behind the shale bank, careful not to touch him. Then they set the trap in the entrance to the enclosure.

They kept the flock up in the top corner of the field all night. It wasn't easy because it was dry and the merinos wanted to browse in the moonlight. There was absolutely no question of getting any sleep.

'Does a jackal ever come back to a lamb?'

'Maybe . . . if there's nothing else going.'

But when morning came, nothing had been touched.

'We'll have to use a live lamb. There's no choice.'

'Another one. What will Dad say?'

'We have to try. Every lamb born is jackal-fodder these days.'

'Dad will beat the living daylights out of us.'

At sundown they drove a stake into the middle of the enclosure, caught a two-day-old lamb and tied him like a sacrifice to the stake.

'Stop that ewe. Next thing she'll spring the trap.' The ewe circled the enclosure. They drove her off with some difficulty. But the important thing was that the lamb was bleating. That should attract the sheep-killer.

'Let's drive them to the bottom corner. The bloody ewe will play up all night if she can hear him.'

It wasn't easy to move her. She was like one possessed. Perhaps she could hear something they couldn't. Anyway, she upset the whole flock.

Perhaps she already knew her lamb would be dead, lying in the kraal as if he was sleeping, except for the gravel and dry leaves on his little tongue. The trap was untouched.

The ewe drew nearer to nuzzle the dead lamb, then looked up at them as if they had killed him.

Build the thorn-walls higher, force the devil to come in through the opening, conceal the trap more carefully . . .

'We must hang up the lamb and set the trap right under it. Then the jackal will have to step on it.'

'How are we going to do that? You know it won't come near a dead lamb.'

'A live one.'

'Not another one!'

'Well, what else can we do? You come up with a suggestion.'

'We'll never catch it.'

'So what do we do?'

He hesitated a moment. 'We could drive the flock nearer to the farmyard and then run away.'

The older brother looked at him, and because the same idea had occurred to him, he said, 'Remember, the Griqua told us: "What lives must die." '

'What lives must die.' He laughed scornfully. 'Don't give me that.'

A heavy silence. After a while: 'And how will you hang up the lamb?'

'We'll make a harness of sacking.'

'How will you join the pieces?'

'We'll just cut holes in it. I'll show you how.'

'Will it hang there all night?'

'What else can we do?'

'Let it stand on its own feet when the jackal comes. It isn't so cruel.'

'I wish we could catch one. Just one.'

That afternoon they found a suitable place. There were only a few of the hardy shepherd's trees that were tall enough.

They wanted to be sure the jackal would have to jump up to get at the lamb. Not just once either. It mustn't miss the trap.

Deadly earnest, they made a hollow and set the trap in it. They tested it with a stick, wishing it was a red jackal's leg it was snapping like that.

As a concession to mercy they took the lamb from the flock at the last minute.

Unfortunately the tree was so placed that they couldn't really get the flock out of earshot of the bleating. On top of this, the wind kept on carrying the sound towards them.

They kept the flock together, stumbling about, even when there was nothing to do. Jesus, anything to keep their distance from that misery.

The pestilent wind kept churning about all night, this way and that, like a sheep with brain fever. With this crazy wind you couldn't tell if the lamb was still alive or not.

No, the ewe was calling again. But she was probably only prompted by her full udder. Prick your ears and try to hear what she can hear. The night was alive with jackals, there were so many of them that they dislodged stones on the slopes and beat a hasty retreat while the grey shadows came racing along with them. They hovered somewhere between sleep and wakefulness. Down here they just had to keep on moving. (What is she up to now? Who are you waiting for to stop that horned sheep?)

The sinking moon was curved like a trigger and they wished they had a gun instead of just a trap with a weak spring and a small tab the devil must step on to set it off. The night was so dark a bare patch looked like an ant-heap and an ant-heap looked like a bare patch and the sheep were milling around again uneasily.

The lamb was still hanging, that was the first thing they noticed. Its neck was bent to one side. The neck swung to the other side right against its body. Stiffly. But it was still alive.

Half-surprised they checked the hollow in the ground. But that was where the trap should be! Then the beast leaped up like a nightmare bird. As a shining streak yanked it back again, they knew: 'We've got him! We've got him!'

Suddenly they felt dumb.

The creature leaped again and again. The red dust matted in its fur.

Above it the lamb's neck swung like a pendulum this way and that. The butt of a whip swung up.

'Watch out, he'll pull himself free.' They remembered that weak spring.

The animal was exhausted. Its jaw was drooping.

This was not a red jackal.

The wildness of its leaps in the red dust and the white teeth should have told them that at once.

This was no red jackal. The long mane and the stripes. This was an aardwolf.

'A bloody old frog-eater!'

'They don't take lambs.'

'Well, what else was it doing here?'

'It's probably spoilt.'

Bitterness seeped from them like aloe juice.

'Spoilt!' When the spent dusty bundle bared its teeth once again, the older brother thrust his whipstock right into its mouth, stepping on its neck at the same time so its head was pinned to the ground.

'Bring your whip. Tie up its jaws! Tie up its jaws! Stop fumbling. Make sure the handle stays inside. Let it bite on it.'

'How can I fasten the handle in its mouth? It'll slip out.'

'Don't you have a knife? Cut a hole in the skin here on the neck behind its ear where I'm treading. Then draw a whip through it.'

'What are you going to do?'

'We're going to skin the bastard. Let him see how it feels.'

They tied the aardwolf down with the ships and a riem. It was only then that they remembered the lamb still hanging in the piece of sacking. It was stiff and when they put it down, it couldn't walk.

'It's going to die.'

The older brother took the knife from the younger. In perfect accord, their hands worked together as they did when they slaughtered a sheep. The older brother went down on his haunches and the other moved over to the other side.

Instead of the normal way, they began up near the paws. The aardwolf's whole body went into a spasm almost as if it was trying to run on its back. It was difficult to work on the shuddering paws. But there was no hurry.

The paws still moved, however tightly they tied them. A strong forefinger worked better in some places, specially near the paws, than the knife. When you stuck your knuckles in between the hide and the warm body, it went faster.

Suddenly they became aware of a danger they hadn't thought of.

'It's going to die. Hurry up.'

It mustn't die. Not yet. There was a lot of blood, and getting more all the time.

With a few quick strokes of the knife the older brother cut the loose hide off. Much of the hide on the back and flanks remained.

'Let go.'

First the trap. Then the riems, all at once.

Was there still life in the creature? It lay very still. But when they pulled the whip handle from its jaws, the front part of its body staggered upright and the forepaws scraped at the ground.

'Come on.' It took some restraint not to kick it.

It actually got to its feet and struggled over the lamb that opened its mouth without managing to utter a sound. They'd completely forgotten about the dying lamb.

The mane looked long and wild on the skinny white legs. It staggered awkwardly to the nearest bitter scrub. Branches scraped against its legs.'

'Kik-kik-kik,' the aardwolf whimpered. 'Kik-kik-kik.'

It was getting redder and redder. But before it went completely red under the saddle on its back, it collapsed.

The two brothers stared at each other over the heap of livid flesh. They picked it up by the limp paws and buried it with the lamb as deep as they could dig into the barren earth.

Translated by Catherine Knox

T. T. CLOETE

Disaster

We were on holiday in Hout Bay when my wife fell seriously ill. The only doctor in the area was a retired GP who couldn't do much more than hold her hand, as my wife put it. When her condition deteriorated, I sent for a doctor from Cape Town, at great expense. He diagnosed a bleeding gastric ulcer. He said my wife could not go home until her condition improved, and then she must fly. The drive home to Port Elizabeth would be too tiring. We learned late-ish on a Sunday afternoon that there was a seat for her on an early Monday flight. I arranged for a taxi to take her to airport in the morning, and on the Sunday evening I set off in the car for Port Elizabeth with our small children.

I would have to drive pretty smartly through the night to reach Port Elizabeth airport in time to meet my wife's flight in the morning.

The children were very tearful, specially the two youngest. They were all convinced their mother was going to die and that this journey home without her heralded a major disaster. I did my best to comfort them, and as I drove along I thought exasperatedly: The things one has to cope with!

By the time we reached Swellendam, the youngest had developed a fever. I dosed her with the aspirin I was carrying.

The things one manages to cope with!

The journey was trying. After sunset we hit a sudden hard downpour with a strong head wind coming off the sea. The coast road winds through a number of passes.

My supply of aspirin had run out by the time we reached Humansdorp. The only waking soul we came across was a petrol pump attendant. He couldn't tell me where to find a doctor or a pharmacist. So there was nothing for it but to race along the home straight faster than the child's temperature rose.

At Jeffreys Bay a steenbuck ran into the road. There was a loud thud but I drove on because it didn't seem to cause any damage to the car. But the fright woke the children and they wanted to know what had happened.

'Nothing serious, just a little steenbuck that ran in front of us. The car's probably a bit dented but the engine's fine and the lights still work. A silly little accident. I'm sorry about the buck . . . But it was just one of those things.'

The children soon dropped off to sleep again.

The things that can happen!

A few kilometres further on, the warning light on the dashboard suddenly flashed red. I stopped. The engine was red hot. When I hit the buck, the radiator had been forced out of alignment against the fan which tore it open a quarter circle at one place. The water had all leaked out.

Now fate really had it in for us.

There we sat. It was raining steadily and a strong wind blew low clouds over us. We could hear the sea a long way off. It was two o'clock. The children were crying again – the older ones sobbed quietly, the younger ones howled. The smallest was so feverish she hardly knew what was happening.

There was very little traffic at that hour of the night and the vehicles that did go past ignored my frantic gestures. In the blinding rain, they probably couldn't even see me properly.

In no time I was soaked to the skin and freezing cold.

When I heard another vehicle coming from Humansdorp, I hit on the idea of getting my oldest son to help me. Surely they'd stop when they saw the child?

That did the trick. A small yellow Mini station-wagon pulled up. The driver got out. He didn't say much as I told my story. He obviously didn't quite trust the situation. Listening distractedly to me, he flashed his torch into my car and then he saw the other children. He was particularly struck by the sick one, producing an aspirin for her.

The emergency was over!

He took my arm and led me to his car, showing me without a word that there was no mother in his car, either, and three young children lay asleep in the back.

Then he began to speak.

'I'm more than willing to help you: I can go back to Humansdorp and get a tow truck. Rest assured: I won't leave you in the lurch.'

The hours passed as slowly as centuries. Finally my good Samaritan reappeared with the tow truck.

I asked to be towed to Port Elizabeth even though Humansdorp was closer.

Relief or sheer curiosity had the three of us peering into my car's engine again. We all leaned forward. When I raised my head, I bashed my unknown benefactor on the nose. His spectacles slipped and smashed into smithereens on the tarmac.

The trouble was beginning again . . .

Day was about to break by the time we'd hitched my car to the tow truck. I wanted to reward the man who'd done so much for me, but he refused to take anything.

'Well, at least let me pay for your spectacles,' I insisted.

'No, I don't want a cent. If I accepted something from you, in some other way it would be taken away from me in greater quantity. I'm glad I could help you.'

He said goodbye. As he left I asked him what his name was, but he didn't answer.

He was already on the road, ahead of us. He travelled faster than us, naturally – off into the dawning day.

The end of our tribulations was at hand. (It had even stopped raining.)

The man in the tow truck drove recklessly fast and I had to focus all my attention on the tension of the tow rope between him and me. Meanwhile I was thinking: I could have taken the yellow Mini's registration number and used that to track the man down and repay him once everything was back to normal . . . But in the heat of the moment I hadn't thought of it.

A thick mist rose off the sea. It was hard to make out the road. Luckily I had the tow truck in front of me. The difficult conditions had slowed him down a bit.

We went round a corner on van Stadens Pass and suddenly came upon a small yellow car lying upside down on the side of the road. The wheels were still turning, as the saying goes. Three crying children stumbled about in the wet grass and scrub. The man lay on his back, stretched out, dead still. It was clear there had not been a collision with another vehicle or an animal. There was nothing else: just the crying children, the silent man, and the small yellow car. He must have gone off the road on the corner in the mist.

It was nearly day but the mist was very thick now.

I felt his pulse. His heart had stopped. I shone my torch in his eyes. He stared straight ahead, past the torchbeam, fixedly, as only the dead can stare.

The eyes mesmerized me in the brown face – tanned like a farmer's or someone who works in the sun a lot. The skin around his eyes was as pale as the skin around weak eyes accustomed to thick-lensed glasses that shade them from the light.

Translated by Catherine Knox

INA ROUSSEAU

Do You Remember Helena Lem?

Do you remember Helena Lem? This is a sentence in a letter which a woman has just received from her fiancé, a bassoonist in the symphony orchestra of a city in another province.

Do you remember Helena Lem? A girl with peculiar pale blue eyes who used to play with us in the quarry when we were children? I am sorry to have to tell you she lost her eyesight about two years ago. I went to the dentist's yesterday and she was sitting in the waiting-room when I arrived. She looked vaguely familiar but only when the receptionist addressed her as Miss Lem did I recognize her. If I remember correctly she is younger than you, but now looks older than both of us. She said she remembers you. There is an operation in the offing for her which might restore her eyesight partially, but I gather that the chances of success are slim. Do hold thumbs for her.

Helena Lem.

The name splits up into four slippery sounds which immediately merge again and evolve into a memory which links up, not with her ears, but with her eyes. The visual image which emerges from the sounds is so vivid against her closed eyelids that it could have been the after-image of something of a mere second ago rather than the reappearance of something from the distant past.

This is what the woman sees against her closed eyelids:

A butterfly with tremulous indigo-blue wings is clinging to a back-drop of corollae and foliage.

A hand approaches from the right and slowly breaks up into five spatulate fingers: the finger of Helena Lem.

Then two of the fingers – a pair of pincers – take the butterfly wings between them and tear them up with two fingers of the other hand.

'Why did you do that, Helena?'

'Because I felt like it, of course. Why else?'

What remains between the fingers – little tatters joined to some-

thing living – is held aloft for a few seconds and then discarded like garbage. A sudden blast of wind pushes it forward in the sand and then it stays put. But it does not lie still: the residual life trapped inside struggles violently to free itself – until Helena Lem puts her foot on it.

The woman in the garden opens her eyes wide, as though trying to waken herself from an oppressive dream.

The colours of the summer afternoon try to enter in through her open eyes, but what she has just seen against her lids bar the way.

She fetches her writing-pad and pen, and there in the waning sunlight she starts to answer her fiancé's letter.

This is the beginning of her third paragraph:

My memories of Helena Lem are not happy and I am not well-disposed to her. I hope the operation will be unsuccessful, because –

And now her pen takes charge and automatically pushes the words on to the paper, one word after another, an avalanche of words:

it is my wish that, just as she has been unable for the past two years to see the wings of a butterfly – the wings which he carries over him like a little firmament; the wings like little open Chinese rice-paper fans; the wings spattered with dots which shake together like confetti when he moves, but become like the stained glass of cathedral windows when he is motionless; the wings with scalloped edges bound with black rickrack braid; the wings covered with a mesh of gossamer-fine embroidery thread; the wings which he opens and shuts like a little picture-book – that, just as she, Helena Lem, has been unable for the past two years to see these wings, she will not be able to see them in the years ahead either.

In the days that follow a feeling of oppression takes hold of her every time she thinks of the child Helena Lem; but then she remembers what happened to the woman Helena Lem and her disquiet makes way for a sense of satisfaction.

She awaits her fiancé's reply to her letter but, like his regular bi-weekly telephone calls, it fails to materialize. Then she starts dialling the telephone number of his flat at short intervals, but every time the bell rings in vain. Eventually, in her desperation, she sends him a telegram commanding him to write to her, and three days later she opens the envelope of his letter.

He had always found it rather difficult to express himself when in the grip of an intense emotion, and the letter is a battlefield of demolished words, particles and phrases. As though he had stuttered with his pen, she thinks, the way he sometimes stuttered with his tongue.

He writes:

Helena Lem will never again be able to see, nor will she ever again be seen by anyone. I hope that ~~makes you hap~~ satisfies you.

Your description of what she did to the butterfly didn't shock me. I can assure you that most children commit deeds far ~~wor~~ crueller than that. Destructiveness is common among children.

What you can't forgive Helena Lem is not that she was destructive but that she destroyed something you thought was precious to you.

~~In flowery language With In high sounding langu fustian With purple wr With preciosity Bombas Flashily~~ In flowery language you describe at length the ~~wi~~ butterfly's wings, comparing them with all kinds of other things which you consider ~~preciou~~ pretty. Had it been a fly, or a worm, or a flea, or a louse, or a mosquito which she ~~demoli~~ destroyed, it wouldn't have touched you. And do you want to tell me that when she killed the butterfly she was more ~~crue~~ destructive than you were when you wrote that sentence which expresses what you wish on her? And if Helena Lem killed the butterfly simply because she 'felt like it', in a desultory fashion, it ~~proves~~ means that the butterfly did not have the ~~meani impo~~ significance for her that it had for you. ~~And therefore she should not be hel~~

Actually I have something ~~terribly consequential~~ important to say to you, namely: that, just as you do not want to forgive Helena Lem because she destroyed something which was ~~beauti~~ precious to you, I do not want to forgive you for destroying something that was precious to me, and that is ~~our love for each ot the bond between you and me~~ my love for you. In telling me what you hope wish on Helena Lem – with that one sentence – you have totally ~~kill demoli~~ destroyed it and now it no longer exists. In other words, our engagement no longer exists either. The woman I ~~ador idolis~~ loved has stopped existing. She stopped existing the moment I read that sentence. And I will never forgive you for destroying something so ~~beau~~ precious – that which more than anything else gave meaning to my life – with one sentence, the way Helena Lem destroyed an insect with one gesture. I could also list many beautiful objects with which I could compare ~~the lo relationship betwee~~ my love for you, but I am not doing it, because I know that ~~you wouldn't be~~ it wouldn't ~~impress~~ touch you. That you could destroy it so ~~desultorily casua~~ easily, without even realizing that you were ~~destroy~~ destroying a living thing, that you could write down that sentence just like that, apparently just because you 'felt like' writing it at that moment, without considering its ~~likel possib~~ effect on our ~~relat~~ love, proves to me that it did not have the significance for you that it had for me, just as the butterfly did not have the significance for Helena Lem that it had for you. ~~That it was more important to you of greater importance to you at that moment to write that sentence than to preserve our love to express your vengefulness than~~ That the expression of your vengefulness was more important to you at that moment than the preservation of what ~~exists~~ existed between me and you, means that what existed between us now no longer exists, and therefore I never want to see you again. You had no right to reveal that ~~ulcer in your soul black spot on your soul~~ rotten place in your soul to me. Had you not written down that sentence, I would not have known of it and the woman I ~~love~~ loved would still have existed. ~~Perhaps all people carry around deep within themselves something like this~~ Perhaps all of us carry around deep within ourselves something like this. But it behoves us to keep it hidden from those who are dear to us. Perhaps all of us are living behind a ~~veil front~~ façade, and it is only this that makes it possible for us to live close to those who are dear to us. No one has the right to ~~tear the veil violate our façade tear down the veil from ourselves~~ damage our façade in the presence of those who are dear to us. And once the façade has been damaged it is damaged for ever, because once the truth has been unveiled, nothing ~~on earth~~ can ever ~~hide~~ cover it up again. Before the façade is damaged one is aware of the possibility of something ~~unpleasant ugly~~ shocking behind the façade, but one ~~hopes~~ goes on ~~ho~~ believing that this is not so until the façade is damaged and it is proved beyond any doubt that the shocking thing does exist. Thereafter it is ~~totally completely~~ absolutely impossible to be deceived by the façade again. This thing you have done to me and ~~therefore everything between us~~ in doing it you have destroyed for ever everything that existed between us. Do not try to get in touch with me. I do not want to see you again, ever.

It is from this time onwards that the woman starts to deteriorate slowly but markedly. Some people contend that her broken engagement must have given her a blow from which she could never fully recover. Others say that there must be more to it than that. Many try, in subtle ways, but always in vain, to ferret out in conversations with her what the secret is that she is carrying around in her. And then, when she is already old and many people believe her to be in her dotage, she relinquishes the secret to a visiting pastor. She tells him that there can be no mercy for her because the sin that she committed is unforgivable: that as a child she had one day torn the wings of a butterfly, flung him down in the sand and then pressed her put down her foot on him.

Translated by the author

P. J. HAASBROEK

Departure

The train was to depart at 22h00. You all arrived a little early with your families, your girls and a few friends, with your kit-bags and rifles, and stood about on the platform, self-conscious because the train was not there and the wind was blowing so; uncomfortable in brown uniforms amidst the colourful, soft people who have come to see you off. Fortunately you are all spruce again, even those who have come out of the plastic bags. The authorities have at least arranged that properly.

'This will take some getting used to,' you hear Petrus Bosman's father say. 'We had so many plans.' You glance in his direction, because you remember what Petrus had said about his father's plans, and you see how his mother clutches the man's arm in both her hands. 'I'm going to miss him *so*,' she says. 'I can tell what Christmas is going to be like without him. Everyone will come for a swim and a *braaivleis*[1] again. Caro-Anne will probably arrive early to help with the salads. Now I won't even be able to send him a little something any more,' and she begins to sob. 'We'll just have to "*vasbyt*",'[2] says his father.

You feel you could laugh. '*Vasbyt*'! Easily said. Easy army talk. Like '*min dae*'.[2] No, certainly not that. '*Vasbyt*', yes, but not '*min dae*'. You keep a casual eye on the other men, a little surprised at the civilized geniality, the playful bravado – at

---

1 *braaivleis* An outdoor barbecue; a popular and typical South African meal.
2 '*Vasbyt. Min dae*' is an Afrikaans expression common among South African soldiers, used as an encouraging injunction to endure what lies ahead (usually the term of one's military service) with determination. 'Vasbyt' is an imperative meaning 'grit your teeth' or 'bite the bullet'; 'min dae' conveys the assurance (often wishful) that there are but few days left; the trial is nearly over.

how different your companions are amongst their families. It is clear that they want to caress their girls, that they are anxious to comfort and to keep sentimentality at bay, but every now and then they glance at the signal in the distance which has been an unwavering green for the past quarter of an hour.

Even though you are alone, you also wish that the train would come. The station is a no man's land, a place one comes to only to depart for somewhere else. It was not designed or built for people who wish to be together, but for separation. Domestic chats do not belong in these stark, rectangular, open spaces. The dirty concrete and tar, red brick and steel are unfriendly, intentionally unfriendly like the massive pillars and the cold gleam of the tracks in the dark under the electric light. The station is open so that the wind can blow in and snatch at people's clothing to separate them from each other. You tap your pipe against the side of the platform and watch the coals spill out in the dark and die. Why can't departure be just as easy?

You pick up your bag when you see the train light, a sudden star growing, brightening and blinding as it approaches. The pitch-black locomotive passes you with a gnashing of steel wheels on steel. For a moment you see red fire and the white, curious face of the engine driver in his window, and then come the third-class passenger cars. The pale yellow light is like thin oil washing over the crowded commuters. 'Are they actually going to send the Blacks with them?' a man behind you enquires angrily.

You all walk down the length of the train in search of your compartments. The last two carriages are yours. You throw your kit-bags on to the luggage racks and hang your rifles on the clothes hooks. Many get off the train again, but others remain in the passage, leaning out through the window to say goodbye. You sit in the compartment and gaze through the window at the deserted, windy platform on your side of the train, relieved not to have any part in the farewell. The train jerks, and you hear the wails of the people and the comforting words of the soldiers. The station glides slowly by.

They were only shunting. Your carriages now stand alongside another platform, number 6, without a locomotive. The devil alone knows where in the dark night it has been moved to with the Blacks' cars in tow. Fortunately all the people left before you were returned here, and you all are alone; there is not even a railway worker in sight.

Slowly, cautiously, the men begin to question one another: How it had happened, where, on what day and at what time, and are surprised at the degree of similarity, often the exact concurrence, but you keep quiet. Your story is none of their business. Your horror is your own.

In their conversations they return to the border camps surrounded by trenches, and machine-gun installations protected by sandbags, to the sandtracks reaching in endless straight lines to the flat horizons, and the bush where all memories have become indistinct like the haze in the afternoon sky. Whatever may have happened before is no longer relevant. Only that which caused you all to end up on this train. Nothing else.

You have taken the hidden bottles of alcohol from your bags and drink large mugs of brandy and Coke, cane spirits, vodka and beer with great gulps straight from the bottles. Each one has a story to tell, each one knows a joke, and there is much boisterous laughter and comradely backslapping. No longer accustomed to the raw, strong spirits, you are all soon drunk.

Men fall about, cursing. Some pick quarrels and fist fights break out. Petrus laughingly holds a quarrelsome soldier by the wrists, but when he tries to butt Petrus with his head, Petrus flings him off. The soldier staggers into someone else, and begins to swipe wildly at the broad, dense face which confronts him. His fists strike bone, eye-socket, nose and chin, but the sweaty, shiny skin shows no damage; no bruising, no blood, the eyes expressionless, uncomprehending. The soldier abruptly stops his blows, turns and walks out of the compartment, his anger quenched.

You can hear the noise of fighting in the passage and the other compartments too, but you ignore the hubbub. That is just your way of keeping to yourself, and here it is each to his own. You sit with your head in your hands, as you always do, and feel your companions' shoulders against you, their

212

breath warm as blood. Their hands grab at you when they
stumble but you do not look up. Nor do you answer their
questions, trying only to concentrate on the hissing and
heaving of the train, the rocking, rolling and upward rearing.
The loud, shrill voices recede to a soft continuous sigh.

It occurs to you that the authorities have left you here with a
purpose. Were you meant to get drunk and start brawling
before the journey could begin? Were you meant to confront
each other with the meaninglessness of your short lives and
your deaths, or are they allowing you first to reconcile yourselves to the journey? You stand up, suddenly suspicious, and
put your head out of the window.

There is a man crossing the platform. He is carrying a zinc
basin and is elderly; he looks about fifty to you, with his thin
hair and his bent-over, plodding walk. Judging by his khaki
trousers, open-neck shirt and dirty, crumpled jacket, you
presume that he is a labourer. He has either been misdirected
or he has misunderstood, but this cannot be the train he
intends to catch. He pays no attention to the lists of pas-
sengers' names, slogs unsuspectingly by to the door at the end
of the carriage, and climbs in.

You feel you should warn him.

'Oom,'[3] you say, 'you're on the wrong train.'

He looks blankly at you and lowers his little bath-tub on to
the floor of the passage. 'No,' he says, 'I'm going with you.'

'This is a troop train,' you say, afraid of alarming him. 'You
are not a soldier, Oom.'

'I do not mind with whom I travel,' he says. 'This is my last
journey. Don't spoil everything now. Where can I find a seat?'

You wanted to tell him that the train is full, but then it
occurred to you to play a trick on the old man. He would not
know that this train does not stop anywhere. He would have
to make the entire journey.

'Let's put the tub in the toilet,' you say. Maybe he'll still
realize his mistake.

'No, I'd rather keep it with me,' he says.

---

3 A respectful, often affectionate form of address literally meaning
uncle, but used more widely among Afrikaners to address any older
man.

The tub is bulging, covered with a towel and tied with a string. You carry it ahead of him to your compartment.

The others are surprised. 'Jesus, Oom,' says one, 'where do you think you're going?'

'At least I know where I come from,' the old man says and sits down next to Petrus. 'And that's enough for me.'

You nod at the soldier. 'The oom knows', you say.

Someone else asks about the bath-tub, and the old man begins to undo the string. No one stops him. He removes the towel. In the tub is a framed wedding picture, a sheaf of papers, a tool-box and a few articles of children's clothing, neatly folded. He unpacks the contents on to his lap so that he can dig deeper. He uncovers a worn blue overall and a white tie. He hesitates. 'They said I must bring this all with me,' he says. 'It must show who I am. It's easy. Apprentice, carpenter, married, had two little girls. And I was church warden in my day.' His hands fold lovingly around the bundle of possessions. 'My whole life,' he says.

'That's more than we've had,' says Petrus. 'I've not even had a job.' He takes the overall from the basin and holds it up to his chest as though to measure it for size, but you are no longer watching him.

Right at the bottom of the bath-tub are two dolls. A pink rubber doll like the ones children play with in the bath, and a grinning black golliwog with white eyes and checkered pants. Suddenly you remember, you see them, and the blood roars in your ears like an approaching storm. You feel your guts contracting beneath your chest, a miserable nausea rises thickly in your throat, and your body begins to convulse as it did on that day. You vaguely hear someone say: 'Look what we have here. A terrorist!' and someone else adds: 'And sharing a bath with the white baby.'

You see them standing around you in their tattered bush wear, see them dragging you from the hut where you were hiding. You hear them laughing as they shove you with their rifle butts. You had no idea what they were planning to do. The sun pierced your eyes and you found yourself at the split-pole fence, at the high, sharpened corner stake, and you felt their hands. They lifted you. You screamed, but no sound came from between your clenched teeth.

You lift your rifle from the hook and fix the bayonet.

Departure

The old man looks in amazement at the golliwog. 'It's just a doll,' he says.

The blade impales it and you lift it high, higher than the old man's snatching hands. Right up to the light where it hangs like a flopping dead bird against the sun on the point of the bayonet.

The old man shakes his head. 'We are on the point of departure,' he says. 'And you have still not made your peace.'

Then you realize that the old man knows where you are headed. Your destination is also his.

The black locomotive barks abruptly a few times into the wide mouth of the dark, and your journey begins.

Translated by Lynette Paterson

JOHN MILES

Lucy

When I was a child I never noticed that many trees blossom some time in August. There were just trees with leaves and trees without leaves. (Those without leaves I simply do not remember as well, because they had nothing in common with mulberries, loquats and oranges.)

I never knew whether the previous summer had been hotter or not, whether this year's winter had more or less rain than any summer. Everything just was the way it was almost all at once. And if it is impossible for summer and winter to coincide, then it was just that cold knew no other time before it, it was just cold. Or: hot.

That is how it was with Lucy too. She was there. She had always been. Today I can say that for many years, and as far back as my memory recalls, my father and I lodged with the Smiths. Old Smith was Lucy's father.

They fed me and in the evenings I saw my father. I was glad that my father liked to talk. Then I could also stay with Lucy longer, until she was asleep. Old Smith spoilt her a lot and I loved her. (Shh, Dad, Lucy is sleeping.)

I can only remember old man Smith's face from the side. Drinking his wine: it was Lucy's birthday again. (You're eleven today, Lucy, more than I have fingers for. Lucy looks and smiles.)

Of Ma Smith I only see a corpulent walk, down the passage, and the mouth saying, crookedly to the right: Phew. (Lucy and I are sitting under the mulberry tree, it's hot; her trembling head.)

Of my father I especially recall the voice. He used to read to us from the Bible in the evenings, and prayed. His voice I hear, but I can no longer imagine what he said. (Shh, Lucy.) And he must have helped me with my Sunday School exams, but I cannot even remember which mistakes he made. (Never mind, Lucy, I'll be back soon.) He also gave me a hiding because I swore at the closed gate, and once – probably by accident – kicked me because of my habit of wetting the wooden seat in the privy. But I don't know exactly what he looked like when he punished.

Yet I remember him exactly, exactly, the way he brought Lucy and me a milk shake in a brown ginger-beer bottle from work one day. For me it was precisely the brown glass that prevented the flavour of the milk shake from escaping. As a thermos flask does with hot tea. My father stood leaning forward for a long time watching Lucy pour for us. The ends of his moustache trembled (almost like Lucy's hands), for he shaved very carefully so that his moustache would grow only on his upper lip. (Lucy's small hands, and short, plump little fingers.)

The house Lucy and I knew was the one towards the back yard. (We're sitting under the trees and I predict exactly where the next loquat or orange will fall; her head trembles as she laughs.)

Then the time came. We were fourteen when Lucy died. Everything began to change, and is still changing. We spoilt her, but since then the earth has been spoiling her. Today I can understand. She was always much smaller than I, except for her large head, twice the size of mine. She could do almost nothing, for her hands trembled so.

My father bought me a bicycle. And time, which had begun for me, is still continuing, becoming. I left Pietermaritzburg years and years ago, but each year when nature becomes restless and many trees blossom, I smell Pietermaritzburg's trees. Some have leaves. Of others it must be the bark, or the branches.

Pietermaritzburg's trees. A bicycle is standing in the street around a corner and looking as though it is about to slide down. Ma Smith turns around at the front door. And on the verandah my father remains seated with his foot drawn inwards. Next to him sits old Smith, about to swallow, his hand with the glass three quarters of the way to his mouth, his other hand on his spectacles in his pocket. I sit askew on the little verandah wall with just a taste of ginger-beer in my nose.

John Miles

My father keeps his foot drawn inwards, but he's leaning slightly forward. His bare upper lip is trembling. I am struck dumb by my own paralysis because I see him about to whisper: Lucy is dead.

Translated by Laura Jordaan

ELSA JOUBERT

Back Yard

I live on the periphery of an existence which I don't understand.

There are superficial points of contact: a few words to the petrol-pump attendant, good morning to the man who delivers the milk. And there is the Black woman who works in my house.

She is closer to me than a sister, and she is more intimately acquainted with my private life than a sister could ever be.

But I do not know her.

Even the name I call her is a functional title, chosen for practical reasons. It is not rooted in her identity as my name is in mine. I have not been informed of her real name; I would not be able to pronounce it.

She is my link with the unknown, a bridge I negotiate with great difficulty.

My home is my fortress. I know the walls that enclose every room. I move from room to room. I shift a chair, straighten a mirror against the wall, I pick flowers and arrange them in a vase. I caress my house with touch and glance.

But now she is here I am no longer alone.

She came to live in the room in the back yard and her territory is demarcated.

I planted large shrubs to screen the room from my view. In the evening when I close the window that faces her room, I hear voices behind the shrubs, or a rustling sound as though someone has come out of the room to urinate in the shrubbery.

I don't say anything and I don't look out. I draw the curtains closed.

But when morning comes I open the curtains again.

The life in that room in my back yard is bound up with my

life. Without that life, I'm like a body that casts no shadow; my property and my house feel deserted; I wander aimlessly; the flowers droop in their vases and the mirrors on my walls reflect blurred images.

I seek the life in the room in my back yard so I may know it. With the fingers of the blind, I grasp the door which is so firmly shut against me. I cannot see.

For God's sake, just walk in and have a look, my husband tells me. Why the nerves?

He goes to work and I stay behind.

My children go to school and I stay behind.

My visitors leave and I stay behind.

I and the life of the Black woman in my back yard.

It is not a solitary life, but one of multiplicity. This is the first thing I have to learn. Her life is involved with another, and this second life with others, and I, through them, with an amorphous body that has entered my life. Most of the time the room in my back yard surges with the strangers who are entertained there. It seems as though the walls are flexible, they've lost their rigidity and can expand and contract like a canvas bag.

And these strangers have a radar which I don't understand. It warns them of my approach along the nearby garden path, the approach of danger. The noise level drops, the bulging contracts, the buzz, the drone of conversation fades into silence. The walls shrink back into themselves, become solid, the room just a room and the door firmly shut.

If I walked on, if I came along the cement path, turned the handle and opened the door, what would I see? Perhaps a man on the bed, a woman on the chair, a child on the floor, a second child hiding among the clothes behind the door, and another man on a bench at the window – the fat man whom I know.

And they'd gaze at me as if they were carved out of wood.

And the mugs of coffee, or the bowls of cold congealed food, or the children's helpings served on torn-off bits of paper, would also freeze; disappearing in the silence. Becoming nothing before my eyes.

And I would see nothing. I would look at the ceiling and say: Oh, isn't Flora here? Or Emma, or Agnes, or Evangelina. That's what I would say if I went in.

But I don't go in. I walk past the closed wooden door, past the silent fixed walls of the small rectangular room. I tread on a dry twig on the path to make quite sure they're aware of my presence, and turn the hose-pipe on to the fruit trees in this dry patch of back garden. Then, talking to myself, I walk away.

If I was to wait, if I was to wait concealed, I would see the strangers start moving again, and then, as if my coming was a danger signal, begin to leave the room. The black figures would slip away across the back garden behind the shrubs. Those who had more confidence and carried briefcases or wore hats would pass through the side gate back to the freedom of the streets.

As I water the flowers in the no man's land of my front garden, I greet the ones with briefcases and they return the greeting.

And sometimes, in the intimacy of my back garden, I greet the ones who slip away, and they too return the greeting. And they learn to trust and they dare to come from their dark world into mine and say with eyes blinking in the bright light, Help me.

The fat one whom I know stands at the back door.

'Oh, madam . . .' His eyes are shiny, round and empty as marbles. 'Oh, madam.' He digs in his ear with a finger. He lowers his hands and produces his pass from a trouser pocket.

He shows it to me, childlike in his pleasure.

'It's there. Honestly, it's there.' His finger goes back to digging in his ear. 'But it's wrong.'

The pass is tattered. The stamps are not in order. Flora – he's her brother – has been battling to get him to put it right but he won't listen to her.

'They must just catch him and take him away to Bethal,' says Flora. 'He can plant potatoes there. They hit you with the spade-handle there. That'll teach him a lesson.'

He laughs at the idea he should be hit with a spade-handle. His thick lips draw back to show the pink flesh within and the yellow roots of his large teeth. He laughs and shakes his head at himself and his own stupidity.

'But I went there, madam, like Flora said I should. To the permit office, as she said.'

'And I told you to ask for Tebe because he'd help you,' said Flora.

He laughed again and had another dig in his ear. 'I forgot the name, madam, and I asked for Febe, and they told me they didn't know anyone by that name.'

'He's a mampara,'[1] said Flora. 'He just stood there at the office. Wasted my bus-fare.'

I took the pass and paged through it. I read: Work permit and new pass 23 September.

It was now April of the following year. I felt the desperation rise up in me. 'Can't you do what it says here? He's been at home for six months. And here it says you should have come to get a new pass and permit on the twenty-third of September.'

Now Flora too was scratching her ear. She opened her mouth to speak and then shut it again.

He began to laugh again, about his own stupidity, and he mumbled: 'Oh, madam . . .' But I'd seen the darkness fill his eyes and I felt the chill of fear.

It was only then that I realized: like Flora, he could not read.

The old man too had drawn a letter from his pocket. The old man who'd found his way here from the location at dead of night or in the small hours of the morning. The old man who'd used his knobkerrie to heave himself on to his feet from the straight-backed chair in a dark corner of the room in my back yard. The old man who'd steadied himself with a hand on the concrete wall as he climbed laboriously up the steps to my back door.

He didn't say much. He took off his hat as though he was preparing to pray.

'You talk,' he said to Flora.

His eyelids were sunken, he was thin and bowed, his hair was damp, flattened by his hat. There were threads of white in his beard and his mouth was small and meek.

'He is my uncle,' Flora told me.

---

1 *mampara* Idiot.

The old man held his knobkerrie under his arm so he could use both hands to unfold the sheet of cheap thin blue paper. He gave it to me so I could read what was written on it in pencil.

'We have had it read,' said Flora. 'I can tell the madam what it says. It's from his grandchild. Her father and mother are both dead. But her father wasn't from the Cape and when he died, his brother took the girl back to the country to grow up. But now she wants to come back to her grandpa and get work in town. It's dry in the country, she's hungry and there's no work. The old man has been sending her money but he's old now and he can't carry on.'

'Does she have the right papers?'

The old man produced another document. It was a school form, much folded, yellow with age, bearing a faded stamp. I could just make out the name of the school and Patience Makebe, Standard One, but it must have been a while ago and the date was so faded I couldn't decipher it.

I gave them a lift to the permit office.

Flora wanted to find Tebe so she pushed through the queue, obliging us to follow. They let us through because I was there. We came to Tebe's work station. He was a small, lightly built Black man in a suit with a white shirt, a tie, and spectacles. I wondered if he was related to Flora, or perhaps a boy friend, because he stood up the minute he saw her and led us through an even longer queue, through waiting-rooms where people sat as though they'd been there for centuries, patiently, purposefully, organically part of their benches. Some looked at us, others had their eyes closed as though they were asleep.

The White official was tired and irritable. Tebe, bringing yet another bunch of people, made him angry and Flora, who kept interrupting, added to the aggravation. He took out a handkerchief and mopped his brow. There was a wide gap between his desk and the bench against the wall where we sat.

Flora was hardly seated before she stood up again, talking.

'Sit down,' he shouted at her. 'Keep quiet.'

There was an immeasurable chasm between the large

empty wooden desk he sat behind and our bench against the wall. He drew a piece of paper towards him and picked up his pen, waiting.

Flora pulled the letter out of her bodice, unfolded it and put on the desk in front of him. I tried to say something but the official shut me up.

'Does she have papers?'

The old man took out the yellowed form he'd folded up and put back in his pocket.

The official read the form. He read the letter.

He tapped the name on the letter and the name on the form. Nhlanda Rhoda was mentioned in the letter, Patience on the form . . . which one were we talking about?

The old man spoke to Flora in their language, quietly as though he dared not speak over the desk. When he looked up again, his eyes were expressionless, as though any certainty or optimism he might have entertained had waned.

'The teacher was a nun and she gave her another name,' Flora explained.

'And these are all the papers she has, these . . .' Exasperated, he didn't even finish his own sentence. But he took pity on the old man. 'Look, she can't come here without papers. Hasn't she got anything else? A birth certificate?'

The old man shook his head, he didn't know. He reached for the yellow rectangle of paper on the desk.

'This isn't sufficient,' said the official. 'This . . . this Patience. How do I know it's the same girl?' He indicated the letter. 'And even if I knew' – he pointed to the stamp – 'When was she there? Where was it? The school probably doesn't exist any longer.' Then, at the end of his tether: 'How am I supposed to know who you want the form for, or even that Nhlanda Rhoda ever even existed?'

'We'd better go,' I said.

We pushed our way outside through the people. My hands were sweating and the smell of people made me claustrophobic. The steering wheel was stiff under my hands, the car was stuffy and smelly. The old man didn't come back with us. He didn't get into the car, simply took off his hat and bowed slightly as if in prayer.

'I'll just send some more money for food,' he said.

I nodded. 'Yes. Send some more money for food.'

There's a mysterious radar link between my back yard and the back yards all around mine.

There's a network running right through town, invisible lines joining one back yard room to another, joining suburbs, and joining the suburbs to the Black locations. Like a spider-web – invisible until the light catches it, or dust collects on it, or smoke coats it with soot – these lines of communication only became visible in a time of crisis.

Rosy drank.

Rosy, who was relieving Flora. Rosy who wore her dresses long and sometimes asked to go early so she could attend a church service. Sometimes she sang right through Saturday night.

But now and then I'd hear something falling in the kitchen and when I got to her I could see something had snapped in Rosy. Her headscarf would be awry, and when she stirred the saucepan, the food would splash over the stove, because her movements had lost their co-ordination.

Then I'd send her to her room to sleep it off and I'd finish the supper myself.

That was when the weakness was containable, bearable, overlookable.

But when she finished off everything that was strong and piquant in the house (we'd taken to locking up the liquor much earlier) when Rosy grew silent and preoccupied, then we knew something was brewing, just as you know bad weather's on the way when the wind drops, or mugginess rises from the tarmac or the perspective of trees and buildings in the distance is flattened.

Then all we could do was wait.

And one morning Rosy was no longer there. She was gone. She had disappeared somewhere in the limbo which the Black locations seemed to us.

An uncomfortable feeling hung over our house like a cloud. Contact with the darkness, the unknown. A stranger had entered our world of whitewashed walls, swags of red bougainvillaea and shiny verandahs; of laid tables and a warming oven full of dishes ready to be served; of freshly made up beds and a bale of pressed laundry to be put away.

Was the stranger fear, guilt, regret, or love?

We loved Rosy. We shared our food and our clothes with her. We told her of our hopes and fears.

Why then the stranger who came to live with us in our house when Rosy was off somewhere in her own limbo?

I did the housework. I chatted with the milkman. I bought a new vegetable knife. I was busy.

Then being busy made me restless.

And I became aware of the radar that was operating from my empty back yard to the back yards nearby, to far-flung neighbourhoods, over the mountain, as far as the workshops in the industrial area, delivery vans, garage allotments to the unknown darkness of the men's hostels in the Black locations.

And late, after nine on the third night after she'd gone, there was a knock at the door. A young Black man asking, cap in hand, 'Madam, is Rosy back?'

The phone rings ... From whose house? While which White woman is out – just nipped down to the shops, or to get the post? 'This is Agnes, madam. Is Rosy back?'

Or a bleep bleep in the telephone receiver and the sound of a coin being inserted, but the receiver clicks and I hear nothing. And there it is again: bleep bleep, another coin in the slot, the call comes through and gruff male voice asks: 'Madam, I speaking Rosy? Rosy not there?' And then: 'Madam, I find out. I let you know.'

Rosy is part of a peculiar amorphous body that feels her absence, that feels somewhere in its intuitive radar: a line is down, someone somewhere in the network has fallen.

And after another two or three days another Black woman came and knocked at the door. It was late – after ten. Where had she come from? Which kitchen had she to clean first? At which bus stop had she stood and waited? She had a young girl with her.

'She'll help you, madam, until Rosy is back.'

And this young girl, hardly more than a child, who I didn't know, knew me, knew the way round the back to the room in the back yard, and she knew which loose brick in the wall to look under for the key to Rosy's room, and the Black woman said: 'It's all right, madam, you can let her stay in the room.' Rosy's uniforms didn't fit her too well, straining to remain buttoned over her young bosom. I gave her a T-shirt to wear under the uniform. The next day she set to work at the kitchen sink with the confidence of experience. The strong black hands wrung out the tea towels and polished the stainless steel, and once again I saw that special dry shine only a black hand can get on my sink.

Rosy reappeared after a week. She was brought by the some strange Black women. They came in the evening and Rosy hid behind her as they stood in the shadow on the verandah. 'She's not completely fit yet, madam, but she's all right. She'll be able to work tomorrow.'

Rosy was embarrassed, her face was ashen and she'd lost weight. The dress I knew so well looked as though it was hanging on a scarecrow. Even her shoulders seemed narrower.

Later when I had a cup of tea in the kitchen with the Black woman, she told me what had happened.

'We looked for him, madam. He's got his problems too and sometimes they get on top of him.'

I know about Rosy's problems. I gave her school fees for her youngest child in Cradock, the child who'd been living with foster parents from birth. We'd sent food because they'd written that she was thin and wouldn't eat. I told Rosy not to distress herself over the son in Port Elizabeth who wouldn't work. She should stop sending money to pay his fines and bail him out of prison. They wrote to tell her he was to be declared a habitual criminal if he was involved in another stabbing. Couldn't his father lend a hand? I suggested – but she hadn't seen the father for ages and the son was thirteen the last time he'd seen him. He was the child of her youth, and, because she was working, he too had grown up with foster parents. I told her: What can you do? Upsetting yourself doesn't achieve anything.

Until last week when the letter came and I opened it for her because her hands were shaking too much and it said: her son had killed and was to hang.

'It's a good thing we found her, madam,' the Black woman told me. 'They're looking for her at the office. The papers came saying she had to come and see her son one last time before he hangs.

'Madam, I think she's afraid to see this child who is to hang.'

The woman sitting on the edge of the bed in the dimness of the room in my back yard is still a child herself. A child who looks up at me with no fear or self-consciousness in her eyes, but a radiant composure, an unshakeable sense of being. As my eyes grow accustomed to the dimness and she turns to me, I see the great swollen belly resting on her knees.

She wears an overall of Flora's or Rosy's or Agnes's. The shoulders are too wide and drop almost to her elbows. An adult garment on a child's body.

A child's body? She clasps her stomach with her hands. The hands hold the stomach protectively as if they have a primal knowledge which the child does not have yet.

The delicate hands of a child are the hands of the ancients.

Her face is thin and angular. She is wasting away while her baby grows. What source did she draw on for strength to let the baby grow?

Flora had called me from the house to the room. 'Madam, Nhlanda has come back.'

'Nhlanda?'

'Patience . . . she's going to have a baby. The man of the house is dead and the widow doesn't want to look after her so they sent Nhlanda to us.'

It was oddly poetic: the girl who came from nowhere with no papers, and the baby she would bear.

There was an order in the chaos. There was a light in this darkness, and I allowed the brightness of the dark unknown to flood over me.

The advent of the child she would bear was poetic, in spite of the problems she brought with her – where would she be confined, what clinic would accept her at this late stage, which hospital would admit her without papers, who would support the child, buy its clothes?

Even my mother-in-law, who was strict about this kind of

thing and didn't believe in 'spoiling' people, volunteered to provide the nappies.

My one daughter crocheted a matinée jacket and my youngest found a doll she could spare.

Was there ever a child so lacking in papers? Was there ever a life so guilelessly conceived. To be born and set on its way in the world?

We'd hide the baby if they came looking for it.

We'd comfort him with milk if he screamed. We would wrap him up if he was cold and we'd wash him when he was dirty.

Was there ever a baby who would come into the world so uninvited?

We went away for a week's holiday and on our return we found the back yard was deserted again. The cat sat on the high back garden wall and watched us with wild hungry eyes.

The room in the back yard looked strangely small, as though it stood alone on an open space, four white walls and a sloping roof and three steps leading up to the door. It stood abandoned and whitewashed and lonely. The door was tightly shut, the windows too, and the curtains were drawn. Two freshly laundered uniforms and two aprons hung on the line. The pegs had shifted up in the wind so they were bundled wretchedly together against the pole.

The key to the room lay on the table in the back yard. That was all. When we unlocked the door we found nothing but a stuffy smell and the neatly folded bedding.

There was a layer of dust on the newspaper lining the drawer in the small chest. It looked as though it had lain there undisturbed for a long long time – even years. When I drew the curtains, the rings dragged as though they'd rusted from years of hanging in one position. The dark burnt patch on the dressing table suggested someone had used a small stove there.

And the servants from next door came to tell us that they'd packed their things and left with the bundles and boxes on their heads one night. Flora, Nhlanda, a strange man, and boy.

Elsa Joubert

The room in my back yard is empty.

Another Black woman is moving in this afternoon.
I live on the periphery of an existence I do not understand.

Translated by Catherine Knox

KOOS PRINSLOO

Crack-Up

She closes the door and goes to the mirror on the wall. First she checks that the combs holding her hair are still firmly in place before she turns and lights the candle. The bell in the church tower begins to ring loudly. She glances at her watch and moves to the window. She lets the blind down only half-way and puts out a hand to smooth the limp fabric. She goes to her bed and starts leafing through a copy of *Films Illustrated*. Suddenly she flips back two pages. She looks at a picture of Marlon Brando in *A Streetcar Named Desire*.

When a knock sounds at the door, she closes the magazine hastily. But she waits for a second knock before she gets up from the bed and goes to open the door.

'Oh, hello! What a surprise.'

'Good evening.' He presents her with a rose. 'The first rose of summer,' he says, running a hand over his cropped head. 'I meant to pick jasmine, but if I remember correctly, the smell is too strong for you.'

'Come in.' She laughs. 'Not too strong. Just entirely too sweet and sentimental.'

'Not decadent enough?' He steps into the room, closing the door behind him.

'Yes, roses are so ephemeral . . .'

'Is she quoting A. G. Visser[1] now?'

'Verbatim.'

They laugh.

'Be careful, your background is showing.'

'I promise you, there's no cure either for Calvinism or folk poetry,' she says and goes to the bathroom.

'Quite right,' he says. 'How are your parents?'

'Fine,' she replies from the bathroom where she fills a vase

---

1 Early Afrikaans poet of humorous and sentimental doggerel.

with water for the rose. 'Dad is still happily sermonizing, and Mother plays tennis and the organ with a song in her heart.'

He smiles. She puts the rose beside the candle on the small table. 'And your mum?'

'Oh, she's pleased about my seven days – she brags about me to the neighbours. But what can you tell your mother?'

'That you love her.'

' "A Soldier's Home"? Eat your heart out, Hemingway.'

'Or you tell her about the war.'

'When you go home, tell them of us and say, For your tomorrow . . . We gave our today!'

They laugh. The church bell begins to ring again. She looks up.

'This is the second lot of chimes.'

'You can't win,' he says.

'Oh come all ye faithful.'

'What is white and streaks across the sky?'

'Don't know.'

'The coming of the Lord.'

They laugh and then remain silent until the bell stops ringing.

'Sit down,' she says.

'Thanks,' he says. He seats himself on the sofa.

'How about something to drink?'

'That would be nice. What's on offer?'

'Coffee or tea.'

'Tea,' he says, smiling.

She gets up and goes to the kitchen. He looks around the room. There is a picture of a man in a simple wooden frame on the chest-of-drawers next to her bed. He gets up to examine it more closely. When she returns from the kitchen, he sits down on the sofa again. She puts the tray on a small table.

'Milk and sugar?'

'Thanks.'

She hands him a cup and offers him biscuits on a plate. He takes two. She pours herself some tea and goes to sit on the bed.

'You've put on weight,' she says.

'Yes, the army knows how to look after you,' he says and bites into a biscuit.

She takes a sip of tea and then puts the cup down beside the rose and the candle. He holds out one foot. 'How do you like my cowboy boots?'

'Not very patriotic, are they?'

' "They've all come to look for America",' he says, chewing the second biscuit.

'Vietnam? And he probably wouldn't mind becoming one of America's forgotten warriors – his South African *Pro Patria* medal and all.' She takes another sip of tea.

He looks around the room again. 'I like your place.'

'Thanks.'

'The candle-light is very romantic.'

'Soft light is more flattering,' she says and gets up. She goes over to the hi-fi set and snaps a tape into the cassette deck.

'Did you know they used only natural candle-light when they filmed some of the scenes in *Barry Lyndon*?' she asks, sitting down on the bed again.

He doesn't answer. There is a long silence. He finishes his tea and puts the empty cup down on the tray. After a while he gets up from the sofa and goes to sit beside her on the bed.

'I like your perfume.'

'Halston.'

He takes a cigar from his pocket and lights it on the candle. 'All right if I smoke?'

She doesn't say anything.

'Do you still play the piano?'

'Sometimes.'

'I wrote to you,' he says.

'When?'

'When I heard you were engaged. I wanted to congratulate you.'

'I didn't receive anything.'

'I didn't post the letter.'

He lies back on the bed. She puts her cup down in the saucer.

'Well, tell me then,' she says.

'First tell me about your chosen knight in shining armour.'

'He's an engineer – interested in music and sport . . .'

'And he's very good-looking.'

233

'Yes.' She smiles. 'What's it like on the border?'

'What do you want to hear about?'

'Anything.'

He puts his hands behind his head.

'Our RSM wears one of those Afro-print shirts to our Saturday braais.'

'Charming.'

'Peter, one of my buddies, told him one night: "Dig that caftan, man." '

She smiles again.

'Or do you want to hear about the war? *Contact* – from the diary of a young soldier.'

'Come on,' she says and lies down next to him.

'I thought you wanted to hear about the war.'

She stares up at the ceiling.

'Since when have you been smoking cigars?'

'Since I've been wearing cowboy boots.'

He blows a smoke-ring to the ceiling.

'You become isolated and then you want to fuck up everything but it's not serious.'

'Not?'

'In fact, it's boring. Last week a troopie yelled out in the pub: "Guys, I've got something to show you!" and he stuck an R1 in his mouth. Anyway, traumas are boring.'

'What happened then?'

'Nothing. That type of guy seldom pulls the trigger.'

'Seldom?'

'Well, one chap did. Oelofse – an ugly bastard with pimples. In any case, he looked better afterwards. I saw the body before they zipped it into a body-bag and posted it back to the States.'[1]

'Why did he do it?'

'Probably a Dear Johnny or his wife who fucked around.'

She keeps quiet.

'Haven't you got any music with a stronger beat?'

'No,' she says.

They stare at the ceiling. He sits up and leans over her to

---

1 *States* army slang for South Africa.

the ashtray where he stubs out his half-smoked cigar. Then he puts his hand on her breast.

'It's a pretty blouse.'

'Thanks.'

He kisses her. She doesn't move.

'Please lock the door,' she says.

'Why?'

'My Calvinistic background.'

He gets up, locks the door and pulls the blind down to the window-sill.

'Is that better?' he asks.

She just lies and watches him.

He goes back to the bed and takes a packet of crêpe-de-Chine out of his pocket.

'That's not necessary,' she says. 'I am engaged.'

But he tears off the wrapping and drops it on the floor.

'Let me,' she says.

He lies down next to her and runs his hands down her body. He kisses her neck as he works open the zip of her jeans. Then suddenly he grips her in a close embrace.

'What's wrong?' she asks.

He takes a long time to answer.

'Confucius says: "Man who fucks plastic bag comes in a jiffy".'

'He also says: "Woman who stands on head must have crack up",' she says.

He gets up and goes to the bathroom.

She hears him flush the toilet.

The taps run for a few moments. When he comes back into the room, he goes to the tape deck and presses *Play* and *Record*. With his mouth close to the built-in microphone, he sings quietly over the recording.

She gets up off the bed. She goes to the mirror on the wall. She replaces the combs securely in her hair and then goes to the bathroom.

Translated by Catherine Knox and the author

FRANSI PHILLIPS

Clown Stories – *Fragment*

1

A woman becomes pregnant and gives birth to a little boy. The little boy becomes a clown. The woman wants to keep the clown on her lap, but he travels through the streets and holds performances. The woman does not know what to do about it.

Another woman gives birth to a cat. She feels much relieved after the birth. The doctor tells her that she must give birth to yet another cat, but she tells the doctor she is too lazy.

2

A woman becomes pregnant and gives birth to a cat. She feels much relieved after the birth. The doctor tells her that she has to give birth to yet another cat, but she tells the doctor she is too lazy.

The unborn cat is left behind in the dark along with the absences, the untruths, the hunger pains, the ideals still unrealized, the needs still unsatisfied and the longings still unfulfilled.

3

The clown travels through the streets and holds performances. At one of the performances the clown plays a little piece on a silver flute for the people. Beautiful sounds come out of the flute. The sounds change into memories and the memories change into dreams.

One of the dreams changes into a block of flats. In the block of flats a woman cuts bread with a knife. The woman begins to play the flute on the bread-knife. Beautiful sounds come out of the bread-knife. The sounds change into memories and the memories change into dreams.

4

One of the men in the streets gives the clown a silver coin. The clown takes the silver coin and goes to Checkers. At Checkers the clown takes a basket and fills it with eggs. He goes and stands in the queue and waits to pay. In front of the clown a pregnant woman stands and waits.

The clown waits in the queue for a very long time. The minutes change into hours, the hours change into days and the days change into weeks and months. The child grows large in the pregnant woman's stomach. Finally the woman gives birth to a little girl.

The months change into years and the years change into decades. The little girl becomes a woman. The woman becomes pregnant and gives birth to children. Generations are born and die.

The clown waits in the queue for ever.

5

Outside Checkers there are two clowns. The one clown holds a melon in his hands. The melon looks just like the clown's head.

The other clown holds his head in his hands.

6

Outside Checkers there is a butchery. The clown goes to the butchery to buy a dead rabbit. In the butchery window he sees two goat's feet hanging. He looks at the goat's feet and walks on through the streets. The goat's feet change into memories and the memories change into dreams. That night the clown dreams of the goat's feet.

The next day the clown walks past two boys who are having a fight. He looks at the boys and walks on through the streets. That night the clown dreams that the boys grow goat's feet.

The clown grows horns while he dreams about the boys.

7

One of the men in the streets gives the clown a silver coin. The clown takes the coin and puts it in his mouth. He dreams of a silver butterfly. When he wakes, the coin has changed into a butterfly.

The butterfly starts to lay eggs in the clown's mouth. The eggs change into larvae and the larvae change into pupae. The pupae in turn change into butterflies.

The clown's mouth, throat and stomach become filled with butterflies.

8

One of the men in the streets gives the clown a silver coin. The clown takes the coin and puts in his mouth. I tell the clown to take the coin out of his mouth because it is full of germs, but the clown keeps the coin in his mouth. The clown's mouth, throat and stomach become filled with germs. Thereafter the clown's mind also becomes filled with germs.

If I ask the clown to sing me a song, he sings a song about germs. If I ask him to write me a story, he writes: germs

germs germs germs germs germs germs germs germs germs
germs germs germs germs germs germs germs germs germs
germs germs germs germs germs germs germs germs germs
germs germs germs germs germs germs germs germs germs
germs germs germs germs germs germs germs germs germs
germs germs germs germs germs germs germs germs germs
germs germs germs germs germs germs germs germs germs
germs germs germs germs germs germs germs germs germs
germs germs germs germs germs germs germs germs germs
germs germs germs germs germs germs germs germs germs
germs germs germs germs germs germs germs.

9

The germs become divided into molecules and the molecules become divided into atoms. The smallest atoms become divided into waves and dreams. The dreams become filled with germs.

10

One of the men in the streets begins to sneeze. While the man sneezes, germs jump out of the man. The germs change into infectious diseases which settle on the clown. The clown gets mumps, chicken-pox, measles, smallpox, whooping-cough, diphtheria and scarlet fever.

The clown is taken off to a hospital. Some of the people in the hospital have leprosy. The other people have shrivelled hands, fever and moon-disease. Foam comes out of the people's mouths. Some of the people die.

The sick people's germs jump on to the clown. The clown catches the people's diseases. The infectious diseases go on for ever.

The clown dies.

Translated by Laura Jordaan

ETIENNE VAN HEERDEN

My Cuban

I have a Cuban on a leash. As we were taught to do at the South African Defence Force Horse and Dog School in the powdery red dust of Voortrekkerhoogte, I loop the lead loosely over my left wrist. The choke-chain round the Cuban's neck doesn't hurt him when I jerk it – it's just a sharp reminder that he must toe the line.

Barbara Woodhouse, in a pastoral English setting, explained elementary basics like this to our people. First principles known to every corporal in the Dog Division.

I have not yet cut off the Cuban's ears. This will take place later – an ecstatic deed with its mythology rooted in the Americas (closer, after all, to the Cuban's heartland than rank, defiled Angola). Like a Red Indian, I will only claim my trophy at the end, the very end. I will salt the ears carefully, pack them in cotton wool and send them by Air Force freight to Bellville, where my family will store them in formalin for display to amazed Sunday afternoon visitors, or, at my request, nail them to the front door jamb.

So they who have ears to hear, may hear.

It sounds cruel. War is like that. But on the other hand, love is also cruel.

I am not trying to digress.

Six weeks' bush patrol and only now do I understand what the newspapers and the weather reports mean when they refer to searing heat. That word carries a wealth of meaning: the shrill note of the cicadas that shoots through everything like radio waves, through flesh, through bone, through marrow. Also: the beads of sweat that hang on your eyebrows. If you look up for a second (through you dare not) you can see the droplets.

The green bush, the green fatigues, the shadows of other bodies, the light that shifts and splashes, the sun that breaks

and you plodding on with the only body that you have.
Searing.

So I am not digressing. I am coming to my peculiar relationship with the Cuban. Naturally, we had to find one
another first, as in the slave trade of old. (They say Portuguese girls – some distinctly coloured, unfortunately – are
now for sale just north of the Rooikat area. We never went
that far, but apparently the recces bugger around there sometimes.) I looked him over carefully first. His molars were
sound. His front teeth were slightly discoloured by the Havana cigars he'd smoked. But his nostrils were pleasing, finely
chiselled. His hands were slim. On the whole, I couldn't
complain.

As for what the others got . . . . Oh well!

I took my Cuban with me everywhere. That was the golden
rule. Never leave your Cuban, the commandant said.

Because Total Onslaught demands Total Defence.

I and my Cuban talk.

I: What's so special about Castro?

He:

I: Would you rather be killed by a mortar, a Stalin-organ, an
AK-47, or a bayonet?

He:

I: The Swapos do it another way too: they tie you to an
anthill. The ants go for the soft damp places first – the orifices
and other openings. People are like that too: we start with the
cherry on top. But the ants are innocent. They don't know
what they're doing. In the final analysis they don't even
know what pain is. The victim's writhing, shrieking body is
just food. They don't know it holds life, precious life. Intelligence has no value for them. The spark of personality is
nothing to them. Nor are individual features. In short: you
are just a meal to them. They are motivated only by a mute,
mindless, innate drive. They eat and they march with a
ruthless instinctive compulsion bred into them for generations. I do not blame the ants. Whom do you blame?

He:

I: Perhaps we should explain to the readers how I came
upon you. We do not want the readers to feel, as we do, that
they are up in the air, puppets on strings that make ridiculous

jerky movements when someone somewhere lifts a finger. Most important of all, the reader must not feel like a yo-yo, repeatedly hurled into a dangerous borderless void. Better that we seduce him with familiar things and see if we get anywhere.

He:

I: Come, sit quietly now. Tonight I'm going to tie you up outside again, like the others do sometimes. In the rain. If it rains. Do you think it is going to rain?

He:

I: It was long after the Bridge 14 episode. Or saga. Or victory. I mention this to orientate the reader. Al Venter had just been here to shoot 'Into Angola' for SATV. He was selective about what he filmed. From the shade I watched the crippled children hang around him, vying with fat nurses for a spot in the picture. And the readers probably also saw the scene where they unloaded the meat, pre-wrapped supermarket-style.

As cruel as love, that's what war is. As I have remarked already.

The parachutes drift like scraps of down with a dot hanging beneath each one. They drift like thistledown with its seed. Nature's wonderful dynamics. The breeze carries the seed with its downy parachute to a patch of ground where it falls and germinates and lives.

I am one of the thistle seeds. Oh how we float, the flower of the Republic's youth. Green our uniforms, red the flush on our cheeks, fresh the wind, Africa an open hand beneath us . . . And away, away drones the aircraft, below, even lower than we are, the helicopters with their red crosses churn. We sink easily in the sun, in the wind. My God, I am so near, and yet so far. Everything can change in the wink of an eye. Death/life. Just like that, with the borderline between the two as fine as the siting on a gun.

Thistle seeds, heroes' deeds, Sons of the Republic. Africa is ours, the white, white down feathers.

Keep still, Cuban: no food for you today. Listen to the metallic clatter of the mess-tins in the sink. A crippled ex-Swapo does the washing-up. He stands on one leg and stares with one eye

242

into the dirty water as the shiny mess-tins slide into it. He stands under the tarpaulin near the lone tree and sees the leftovers thrown in a drum, the overflow trampled by aimless boots as the men go to lie in their tents like young dogs, panting, shirtless, fondling photographs of their sweethearts, or carrying them off to the latrines.

Love is cruel. Sometimes just as cruel as war.

It was shortly after Al Venter and SATV's last visit. Operation Kudu was still in the planning stage. We didn't know about it for sure, but we had heard. (The camp grapevine runs through all the tents.) The whispers grew into rumours, the rumours turned to news, the news was promulgated as fact and became common knowledge. It wasn't so yet, but it was so: we would go in deeper than before – deep, deep into the torn land, past the ruins and abandoned tractors and cars and delivery vans, past gutted Portuguese shops and past groups of the dispossessed who wait with staring, hysterical eyes for the jeeps and Bedfords to come and go. We would break through, through Savimbi's land and over the savannah, almost to – or, yes, right to – Luanda.

All the units would become one great unit: one machine. The idea of penetration was exciting, understandably.

Or like with Jamesy . . . hey, Cuban, listen. Like with Jamesy.

Jamesy was half-Dutch, the cheese-eater of the camp. He still had one foot in the Netherlands. On patrol, he'd take out Gerrit Achterberg or Nijhoff,[1] which I found hilariously funny – the cosmic revolt and 'Voor dag en dauw' in the Angolan bush. We were over the border – his Netherlands a mild little country somewhere beyond our collective subconscious.

They rolled him up in a fresh cowhide and the women sewed him into the wet cylinder. By the time the hide had dried under the tree, the gang was long gone and we found Jamesy with his tongue lolling on to his chest with a swarm of bluebottle flies on it. (How long does it take a hide to dry and shrink in the Angolan sun?) We buried him like that; just like that, inside the dry cowhide coffin.

So died Jamesy Zeeman from Amsterdam of cowhide shrinkage.

---

1 *Nijhoff* Dutch poet.

What happened to the conversation with my Cuban? He didn't answer, and even if he had ... well, I don't understand his language. I wonder what he speaks? Does Cuba have its own language? We were never told. Their cigars are good, anyway. They lay among the bodies in underground bunkers or smouldered between dead fingers. There was still smoke in the warm lungs when we dragged them out of the bunkers. We threw them on the Bedfords like laundry bags, and as they thumped down dead chests coughed out blue smoke.

Their souls had been in Cuba for ages already, I decided.

Anyway, we'd been instructed not to talk to the Cubans too much. They'd probably also had the classic command: name, rank and number, say nothing more. Even if they treat you like a dog. Or tie you on an anthill.

Operation Kudu was still forming on paper and in the brilliant minds of the strategists: a Disneyland of power and explosions and violence and bucking jeeps and rattling firearms and flesh that suddenly thrusts out through skin and the shock of white bone splinters. I'm not just saying it. I was there.

Others weren't there. Some of the guys – and not just lefties, note – who were at Bridge 14 and after that, had awoled. Not again, they said. The territory was too alien. They came from cosmopolitan Sea Point, for example. They'd lived there always. Now they landed up in Angola. They ... oh well, I understand. It was like Jamesy Zeeman: there was a short circuit somewhere.

Many awoled. Bad food was supposed to have caused it in one camp. We knew that it was Operation Kudu: but the top brass didn't know that we knew. Everyone from rifleman up to first lieutenant knew that we knew. The higher ranks thought that only they knew – the carriers of swagger-sticks who strut around the mess at night.

We knew and we prepared ourselves. How does a soldier prepare himself? He takes leave of things which cannot be left. He isn't like a man on Death Row because he doesn't know for sure. He says goodbye to certainty. Saying goodbye to certainty takes a long time. It takes many nights. It takes a lot of thinking or a lot of blotting out. Some guys blot it out.

They go crazy, the camp goes crazy before an operation. The men drink and fight like tigers. They swear and vandalize the latrines. They steal Bedfords and dice through the refugee compound. They strip the queers naked and tie them on the bonnets of jeeps and race off to town with them. They drink, drink, drink.

The other guys who just think . . . Some of them run away. They awol. They can't go home because that's the first place they'd be looked for. They awol to the YMCA in Durban, Port Elizabeth, Cape Town or Johannesburg. But eventually they can't go there either. The top brass keeps a permanent watch on the YMCA. Could you say a whole generation awoled? What do you think, Cuban?

He:

I: Awoled from a war that didn't make sense? And you: you're from an island and you're fighting in another place, another continent. Or is your homeland just a concept?

He:

I: Operation Kudu is announced with the daily orders. The officers want to prepare us so on the big day they inform us quietly that we are to go in. But we know already. We are prepared.

It was a long time ago. Ever since then I've had my Cuban. He is the result of everything that's happened in between.

My whole life changed when I got this Cuban. I can't leave him alone. He is always with me. Part of me, you could say. We are, so to speak, one. When I go to the latrines, he must come too. If I take a shower he must share the private moment with me. He is so close to me he knows my dreams. He almost knows how I think.

I: Hey, Cuban, do you agree? Isn't it so?

He doesn't answer, he doesn't look at me, like a cowered dog too frightened to look at its master. I clank the choke-chain. Its sounds like something out of a medieval dungeon, or a Barbara Woodhouse programme.

People felt it. Each one felt it: his life would never be the same again after Operation Kudu. Some came to this conclusion melodramatically. Some faced it calmly. I knew it instinctively, more completely than the others.

The short patrols into the bush (which I mentioned earlier) began to seem like Boy Scout expeditions to the Vaal Dam or Chapman's Peak. Something bigger lay ahead, my Cuban, something that provided me with you, something that brought you to me, so that I have you with me now like one would carry shrapnel in your thigh – you're never without the dull pain, the reminder.

Thistle seeds. Heroes' deeds. In the aircraft the drone of the engines deadens other sounds. It always makes me think of insects: the big netted helmets, the backpacks with small arms, water-bottles on hips, painted faces. Like insects in the belly of a bigger insect. At a time like this one also goes for the soft damp places. There are things you think about, things that haunt you. And it is now that love becomes crueller than war. On the surface there's no more fear. The plains that shift beneath you are no more than the chart they drummed into you at base before take off. You are a drawing-pin: if your moves are tactically correct, the blue drawing-pin will become a little flag on the map. If you or someone in your platoon makes a mistake, the pin will be pulled out, leaving only the little puncture in the map.

You no longer know you are life, precious life. This is the magic power of the uniform, the tribal dance, the marching platoon, aircraft in formation.

Thistle seeds, heroes' deeds. In the aircraft Africa's wind does not smell of Etosha's mud or the humid tropics, it does not smell of fresh dung and grass and early mornings. This smell – a blend of machine oil, sweat, leather, boot polish, clothing, canvas, rubber, sperm, bodies, blood, and the sharp stink of adrenalin – this is the new smell of Africa. It is the breath, the new breath of the continent.

Soon we know we must make ready. The engines are throttled back, the red light flashes on. Quickly, too quickly, the time has come. The cabin door gapes, mouth to a dark wilderness below. The smell is suffocating. The smell of Africa. Our sweat . . . Our sweat and the camouflage paint smears off on the back of our hands. You want to jump, to get out into the air, into the freefall where there's no turning back. You want just to fall and fall like a bullet, a missile to the centre of the earth.

I must jump. The wind drags at my cheeks. My mind is empty.

246

All my concentration is on the jump, the mechanics drilled
into me at Parachute School. I am free of the aircraft, the
great steel bird that's suddenly gone; I can see its shadow
slipping by on the bushes to the left below. Beneath me
a pair of open parachutes bloom white. I see ruins and a
rusted tin roof that still catches the sun. I yank my parachute and slide into a restful drift. I am now in the no man's
land where all certainty has gone. No ground under my
feet, no propeller to drive me away, no knowledge of what
waits down there.

I drift like thistledown at the mercy of the wind, or
chance, and – according to the chaplain – Divine Providence.

I will be completely alone until we marshal again on the
ground after extricating ourselves from our parachutes.

I must control my fear. Think of the operation. Think of
every movement. Mentally check my firearm. Try to steer
my parachute. Keep a look-out for an enemy patrol. The
alien land comes closer and closer. I fall like a seed with life
or death in it.

I didn't expect the Cuban. I didn't ask for him. He was
forced on me by the times, by history, particular political
circumstances. But how *he* came to land there . . . By fate or
by providence? The fact is when I touched down in a swirl
of air, half skew in a bush that stood almost man-high, with
my parachute billowing out to one side in the breeze and me
tugging and struggling and swearing while I looked around
for the other men . . . then the Cuban was there.

Yellow as an islander, foreign, with chiselled nostrils, sen-
sual nostrils, he stepped out of the shade into a patch of
sunlight, his cream uniform brand new and ultra-correct on
his body. Did he smile at me? Swearing, I tried to drag
myself out of the parachute harness that bound me to my
winged anchor. At last I was free, the short carbine warm in
my hand because the sun had already penetrated the metal.
I fell half into the bush and the carbine began to chatter
under me and small puffs of dust leaped up around the
Cuban's feet but still smiling he kept coming and I cursed
him his race his whore of a mother and his island and he
kept smiling and coming but he never reached me where I

lay sobbing and firing until my carbine was empty, still half in my harness, with the parachute to one side, gently rising and falling with the breath of Africa.

Translated by Catherine Knox

NOTES ON CONTRIBUTORS

Part One

JEREMY CRONIN (*born 1949*), educated at the University of Cape Town and in Paris. Jailed 1976–83 under the Terrorism Act. At present a tutor in philosophy at the University of Cape Town. Author of *Inside* (poems, 1983), from which the selection is taken.

MODIKWE DIKOBE (*born 1913*), after elementary schooling, worked as newspaper vendor, hawker, clerk, book-keeper, trade unionist, night-watchman. Retired to Bophuthatswana in 1977. Author of *The Marabi Dance* (novel, 1973) and *Dispossessed* (poems and prose pieces, 1983), from which the extract is taken.

AHMED ESSOP (*born 1931*), a secondary-school teacher until 1974. Author of *The Hajji and Other Stories* (1978), from which 'Dolly' is taken, *The Visitation* (1980) and *The Emperor* (1984), novels. *The Hajji* won the Olive Schreiner Award.

NADINE GORDIMER (*born 1923*), author of eight novels – including, most recently, *Burger's Daughter* (1979) and *July's People* (1981) – and seven volumes of stories, for which she has won numerous international awards. 'A Lion on the Freeway' is taken from *A Soldier's Embrace* (1980).

CHRISTOPHER HOPE (*born 1944*), educated at the University of the Witwatersrand and the University of Natal. Now lives in the UK. Author of *Cape Drives* (poems, 1974), from which the selection is taken, *A Separate Development* (novel, 1980), *In the Country of the Black Pig* (poems, 1981), *Private Parts* (stories, 1981) and *Kruger's Alp* (novel, 1984), for the last of which he won the Whitbread Award.

MAZISI KUNENE (*born 1932*), educated at the University of Natal and the School of African and Oriental Studies, London University. Proscribed in South Africa under the Suppression

of Communism Act. Professor of African Language and Literature at the University of California, Los Angeles. Author of *Zulu Poems* (1970), *Emperor Shaka the Great* (1978), *Anthem of the Decades* (1981) and *The Ancestors and the Sacred Mountain* (1982), from the last of which the selections are taken.

BEN J. LANGA, an office-bearer in the South African Students' Organization, who died under unexplained circumstances in 1984. The poem is taken from *Staffrider*, February 1980.

JOEL MATLOU (*born c. 1957*), a factory worker. The extract is taken from *Staffrider*, November 1979.

MTUTUZELI MATSHOBA (*born 1950*), educated at the University of Fort Hare. Author of *Call Me Not a Man* (stories, 1979), from which the selection is taken, and *Seeds of War* (novel, 1981).

GCINA MHLOPE (*born c. 1960*), well known as an actress. A collection of children's stories due to appear in 1986. 'Nokulunga's Wedding' is taken from the collection *LIP: From Southern African Women*, ed. Susan Brown *et al.* (1983).

OUPA THANDO MTHIMKULU. The poem is taken from *Staffrider*, March 1978.

MIKE NICOL (*born 1951*), educated at the University of the Witwatersrand. Journalist and editor of *African Wild Life*. Author of *Among the Souvenirs* (poems, 1978), which won the Ingrid Jonker Prize. The poem is taken from *Contrast*, July 1983.

MOTSHILE WA NTHODI (*born 1948*), studied fine art in Paris. Has exhibited widely. Author of *From the Calabash* (poems and woodcuts, 1978). The poem is taken from *Quarry*, 1976.

SHEILA ROBERTS (*born c. 1940*), has lectured in English at the University of Pretoria, the University of the Western Cape and, since 1977, Michigan State University. Author of *Outside Life's Feast* (stories, 1974), which won the Olive Schreiner Award, *He's My Brother* (novel, 1977), *The Weekenders* (novel, 1981) and *This Time of Year* (stories, 1983), as well as poems and plays.

MARIA THOLO (*born c. 1935*), at the time of the 1976 uprisings, was living in Guguletu near Cape Town and acting as
informant in a sociological survey. Her *Diary* (1980) was compiled by Carol Hermer from tape-recorded interviews made in
1976.

CHRISTOPHER VAN WYK (*born 1957*), editor of *Staffrider* and
author of *It is Time to Go Home* (poems, 1979), which won the
Olive Schreiner Prize, as well as of a novel for teenagers.

STEPHEN WATSON (*born 1954*), educated at the University of
Cape Town, where he now lectures in English. Author of
Poems 1977–82 (1983).

Part Two

HENNIE AUCAMP (*born 1934*), senior lecturer in the Education Department at the University of Stellenbosch. Highly
acclaimed as a leading short story writer since the publication
of his first collection in 1963, admired especially for his exploration of the 'private ache'. In recent years he has devoted much
time to the writing of cabaret texts. Received the major award
of the Afrikaans literary establishment, the Hertzog Prize, in
1982. An English anthology of his work, *House Visits*, was
published by Tafelberg Publishers, Cape Town, in 1983.

PIROW BEKKER (*born 1935*), on the staff of the Human
Sciences Research Council in Pretoria, has published several
volumes of poetry and short stories as well as three novels. His
most successful texts are those in which the innocence, disillusionment and cruelty of childhood are evoked.

M. C. BOTHA (*born 1954*), freelance journalist (after editing for
several years a small country newspaper in Hermanus on the

Cape south coast) and a prominent figure among young Afrikaans writers who made their début in the 1980s. Has already published four volumes of short stories – several of them in the vein of 'magic realism' – and a full-length play.

T. T. CLOETE (*born 1924*), retired academic at Potchefstroom University. Known primarily as literary critic, he surprised reviewers by beginning to publish poetry in 1980, followed by a volume of short stories in 1984, and a play. He has been awarded some of the most prestigious South African literary prizes for his poetry.

ABRAHAM H. DE VRIES (*born 1937*), leading exponent of the short story in the generation known as the 'Sestigers', lectures in Afrikaans literature at the Cape Technicon. After concentrating in his early work on characters demonstrating an existence *in extremis*, he reveals in several of his more recent stories an overt concern with the South African socio-political situation.

JEANETTE FERREIRA (*born 1954*), lectures in Afrikaans at the University of Zululand after a stint as editor for a Johannesburg publisher. A volume of poetry was followed, in 1985, by the short novel *Sitate Rondom 'n Revolusie (Footnotes to a Revolution)* in which the private agonies of a woman in love are paralleled by a political situation of strife and division.

P. J. HAASBROEK (*born 1943*), who lectures in Economics at the University of Pretoria, has published four volumes of short stories since the mid-1970s and is known especially for his exploration of violence as an individual and social phenomenon.

ELSA JOUBERT (*born 1922*), has consistently explored her relationship with Africa in several travel books and notably in her novels. The documentary novel *Poppie Nongena* (English edition 1981), on the private and public life of a Black woman trying to survive as an ordinary human being in South Africa, was published in several languages and also adapted for the stage. In 1984–5 she was president of the Afrikaans Writers' Guild. In South Africa her work has been acknowledged with several awards (including the CNA Prize), and in Britain with the Royal Society of Literature Prize.

Notes on Contributors

E. KOTZÉ (*born 1933*), a farmer's wife who has spent all her life in the barren West Coast region of South Africa, has published her short stories in a variety of magazines and is known especially for the collection *Halfkrone vir die Nagmaal* (*Half-Crowns for Communion*) published in 1982, in which the rich ethos and the mythical substratum of a rural world is dramatically re-created.

DALENE MATTHEE (*born 1938*), a descendant of Sir Walter Scott, has spent her whole life on the South-Cape coast and began her serious writing career at a mature age with *Kringe in die Bos* (*Circles in the Forest*, 1984) a novel translated into several languages.

JOHN MILES (*born 1938*), who lectures in Afrikaans literature at the University of the Witwatersrand, established his reputation with the collection of short stories *Liefs Nie op Straat Nie* (*Preferably Not in Public*) in 1970, followed by three novels which all offer highly inventive explorations of violence, notably that unleashed by apartheid. Two of his books were on the banned list of the South African censors.

FRANSI PHILLIPS is a young freelance journalist and art critic in Johannesburg, and has already published her highly experimental fiction in a volume of short stories and the collection *77 Stories oor 'n Clown*, 1985; the latter has also been adapted for the stage.

KOOS PRINSLOO (*born 1957*), journalist and short story writer, spent his early childhood in Kenya; in 1982 he made an impressive début with *Jonkmanskas* (*Wardrobe*).

INA ROUSSEAU (*born 1926*), published her first volume of verse in the Fifties and is regarded as one of the leading women poets in Afrikaans, admired for the deceptive simplicity and subtlety of her work. She has also impressed critics with a handful of short stories published over the years, some of which were collected in the volume *Soutsjokolade* (*Salt Chocolate*), in 1979. After spending many years in Natal she now lives in Cape Town.

ETIENNE VAN HEERDEN (*born 1954*), Afrikaans lecturer at the University of Zululand after spending a year as bailiff in

the Cape, is one of a young generation of Afrikaans writers exploring the South African military experience in their work. His volume of short stories, *My Kubaan* (*My Cuban*) was awarded the highly regarded Eugene Marais Prize for young writers upon its publication in 1983.

JAN VAN TONDER (*born 1954*), a freelance journalist, drew heavily on his previous experiences as a prison warder for the short stories in the collection *Aandenking vir 'n Vry Man* (*Souvenir for a Free Man*, 1985), from which the text in this volume has been taken.

LETTIE VILJOEN (pseudonym of Ingrid Scholtz, *born 1948*), lecturer in Fine Art at the University of Stellenbosch, made a startling prose début with *Klaaglied vir Koos* (*Lament for Koos*) in 1985, in which the disillusionment of a recent divorce is explored against the increasing political polarizations in South Africa.

GEORGE WEIDEMAN (*born 1947*), made his début as a poet in 1966, drawing deeply on his experience in the North-western Cape and Namibia. He has published one collection of short stories, *Tuin van Klip en Vuur* (*Garden of Stone and Fire*) in 1982, offering moving and disturbing views of the loss of innocence. Lectures in Afrikaans at the Academy for Tertiary Education in Windhoek, Namibia.

ACKNOWLEDGEMENTS

For permission to reprint copyright material the editors and publishers gratefully acknowledge the following:

Bateleur Press for an extract from *The Weekenders* by Sheila Roberts; 'Freedom' by Stephen Watson.

Jonathan Cape Ltd and A. P. Watt Ltd for 'A Lion on the Freeway' by Nadine Gordimer from *A Soldier's Embrace* and for an extract from *Burger's Daughter* by Nadine Gordimer.

Contrast magazine for 'Choosing a Cottage' by Mike Nicol.

Ad. Donker (Pty) Ltd for 'South African Dialogue' by Motshile wa Nthodi from *A Century of South African Poetry* (ed. Michael Chapman); 'It is Sleepy in the "Coloured" Townships' and 'In Detention' by Christopher van Wyk.

H.A.U.M. Publishers for 'Dube Knew' by Jan van Tonder (trans. André Brink) from *Aadenking vir 'n vry Man*; an extract from 'Clown Stories' by Fransi Phillips (trans. Laura Jordaan) from *77 Stories Oor'n Clown*.

Heinemann Educational Books Ltd for 'The Rise of the Angry Generation', 'Changes', 'After the Death of Mdabuli', 'On the Nature of Truth' and 'In Praise of the Ancestors' by Mazisi Kunene from *The Ancestors and the Sacred Mountain*.

Human & Rousseau Publishers for 'The Fisherwoman' by M. C. Botha (trans. Anna de Wit and Peter Lilienfield) from *Die einde van 'n kluisenaar se Lewe*; 'Tin Soldiers Don't Bleed' by Abraham H. de Vries (trans. André Brink) from *Bliksoldate Bloei Nie*; 'The Animal Tamer' by Dalene Matthee (trans. Catherine Knox) from *Die Judasbok*; 'Departure' by P. J. Haasbroek (trans. Lynette Paterson) from *Verby die Vlakte*.

Acknowledgements

London Magazine for 'The Flight of the White South Africans' by Christopher Hope from *Cape Drives*.

Perskor Publishers for 'Under a Shepherd's Tree' by Pirow Bekker (trans. Catherine Knox) from *Vangs*.

Ravan Press (Pty) Ltd for 'Walking on Air' by Jeremy Cronin from *Inside*; 'Episodes in the Rural Areas' by Modikwe Dikobe from *Dispossessed*; 'Dolly' by Ahmed Essop from *The Hajji and Other Stories*; 'Man Against Himself' by Joel Matlou from *Staffrider* magazine (1979); 'Call Me Not a Man' by Mtutuzeli Matshoba; 'Nokulunga's Wedding' by Gcina Mhlope from *LIP: From South African Women* (eds. Susan Brown, Isobel Hofmeyr and Susan Rosenberg); 'Like a Wheel' by Oupa Thando Mthimkulu from *Staffrider* magazine (1978); an extract from the *Diary of Maria Tholo* (ed. Carol Hermer); Ravan Press (Pty) Ltd and the Estate of Ben J. Langa for 'For My Brothers in Exile' from *Staffrider* magazine (1980).

Tafelberg Publishers for 'Day of Blood' by E. Kotzé (trans. Catherine Knox) from *Halfkrone vir die Nagmaal*; 'The Afterthought' by George Weideman (trans. by the author) from *Tuin van Klip en Vuur*; 'For Four Voices' by Hennie Aucamp (trans. Ian Ferguson) from *Volmink*; 'Disaster' by T. T. Cloete (trans. Catherine Knox) from *Die Waarheid Gelieg*; 'Do You Remember Helena Lem?' by Ina Rousseau (trans. by the author) from *Soutsjokalade*; 'Back Yard' by Elsa Joubert (trans. Catherine Knox) from *Melk*; 'Crack-Up' by Koos Prinsloo (trans. Catherine Knox and the author) from *Jonkmanskas*; 'My Cuban' by Etienne van Heerden (trans. Catherine Knox) from *My Kubaan*; Tafelberg Publishers and Buren Publishers for 'Lucy' by John Miles (trans. Laura Jordaan) from *Liefs Nie op Straat Nie*.

Taurus Publishers for an extract from 'Lament for Koos' by Lettie Viljoen (trans. Ingrid Scholtz) from *Klaaglied vir Koos*.

Tydskrif vir Letterkunde magazine (August 1983) for 'The Lover' by Jeanette Ferreira (trans. André Brink).